L.J. KERRY

LISTED

Copyright © 2020 by L.J. Kerry

All rights reserved. No part of this publication may be reproduced, stored or transmitted in any form or by any means, electronic, mechanical, photocopying, recording, scanning, or otherwise without written permission from the publisher. It is illegal to copy this book, post it to a website, or distribute it by any other means without permission.

This novel is entirely a work of fiction. The names, characters and incidents portrayed in it are the work of the author's imagination. Any resemblance to actual persons, living or dead, events or localities is entirely coincidental.

L.J. Kerry asserts the moral right to be identified as the author of this work.

L.J. Kerry has no responsibility for the persistence or accuracy of URLs for external or third-party Internet Websites referred to in this publication and does not guarantee that any content on such Websites is, or will remain, accurate or appropriate.

First edition

ISBN: 978-1-83853-738-8

This book was professionally typeset on Reedsy.
Find out more at reedsy.com

*To everybody who supported me on this journey.
Thank you.*

Acknowledgement

Where do I begin. Well first off, I want to thank all the readers again for reading my book, you're all incredible and I truly hope you have enjoyed *LISTED*.

Thank you to my mum, Margaret, for supporting me every step of the way to try and get published, it's been a very bumpy road to get to this point but I finally did it! Thank you for always encouraging me to become a huge bookworm from an early age, without you I wouldn't have found so many books that have sucked me into their worlds and inspired me to create my own. Also a huge thank you to my sister, Emma, for also supporting me and helping me come up plot points.

To my brilliant team of editors: Dan, Denise, and Dee for all your enthusiasm to work on *Listed*, providing advice on ways to improve the final product, your amazing comments of praise and without your hard work the book wouldn't be what it is today. It's been an honour to work with you.

Thanks to all my amazing beta readers who have helped me from my awful first drafts, to the final product. Your advice has taught me things about writing I didn't know beforehand, grew my confidence with writing, and made *LISTED* well and truly grow up from an idea to an actual novel.

To Logan thank you for listening to me talk about the plot and characters for hours, it brought them to life and made them seem real.

A huge thank you to Judas and Nadine for compelling me to write their story, *LISTED* wouldn't be here if it wasn't for you guys.

Lastly thank you to everybody who has supported me for all these years trying to get published. I'm so happy a book of mine is finally in your hands.

WARNING

Some scenes in this book may be upsetting for some readers. This book contains scenes which include topics such as: suicide, sexual harrassement, hate crime and violence.

1

Judas

It was 7:30 a.m., and I had just completed Task 105—Church Service. I filtered out of the church alongside my younger siblings with the sound of the organ playing, joining the sea of people in government uniform: blue overalls, white T-shirt, and beige boots. The fall air smelled earthy, and when the wind blew, it sent chills down my spine. I sighed as I felt heat rising in my body, my stomach churning until I felt sick, my ears feeling like they had been set on fire. The proper tasks that involved slaving away were about to begin, and I just wanted a break.

Walking down the street with everybody else, I glanced at Gabrielle, who was braiding her black hair and Michael, who stayed focused on the ground, his hands shoved into his overall pockets. I could tell he was biting the inside of his cheek to stop from talking. Lately, he was crossing some boundaries as the rebellious teenage phase kicked in, so it was best for him to stay quiet. Michael was the youngest sibling of our trio at fourteen years old.

Gabrielle stretched her arms out and said, "Our Leader has graciously given me Task 16 to complete today."

I stifled a laugh. She was deluded and didn't understand why our

Task system was in place. Yet, she smiled as she braided her hair, and if I laughed, I would take the happiness from her.

"Our Leader has summoned me for Task 3 today," Michael interjected.

"You say *summoned* like Task 3 is a terrible thing. Our Leader has given you the task to keep us clean and smell fresh," Gabrielle spat back. I remained silent. Task 3 was a terrible thing; nobody should do laundry for a town of 800 people, including their underwear.

But I pushed my black hair out of my face and said, "I would like to thank my gracious Leader for giving me Task 72 on this perfect day." The sarcasm was strong, and Gabrielle noticed, because her jaw fell open.

Yet we had to part ways from 6th Street. Both Michael and Gabrielle went down North Main, and I went straight on toward the courthouse.

* * *

I was in line for Task 72 check-in. A guard in green camouflage was sitting at a folding table with a clipboard and a barcode scanner. Almost every citizen of The Republic of Denmé was branded with a barcode tattooed onto their right arm. I rolled up the sleeve on my blue denim jacket, ready to be scanned. Despite having done this task hundreds of times, knots formed in my stomach nonetheless. I stared at the two groups they would separate people into: Group One or Group Two.

"Next," the guard instructed, pulling me out of my daydream. I stepped forward and put my arm through the arm cuff. It flashed green and said, "ID 498763, Group Two." The guard circled my ID number on his clipboard.

I walked over to the group of people where a bald guy held up a wooden sign with *Group Two* written on it. Next to this guy were rolls of posters dedicated to Our Leader, ladders, and even paste that always made me feel dizzy. As I sat on the grass and waited for everybody else to check-in, a guy with mousy brown hair approached me. I could tell he was young from the light in his eyes—a glimmer of innocence he still possessed. Soon enough, that light would be extinguished by the regime. I'd give it a year until he looked like he'd just been through hell and lived to tell the tale.

"Hello, I'm Richard. ID 496001," he said.

I nodded and looked at the final three people checking in. "Joseph, ID 498763," I responded.

"Today is my first task. I'm very excited," Richard explained.

So, he was around thirteen or fourteen—shit.

"Task 72 already? Wow. Our Leader must love you." I rolled my eyes.

Richard beamed, missing my sarcasm. His naivety would get him killed; I glanced at the last person who got checked in. Let Task 72 begin, I suppose.

* * *

I got paired with Richard, and after showing him the ropes, Richard was acting like he had been doing Task Seventy-Two for years, despite being slow. I had to make sure the guards didn't see my impatience. I had to keep my cool.

"Come on, Richard, you need to get this right." I huffed as I led him to a small shopping area that ran alongside Newton's river, the wooden ladder under one arm while he carried the posters. I stopped at a bookstore.

Unfolding the ladder and placing it directly under a faded poster, Richard was already up the ladder like a rat running through pipes. The things I had learned about Richard: he was a fast learner, which was unfortunate; the guards were too good at knocking the personalities out of people that were deemed different.

I waited at the bottom of the ladder as Richard carefully took down one of the most terrifying posters of Our Leader that The Republic of Denmé had. Our Leader's boney face enlarged, her evil dark eyes staring into your soul and in golden writing at the bottom *"17 Years of Safety."*

I was six when The Republic of Denmé and the regime came into existence. That was the age I lost my freedom. Everybody born into the regime was told Our Leader came to save us from the apocalypse that never actually happened. It was a 9.9 magnitude earthquake which destroyed what is now known as Zone 13, 5, 6, and 11.

As Richard handed me the old poster, I handed him a new one. I threw the creepy one in the discard pile and looked around the street. A guard stood close by, watching us, all of them looked the same, so I never bothered trying to differentiate them. All of them wore camouflage, all of them were white, all were muscular males. No regular citizen was allowed to know their names.

I jerked my head up at the sound of tearing, and my eyes widened. Richard had torn an entire corner off the new poster by accident. His hands shook as he tried to stick the poster back together.

I grabbed hold of the ladder. "Get down, Richard. Quick."

I tensed as the gunshot boomed around the shopping area. I gripped hold of the ladder until my knuckles turned white. My heartbeat thumped against my ribs. I clamped my hand over my mouth to muffle a scream as Richard fell by my feet with a smoking bullet hole in his chest—*seventeen years of safety*, my ass.

Feeling a tap on my shoulder, I turned around to see the guard looking at me. He handed me a new poster, which I took with trembling hands.

"ID 498763, put the poster up," the guard demanded.

I nodded, and despite my trembling legs; I made the climb up the ladder.

* * *

After the nightmare of Task 72, I walked down the back roads of my town of Newton. I was headed to a secret underground world in The Republic of Denmé that the government had next to no idea about—The Rebellion. I needed alcohol to cope, and I could only get that down there. The only place I was free. Even though the government knew The Rebellion existed, they had no idea where it was or how many of us were part of it. Previous Leaders of The Rebellion had worked tirelessly to keep this world well hidden, most entrances in Zone 14 were down forgotten alleyways hidden in the shadows.

I stopped in my tracks as a military vehicle pulled up on the side of the sidewalk.

Oh no, did they find out my secret?

My heart raced as the door opened. The guards dumped an unconscious woman on the side of the road like trash on Task 15 day. She had crimson hair—*illegal.* She was wearing a purple hoodie with grey gym leggings—*again, illegal.*

A guard poked his head out of the vehicle, scanned the street, then his gaze fell on me, and he smiled.

"Hello. Would you mind helping us put this woman in a crowded location where there are lots of other guards?" he requested. I had a bad feeling about their intentions.

"Why?" I asked. It was normal for the guards to be weird, but this was too much

"She's a Zone transfer from Zone 8. We want to give her a genuine welcome into Newton, Zone 14," the guard explained.

I scratched behind my ear then folded my arms across my chest. It was prohibited in all eighteen Zones to dye hair or perform any acts of body modification, even not wearing a uniform was punishable.

"Okay," I lied.

The guard smiled as he disappeared back into the vehicle. The tyres screeched on the road, and the car sped off, leaving a trail of dust behind.

I gaped at the woman and then bit the inside of my cheek. After looking around the street, I approached her quickly, even though the butterflies from this morning came back as a bad feeling washed over me. I was starting to feel sick.

Placing the back of my hand underneath her nose, relief flooded me when I felt her breathing. Gently, I pushed her shoulder; the hoodie was soft to the touch.

"Hello? Are you okay?" I asked.

Her eyes flew open, and she gripped the straps of my overalls, fear in her eyes. Taken aback, I held onto her hands to try and free her grasp; I hated being touched by strangers.

"Please help me! Ignore what they said!" she exclaimed.

I pressed a finger to my lips and looked around the empty street.

"They chased me for thirty minutes, then they grabbed me." She started sobbing into her hands.

"You're not safe here, follow me." I took her by the wrist to help her stand, letting go of her, and holding my hands up to signal I didn't pose a threat. "Keep up, we need to get you out of sight." I turned and walked towards the alleyway.

Shadows blanketed the alleyway. I moved my hair from my face as the wind picked up, we walked until I could just make out a red line of paint on the wall—it was almost invisible unless you knew to look for it.

Fumbling around in the dark, I searched for the indentation in the floor. Once I found it, I lifted up the section of concrete to reveal stairs leading down into sheer darkness, cold air travelled out of it.

"Down here," I said.

"What's down there?" she asked. Her accent sounded strange, a slow lull that was easy on the ears. Perhaps the guards were right about her being a Zone transfer but got mistaken about where in Denmé she came from, I guessed Zone 7 based on her accent.

"Safety. Now get a move on," I responded.

"Really? It looks like a serial killer's play house to me."

"What's a serial killer? You know what, never mind. We don't have much time." I extended my hand out to her. "Take my hand; I'll guide you down. I promise nothing bad is going to happen to you down here."

The woman took my hand after some hesitation; her clammy hand indicated she was understandably anxious. My stomach fluttered, and my heart raced. We took two steps down into the darkness of the underground, then she stopped abruptly and took a step back.

"Promise?" she asked.

"Promise."

2

Judas

At the bottom of the stairs, I came to a stop, it was so dark down here I couldn't see my hand as I extended it out in front of me. My fingers lightly brushed against the wall that housed the secret door to The Rebellion.

Placing my hand on the left side of the wall, it vibrated as it scanned my fingerprints silently, then a hissing noise sounded out as a section of the wall came free. A white light cut through the darkness, and I pushed it open, stepping inside.

The woman slowly came down the stairs, looking back into the darkness that used to surround us, her hesitation was starting to get on my nerves.

"Hurry, it locks in twenty seconds." I waved my hand to hurry the woman into the facility.

She finally slipped through just in time for the door to seal us in. Her eyes scanned the area, and her jaw fell open.

We were in a concrete room that housed a maze of metal staircases, I knew where we were going from here. Most of the stairs led to false rooms, and only one set of stairs led to the actual Rebellion.

Making my way down the stairs, my boots made a loud pinging

noise as they hit the metal, hers made a slightly quieter sound.

"So, how was Zone 8?" I asked her.

"I'm from Olympia," she admitted. I stopped at the bottom of the first staircase and turned to look at her. My stomach dropped like a heavy weight had been placed in there.

"What do you mean you're from Olympia?"

"I know I'm in Denmé, but those men dragged me from Olympia," she said quickly. "I don't know what they want." The woman shoved her hands into her pocket.

I turned my back to her and resumed our walk down the staircase, the bad feeling I couldn't shake was getting more intense. This didn't seem right, Olympia was the neighbouring country, and international travel was banned for regular citizens. Guards could travel, so this situation must be the work of The Educators.

"We need a serious talk, pick up the pace, don't fall behind," I demanded harshly.

All I heard was our footsteps echoing against the walls for the rest of the journey into The Rebellion.

* * *

The only place I could appropriately take this woman was to The Rebellion's jail. It was a place just out of reach of the actual facility, but not enough to reveal our secrets. Like any place, there were rules to follow, and The Rebellion followed the laws of the old country.

As I handed the woman a cup of coffee from the vending machine, she was shaking and pale, even though it was never cold down here. Every single noise made her jump, as I sat on a swivel chair, I leaned forward and looked into her hazel eyes.

"Above ground, my name is Joseph, but down here everybody knows me as Judas," I explained to her as I leaned back on my chair, putting my feet up on a stack of documentation which sat on a large desk.

"Nadine Ellis," she mumbled as she took a drink. My eyes widened at her unauthorised name; it appeared she was telling the truth about being from Olympia.

Most authorised names in The Republic of Denmé were Biblical or something to make Our Leader look good. Even though my birth name—Judas—met these criteria, we knew him as a traitor in the Bible, so the government forced my parents to change it to Joseph.

"So, Nadine from Olympia, what exactly happened?" I asked, rolling a pen between my fingers to give me a distraction, as I looked at the red brick walls.

"It was 7 a.m., I always go on a daily run. But I noticed men in green camouflage following me, so I ran faster." Her breathing became heavy, and she took a drink. "They grabbed me and put me to sleep with a rag over my mouth. When I woke up at the border, I pretended to be asleep. They hid me under a tarp, and I came alive when you asked me if I'm alright," Nadine admitted, taking another drink. Now it was even more clear this was the work of The Educators.

I couldn't even begin to image how terrified she was. As Archie walked into the room, I placed the pen down, he was holding a burrito which made the room smell like beef.

"Hello, Nadine," he announced while taking a bite.

Her jaw fell open, and her eyes clouded with worry. Nadine looked at me, then at Archie, while she shifted in her seat. I knew him well enough to know he moves like a cat, and was mostly likely stood behind a wall listening to our discussion.

"Archie, Nadine. Nadine, Archie," I said. Archie bowed. "Please don't scare her more than she already is." Archie laughed with his mouthful, I cringed at seeing rice in his mouth, then his twin Adriel walked into the room.

JUDAS

They were almost identical, the only difference was that their personalities were polar opposites of each other—Archie was the sarcastic one. Currently they were wearing the same black suit, and had their brown hair styled the same way. Adriel didn't even bat an eyelash at Nadine as he came over to the desk and tapped my feet. I moved, and he grabbed the pile of paperwork that my feet were resting on.

"Adriel, we have a guest, introduce yourself," Archie said.

Adriel glanced at Nadine while flicking through paperwork. "Hello, outsider, you're not supposed to be down here," he said sternly and glanced at his brother and me.

"The Educators got her," I informed him. Adriel tensed up.

"Explains a lot," Adriel drawled. "Meeting Room Two, please," he instructed while reading information.

I pushed myself out of the chair and watched Nadine also stand up. We both walked down the corridor being monitored by Archie, who was still invested in eating his burrito.

Archie took some keys out of his pocket and unlocked Meeting Room Two. He opened the green door and escorted us in. The room had red brick walls like the entrance, false windows that projected a city skyline. I loved watching cars drive past like these were actual windows. In the middle was an enormous conference table and a projector screen on the back wall. Nadine gasped at the windows; she knew she was underground so it must be weird to see. I watched Archie place his burrito on the table then pull a chair out.

"Ma'am," he said. He showed her the chair as he picked up his burrito.

A few pieces of rice and beef had fallen onto the table, which he picked up and ate. I gave him a disgusted glance. Nadine sat down in the seat he had offered her, and because I was the hero in this situation I tried to sit in the seat opposite to hers.

"No. You sit over there." Archie pointed to a chair in the middle of the table on the same side as Nadine. "This space is reserved for moi, Taylor, and Carlos."

With a roll of my eyes, I sat down where he requested and waited.

Ten minutes later, the entire reason I had joined The Rebellion walked into the room. Carlos Peres—Zone 14's Rebellion Leader and my secret boyfriend of three years. Brown hair, tanned skin, and brown eyes with flecks of green. Handsome inside and out. I smiled at him as he made a bee line over to me. Closing my eyes as our lips met with a long awaited kiss, he had been away for the past three days after being assigned Task 1, getting back this morning in time for Task 105.

"Exsqueeze me, we are in a professional environment," Archie exclaimed.

I opened my eyes when Carlos pulled away, he flashed an apologetic smile as he ran his hands through his hair, then walked to his side of the table.

"Is it true Ramona Sanchez ridiculously outlawed your relationship, during the Great Massacre of Year One?" Nadine questioned with a furrowed brow.

Carlos looked up at her, then laughed. "And she's been killing homosexuals since." He leaned back in his seat, his smile faded to the point he looked sad. "Unfortunately, she hasn't figured out you can't kill how you're born."

Who was Ramona Sanchez? It only appeared to be Carlos and Nadine, who knew who she was. The curiosity intensified greatly.

"Who is Ramona Sanchez?" I finally asked.

"You don't know your own leader's name?" Nadine asked with a slight laugh, like my question was dumb.

"We're only allowed to call her Our Leader, Leader, things like that," Carlos interjected matter-of-factly.

The thought of being more brain washed than I realised terrified me more than anything else. I heard the door open; Taylor walked in, looking stressed and clutching a laptop. Taylor had bright-green hair shaved on the right side; she was beautiful with pale skin wearing a grey pencil dress. Nadine seemed to relax in Taylor's presence.

"Hello, I'm Taylor." She smiled at Nadine while she sat down, opening up the laptop and logged into whatever was on the screen.

I watched Nadine sink back into the chair and smiled as she nodded.

***

Nadine explained everything she told me back to the group. Once she was finished, everybody shifted in their seats, giving each other glances, clearly trying to figure out what to do without actually saying anything out loud. The scariest thing was not knowing if she was lying or being genuine about her story.

"Can you present me with some ID?" Carlos requested. Nadine obliged and handed over an identification card from inside her pocket, it was orange with a hidden phoenix which reflected in the lights. Carlos scooped it up and looked at it.

"Wow, the Olympia identification card is beautiful," Archie said as he looked over Carlos's shoulder in amazement.

"Can I also see your right arm?" Carlos further requested.

Nadine furrowed her brow, but obliged while rolling up her sleeve. I gasped to see her arm completely bare. My stomach tied in knots as Carlos took out a travel pack of baby wipes from the front pocket of his overalls. As he took a wipe out, he ran it along her arm where the barcode was supposed to be whilst gently holding Nadine's hand. As her arm just became shiny with moisture, it became even more obvious she was just like Taylor—Unlisted.

Carlos sucked in a breath, and ran a hand down his face. "What are we going to do?" he muttered.

"Treating her like any other Unlisted is an option," Taylor piped up. "If she chooses to become Listed, she could be a great asset in taking Our Leader down."

"What's Listed or Unlisted?" she questioned as she pulled her sleeve back down when Carlos let go of her hand.

I shifted in my seat, and looked at Carlos as he looked at me. Deep down I knew he was asking if we should show her, in return I nodded. Carlos looked at Adriel, giving Taylor a nudge, she glared at him but quickly understood what had to be done. All three of them rolled up their sleeves, Carlos and Adriel's barcodes on show—in comparison to Taylor's bare skin.

"The barcode is a legal requirement known as Listed, the fanciest of tattoo's. It's the only way you can survive above ground," Adriel explained, then pointed a finger in Taylor's direction. "Taylor's known as an Unlisted, if she leaves The Rebellion she faces execution—just like you."

Nadine gasped and placed a hand to her mouth. "So the gist of what you're saying is that I can never leave whatever this is. And I now have a choice whether or not to have one of those barcode things implanted on my body?" Everybody on the opposite side of the table nodded. She scoffed as she folded her arms over her chest. "Absolutely not. That's barbaric and fucked up in so many ways."

"At the end of the day it is your choice, and while you are in our country we'll work with you to get back home," Carlos explained. "You are more than safe down here."

Nadine looked at me, her eyes were glazed over like she was about to cry she shifted in her seat. Then she let out a breath.

"Fine. I'll think about it," she mumbled as she looked at everybody across the table. "Will I be supported no matter my choice?"

Everybody, including myself, nodded in response. Nobody would care if she chose to keep to herself and stay down here without getting Listed, The Rebellion was a sanctuary. Like Carlos said, the choice was entirely hers.

* * *

Thirty minutes later, in the dining hall of The Rebellion, I bit into a toasted BLT sandwich while sitting with Nadine. She flicked her red hair over her shoulder as she picked up a beef burger. I nervously checked my watch, 1 p.m.— six hours until curfew. Wiping crumbs off my overalls, I watched Nadine's eyes scan everybody, and then she looked at me.

"Explain to me Unlisted, if Listed is a legal requirement, how do the Unlisted exist?" she questioned as she sipped a fizzy drink through a straw.

I took another bite of my sandwich, and looked around the dining hall. Within this space it was clear who the Unlisted were amongst the Listed. Some of the Unlisted had brightly-coloured hair, piercings, tattoos, and the government uniform was non-existent. On the other hand the Listed were all plain looking, with natural hair colours and at this time of day they all wore the government uniform—just like me. However, in The Rebellion, we all lived in harmony.

"Most of the Unlisted exist because they were made orphans before the age of ten, enlistment age. On occasion, The Rebellion rescues these children from extermination camps. Have you heard of those?" I stopped to clear my throat, Nadine slowly nodded as she ate. "These children are then raised in The Rebellion, and then at eighteen they have the same choice you currently have. Some of the other Unlisted exist because they were born down here. And you're new to the mix because you're the first person to be rescued from The Educators." I explained.

Nadine narrowed her eyes at me, and sat back in her seat. "You've mentioned The Educators twice now, and I have no idea who they are," she admitted as she took another drink.

"From what I've heard, The Educators are guards in our country permitted to travel overseas, and they get paid to kidnap people then drag them into any of the eighteen Zones to be murdered. Those unfortunate people are used to educate us on why it's not a good idea to defy the regime," I explained. Nadine's eyes widened, and she stiffened.

"So basically, hitmen?" she questioned.

"What's that?"

"Basically what you are describing is a hitman, somebody actually paid for me to be sent into Denmé to die." She scowled. "Fucking asshole."

I took another bite of my sandwich, still puzzled on her language. She never actually explained what *hitman* or *hitmen* meant, my guess was as good as anybody's. As I decided to drop the subject of finding out what those words meant, I also decided to focus on my lunch and people watch.

Even though I loved The Rebellion, there was a deep ache of guilt about how much better I felt down here. I could be myself and not feel any fear. Could I do what many other Listed people have done and permanently move down here? I never really considered it.

The feeling of hands massaging my shoulders pulled me out of my head, I looked up to Carlos.

"Babe, have you set up accommodations for Nadine?" I asked, taking a sip of my own drink. His hands were sturdy, but they felt amazing on my tense spine.

"Yes, I just gave her the keys while you were in dream land," he said. I could hear the smile in his voice. "So, Nadine. After 7 p.m. we usually won't be down here. If you need anything, Taylor is in Apartment 2A; she's the person in charge after curfew," Carlos explained. She nodded with understanding.

There was something deep within me which hoped Nadine would choose to be Listed in the near future. Just so she could see how desperate everybody was for an escape

3

Nadine

My newly assigned apartment wasn't anything special. It was a small room with a kitchenette to my right, and a single sofa bed to my left which complimented a small flat-screen TV mounted to the wall. It at least smelled clean. As I stood by the wall, I watched as Taylor made my bed, despite being perfectly capable to do the task on my own. On the other hand, Adriel was crouched in front of my open mini fridge and helped fill up its shelves from a grocery bag he carried in here. With a sigh, I slid down the wall and sat on the floor with a thud, Adriel glanced behind his shoulder.

"So, The Educators," I started, Adriel made a noise and Taylor glanced at me. "How do you know they exist if I'm the first one to be rescued?"

Taylor shook a pillow into its casing with a smile. "The Listed who are in The Rebellion see them, people like you, who look out of place. But, it's either too dangerous to approach them or in the small circumstances when it is safe, it's already too late," she explained.

I glanced at Adriel who stayed silent as he listened to our discussion. "So, if it's like a hitman situation as Judas explained, who would hate me so much to call them? My family wouldn't. I only have one friend,"

NADINE

I exclaimed.

Adriel stood up, turned around and leaned on the counter. "What's a hitman?" he asked, drumming his fingers on the counter.

"Basically, you call somebody and pay them to murder another person," Taylor explained for me as she finished on the bed, and smoothed out the comforter.

"Well that's exactly how The Educators work. Except they bring you to this country, and you're murdered for being Unlisted." He returned to stocking up the kitchen. "How did you know you were not in Olympia anymore?"

"I could hear the men talking, and then they hid me under a tarp at the border. It was kind of obvious at that point," I admitted. Knowing the question was an obvious test to see if I was bullshitting my story.

Taylor gave him a warning look as he finished on the kitchen. With a sigh, Adriel grabbed another bag he carried in here and dropped it at my feet, then he produced two different cards out of his pocket. One was a white card, *Zone 14 Rebellion I.D* was written across the top, the other was a green bank card—*Bank of The Rebellion*—was written across the design.

"Carry the ID on you at all times unless you choose to be Listed; if you lose it you're fucked. This does not leave The Rebellion under any circumstances," he said sternly before giving it to me. "Then the bank card has enough to allow you to buy all the necessities to make life comfortable down here. Again, does not leave The Rebellion under any circumstances." Adriel handed it to me, then stood up and started to approach the exit, glancing behind his shoulder to see if Taylor followed him.

Curiosity got the better of me, and I pulled the bag closer to me. Inside I saw some fabric which smelled of vanilla and a cellphone. "Hey, what's this?" I asked.

"I gave you some clothes, and an old phone. You can access the intranet on it to the pass the time, and use the intranet to call or text people," Taylor explained.

"Wait, you guys have the internet?" I raised an eyebrow.

"Intranet," she corrected. "Only way to have access to such technology without detection, same with our electricity; those are solar panel windows from our above ground facilities."

Adriel came back into the room. "You're saying too much," he warned, Taylor's eyes widened at his abrupt attitude. "Nadine, you should sleep, if you leave The Rebellion you're on your own. We have cameras so we will know your movements."

I scoffed at his attitude. Clearly Adriel didn't like me too much. As I heard the front door shut, I pushed myself off the floor and looked around this tiny apartment. Even though this was to be my home for the foreseeable future, I didn't think this would ever truly be classed as a home.

* * *

After I had walked for what seemed like hours, I had found my way to a large dome structure with a floating walkway. With a sigh I sat on the edge, my legs dangling from the platform, and powered up the cellphone Taylor got me. I looked around, realising the dome was a giant screen depicting the galaxy, there were even shooting stars, The Rebellion amazed me at their ingenuity to make the Unlisted comfortable.

Once the phone was powered on, I sucked in a breath and moved it around in my hand. What could this thing do? As I got to the contacts, I dialled in my parents phone number, just to reassure them I was safe. Since Adriel and Taylor left me in my apartment, nobody had bothered to check on me.

I pressed the phone to my ear, and waited for the call to go through while rubbing a hand on my thigh, I didn't know why I was so nervous. There was a weird static noise at first, and then a loud beeping. A lump formed in my throat, and I looked at the phone, it became blurry from tears clouding my vision. I wiped them away, and tried again. The same result, just that loud beeping.

Taylor said something about using the intranet to call or text people, what even was the intranet? Eventually I found out after some research. The results made me want to throw the phone across this weird room I was in, but I didn't. It turns out the intranet was a form of internet which was centrally connected to somewhere in The Rebellion and heavily monitored—no wonder ringing my parents didn't work. I also knew from years of school most technology was banned everywhere else in Denmé. Eventually, I rested my arms on the hand rail of the platform, buried my head in them and broke down crying.

* * *

The Rebellion was a labyrinth of corridors, judging by the hours of walking and discovering how large this underground world truly was, it was evident this place was nothing new to Denmé. So far, I had found a high school which was a huge section of corridor with false windows displaying student artwork, there was another huge section of a different corridor dedicated to the gym with two way mirrors showing all the equipment inside. I had also found a movie theatre, which was just a set of double doors with a neon sign on top.

I stopped at a metal door with a sign above it—Tunnel 14:9. What did that mean? Adriel's warning earlier made me reluctant to open it. Yet, curiosity got the better of me, and I grabbed the handle. I pushed it down, thankful that it gave. Motion activated lights flickered down yet another corridor, unlike the others I had encountered thus far, this one was dirt. Jesus, all these corridors were going to drive me insane.

Sucking in a breath, I took a step forward.

If this did lead me outside, I had come to terms with the fact that I would be on my own as I walked to the other end, where I was met with another metal door. Before even opening the door I knew it would lead to another corridor. Maybe being Listed wasn't so bad, just so I didn't feel so trapped—it was my first day here, and the fact I was already having these thoughts scared me. With a sigh I opened the door, and my eyes widened.

There was literally an underground highway, there was a concrete walk way on either side leading to hundreds of doors, with bridges cutting across the road. Holy shit, this was literally amazing. The ceiling was concrete dirt, I expected those weird screens pretending to be windows or something else instead. As I stepped onto the walk way, I watched the cars zoom past, they must have all been electric—surely—everybody would be dead if they were running on gas.

"You look lost; are you okay?" I turned my head to see a woman with chin-length hair, the right side purple, the other black. It scared me how I already knew she was Unlisted from this small detail.

"How do I get back to the apartments?" I asked.

The woman's eyes lit up. "Oh, you're the girl rescued from The Educators!" I forced a smile and nodded. "Well, I'm Lilith, nice to meet you."

"Nadine, nice to meet you too," I replied.

"Get your phone out and create a new note," she instructed. I quickly did as told, and got ready for her next instructions. "Now, tunnels to remember: 14:7—apartments, 14:8—convenience store, 14:2—food court, 14:12A—supermarket, 14:14—the mall," Lilith said slowly enough for me to understand.

Taking all this information down, I smiled. "Thank you so much. Adriel didn't explain the tunnels, he thought I needed sleep."

Lilith nodded with a smile, then disappeared into Tunnel 14:9 where I had just come from. This was like a hidden world, like a really well-hidden world.

* * *

I knew it was a bad idea to take a detour to the convenience store, but after today, I needed to eat and drink my feelings. Half the bottle of champagne was gone by the time I made it back to the apartment, and I was already crying. I just felt empty, and disconnected from everything.

Unlocking my apartment door, I stumbled into the space, and fumbled for the light as I kicked the door closed.

While walking toward the kitchenette, I took another gulp of wine as I threw a bag of fried chicken onto the bed. I start looking through the cupboards for a pan. *Bingo.* The first cupboard underneath the sink. I filled it with water, then placed it on the single burner and turned it on. I tore into the bag of ramen and poured in the flavour packet, then the noodles.

It took exactly five minutes to cook, and I brought the steaming pan up to my bedside table. Burying my fork into the pan, I sobbed as I ate the rubber tasting noodles while drinking my wine. Honestly, not my proudest moment. The lump in my throat made it hard to swallow anything. With each bite, I kept my hair out of my face. Shaking a piece of fried chicken out of the bag next to me, I ate that too.

How could my life go downhill so quickly? Who rang The Educators on me?

I felt indebted to Judas for rescuing me from them, and I didn't know what to do to repay him. Taylor's words saying I could be a *great asset in taking Our Leader down* echoed around my head as I stared at the kitchenette while eating mechanically. Back at home, in Olympia, I was a nobody. Yet in Denmé they had a sense of hope I could help them regain their freedom. I could be somebody in this country.

I was just a twenty-one year old, the thought of trying to help my saviours regain freedom was completely ridiculous. But something was telling me to at least try, even if it failed.

4

Judas

I held down the trash can as my sister, Gabrielle, shook out the almost full trash bag. She threw it on the ever-growing pile. We were both on Main, checked in for Task 15, one of the most disgusting tasks of them all. In this light, Gabrielle looked mostly like our mum, even though Mum's eyes were green instead of brown. Taking out a fresh trash bag from my overalls, I handed it to my sister and watched her pull it over the metal cylinder. I stepped back as she threw the cover back on.

"Have you heard the latest gossip?" Gabrielle asked, I shook my head. "There's a Zone 8 transfer running around Zone 14, never checked in to get her number changed," she explained in a hushed voice as we walked to the next trash can.

This one smelled rancid. We both covered our noses, and I did everything to not retch. It smelled like sewage, with a hint of mouldy cheese, and sweaty feet.

"Do this one quick," I instructed while cringing.

Gabrielle nodded, as I quickly took the cover off and closed the bag throwing it onto the pile. There's a reason why I, and many others despised Task 15 with a passion.

"Actually, I was part of that," I admitted getting back to the topic of gossiping. Gabrielle looked at me. "Yeah, the guards told me to take her to another set of guards."

"Did you?" Gabrielle asked as she put a fresh bag into the rancid trash can, which still smelled like mouldy cheese.

"Of course," I lied. "However, she was unconscious and hard to carry, so I left her on a bench where guards could see her." Gabrielle gasped, and covered her mouth.

I threw the cover back onto the mouldy trash can, and we started walking next to the next one on Main. Gabrielle was silent for a few moments.

"You did the right thing," she finally said. "I wonder what she did for Our Leader to authorise her to be unconscious during Zone transfer." I shrugged.

Most the time, it was difficult to image Gabrielle being only sixteen years old, almost as old as the regime itself. Yet she was so level headed and independent. As much as I wanted to, I couldn't tell her the guards kidnapped the person in question over blood money. Gabrielle thought Our Leader was too grand. It was sad to see.

Zone transfers were the only good thing Our Leader realistically did, these people had done petty crimes which weren't enough to render them into extermination camps. So she moved them to another Zone to redeem themselves, usually they always came on the supply trains which ran through town on a weekly basis.

* * *

Putting a mop into a bucket of warm, soapy water, I rinsed out the excess by leaning onto the handle in the strainer section. Once satisfied, I put the mop on the ancient wooden floors of the courthouse and cleaned in a side to side motion; the floors shined. Funnily enough,

JUDAS

I liked Task 12; cleaning the courthouse let me think. The smell of bleach was also getting rid of the garbage smell that had accumulated on my clothes.

I stiffened when I heard the familiar wheezing sound which only came from Godfrey McRitchie, Zone 14's Director. He was so fat he could only walk small distances, and needed a custom-made wheelchair to cart him around most places. As I looked over the banister, I was surprised to see him wheezing up the stairs in an ill-fitted grey suit.

Next to him was Zone 16's Director, Alora Thripp, she had wispy grey hair and wore a green dress.

Deciding to focus back on Task 12, I continued to fixate on the floor and make it gleam with water. Only stopping when I put my lips into a straight line as Godfrey McRitchie and Alora Thripp walked through my freshly cleaned floor—Alora left footprints behind, and I tried not laughing at the trail Godfrey left behind, due to his pants dragging on the ground.

"Be careful, Alora," Godfrey wheezed out. "The help is being a nuisance again."

I watched them both disappear into a nearby meeting room.

Dipping the mop into the bucket, I scoffed out of disgust. I pushed my black hair out of my face and shook my head as I squeezed out the excess. How dare Godfrey refer to me as *the help* to Alora Thripp. Pompous asshole. Least I don't have three grey hairs that stick up like they're constantly being rubbed by a balloon.

Throwing the mop back on the floor, I got rid of the footprints to curb my anger.

* * *

That night I was in Carlos's Rebellion apartment, my neck rested on his arm, and I could feel the weight of his other arm around me, our fingers intertwined. His breath was warm on the back of my neck, and his chin felt rough against it. He breathed calmly through sleep.

But I was awake to the sound of movement in the apartment, and I stiffened. My heart rate increased—the sound was coming from the kitchen.

Was it a ghost? I mean, the underground tunnels of The Rebellion were abandoned coal mines which the organisation reinforced with concrete, so it was plausible they were haunted.

I heard more movement, and I squeezed my eyes shut. How could Carlos not hear this?

When I felt a hand on my shoulder that wasn't Carlos, I jumped, he finally stirred after feeling me move.

"Judas," a familiar voice whispered. "Judas, wake up."

Just as I was about to open my eyes, the lights turned on, blinding me. Even the weight of Carlos's arm lifted as he became more awake, and pulled his other arm out from under me.

Sitting up, I saw Daisuke Kim, Zone 18's Rebellion Leader, standing at the foot of the bed wearing government uniform with his arms folded. He had shoulder-length black hair, and a chiselled facial structure. Then I looked at the person next to me—Ezekiel Kenwood—the Head of The Rebellion because of his position in Zone 7, The Capital. His dark brown skin really made his crystal blue eyes pop.

"What the fuck is this?" I heard Carlos groan, then he sat up.

"Emergency meeting about Nadine Ellis, everybody is in Zone 14's auditorium," Ezekiel responded.

"What time is it?" I asked, sitting up with Carlos.

"It's 3:30 a.m.," Daisuke informed me.

"Are you fucking serious?" Carlos spat out as he rubbed his eyes, then moved his brown hair about. He looked more tanned in this light. "Fine."

JUDAS

***

I sat at the back of the auditorium. Realistically, I wasn't supposed to be here because I wasn't a Leader. But Ezekiel insisted I had to be present for meetings lately—even before Nadine came into the picture. My eyes were still heavy from sleep, and I yawned, watching Ezekiel write ideas on how to get Nadine home on a whiteboard while I rested my head on Carlos's shoulder.

One of the popular suggestions was a boat from either Zone Six or Eight, proposed by Lake Boston from Zone 15—the guy in the front row built like a bull. There were six others who liked this idea, especially Sung-Jin Lee from Zone 11—the half asleep guy in the first row, and Thora Paxton from Zone 9—the woman next to Lake with blonde dreadlocks sharpening a knife.

My gaze fell upon the creepiest of the bunch—Samhain Roach from Zone 13. He always wore a black cloak with a goat skull on his head. Currently he had his feet on the chair in front, watching the discussion, then he suddenly raised his hand.

"Yes, Samhain," Ezekiel said with a forced smile.

"Let them have her."

Ezekiel's jaw tensed. "The whole purpose of this meeting is to get Nadine back to Olympia, not get her murdered."

"Fine," Samhain replied sternly. "Fly her over Olympia, then let fate decide if she lives. It'll be a much quicker, and far less painful death than from the war that's going to happen once she returns home."

The whole auditorium fell silent, even I stiffened at hearing him say this, Ezekiel's jaw fell open as he dropped the dry erase marker in his hand. Everybody had turned to look at him.

"What the actual fuck is wrong with you?" Armani Tuscon from Zone 10 spat.

Samhain was silent as he crossed his ankles. I knew for certain he was a sociopath. Other Rebellion Leaders told me he had so many mental health issues, from the trauma of an extermination camp, that he was deemed a lost cause.

"Joseph should keep an eye on his brother," Samhain continued, I lifted my head off of Carlos's shoulder and stiffened. "Both his brother and Nadine will help the fall of Denmé and St. Herculia will rise again."

All eyes were now on me. I hadn't spoken to Samhain enough to warrant him knowing I had a brother. Shifting uncomfortably in my seat, I moved my hair out of my face.

"Don't bring my brother into this, he wouldn't do that," I spat out.

Samahin laughed, and it sent chills down my spine.

"Let's go back to the meeting, thank you Samhain, for your input," Ezekiel announced with hesitation as he picked up the dry erase marker he dropped.

Either way, Ezekiel wrote down *parachute*, then waited for any other input from the team. So far, out of nineteen people to give suggestions, there were eleven on the board. Though some were good, others were a huge optimistic mess which would get The Rebellion discovered. All the Leaders would need to vote soon, causing butterflies to flutter in my stomach.

I was honestly terrified of Samhain's warning. I wanted to know what he meant about my brother, and what the hell was St. Herculia.

5

Judas

My head pounded from the lack of sleep last night. I yawned as I pushed the shopping cart full of new stock down the aisle of the grocery store, clipboard in hand, looking at the inventory. Going down the dairy aisle, I saw the milk was out of stock. Placing the clipboard down on a box of cookies, I picked up the crate of glass milk bottles and placed them in the fridge.

Seeing my clipboard get lifted up, I looked up to see Carlos standing there looking at the inventory, his brown hair messy.

"Are you on Task 5 as well?" I asked. He nodded as he read the clipboard.

"They've decided on The Tunnels," Carlos whispered into my ear. My eyes widened.

The Tunnels were part of The Rebellion, it was a corridor of doors along a series of secret underground highways, and there was an exit to Olympia through Zone 7 and 4. It was heavily guarded by the importers though.

"Oh," I said, smiling at him.

Carlos picked up a crate of yogurts and pushed them into the fridge. The sound of steel-toe boots approaching made me look up to the guard who patrolled Task 5. I glanced at Carlos as his eyes widened, and he stiffed at the sight of them.

"ID 498763, please come with me." I looked at Carlos out of confusion.

"What about ID 494011?" I asked.

"We need to question *you*, ID 498763," the guard announced. My stomach twisted in a sickening knot.

I reluctantly followed the guard while exhaling a breath, glancing behind at Carlos, seeing his throat bob as he swallowed. The guard escorted me out the shop entrance and towards a black car that was parked out front. I could just make out another guard through its tinted windows.

* * *

A hard fist slammed into my mouth, and my head shot painfully backwards. Pain surged through my face, and I tasted the metallic flavour of blood. Wiping my mouth with the back of my hand, it was streaked red just like the guys knuckles, but whether it was my blood or his was anybody's guess. The whole room was spinning, and as the guard paced the room, it was difficult to focus on him.

I knew we were in a brick building inside a field somewhere, evidenced by the smell of cow shit, the farm tools on the wall next to a well, and the concrete floor covered in hay. The smell of shit congealed with the guards cigarette and red wine scent, which made my stomach churn.

"So, ID 498763, where is she?" he asked, stroking his chin.

"Who?" I groaned.

The guard laughed, and licked his lower lip. He stopped in front of me as he unbuckled his belt, and wrapped it around his hand.

"That girl we told you to place in a crowded location!" he shouted, looking like a mad man as his hands trembled while scratching his chin. "There's a lot of money riding on her."

"I did as told," I lied.

The belt came flying at my face, and then the pain struck me. I screamed out and held my face protectively. When the belt hit my back, I screamed out again and groaned.

"Oh, really? Or were you too busy fucking your boyfriend?" The guard approached me, getting so close to my face I could feel his breath on my lips.

"What?" I gasped out of shock, looking into his eyes.

The guard suddenly kissed me with force, I tried to pull myself back but he kept my head in place. My stomach churned as the taste of fish and cigarettes filled my mouth. When he pulled away, I retched until I threw up, then I looked at the guard while breathing heavy—my hands now trembled as I gripped the seat.

"What's the difference between me and ID 494011? I see the way you look at him."

I wiped my mouth, tears now rolled down my cheek as I stayed silent while looking at the guard.

"There is nothing going on with me and ID 494011," I lied. "You're disgusting, I could report you for what you just did."

My head jolted painfully back as he punched me in the nose. I touched my nose, which was also bleeding, a groan escaped my lips.

"Report me, and we'll see where that gets you," the guard snarled, he gripped my chin and ran a thumb against my lips, the creep was giving me a sultry look. "What do you do with ID 494011 behind closed doors?"

I spied the gun in its holster on his other belt, the urge to grab it was getting stronger by the second. He was making my blood boil with anger. When the guard leaned down, and started to kiss my neck, that was the final straw.

With a quick thrust of my knee into his crotch, he slumped forward on me with a groan, and I grabbed the gun. A quick punch in his neck got him off me so I could stand up, the gun tightened in my grip as I breathed heavily. The guard righted himself, then held his hands up; when he took one step towards me, I shot him in the knee.

"Mother fucker," he groaned out as he fell back to the ground.

"Swearing is also illegal," I shot him in the other knee, and he cried out. "Want to break anymore laws?"

The guard was panting as he looked at me, holding both his knees, it gave me a strange satisfaction to see blood flowing between his fingers. I quickly aimed the gun, and shot him in the chest. The guard was dead instantly.

I dropped the gun, and instantly approached the guard. My hands trembled as the reality of what I just did hit me. Oh God, I was in major trouble. If anybody I didn't trust found out about this, I'd be thrown in an extermination camp and executed instantly. Seeing the amount of blood flowing out of his body made me realise how much of a bitch this would be to cover up. Swallowing hard, I grabbed him by the ankles and dragged him over to the well. When his body was slumped over the edge, I pocketed the keys which hung from one of his belt loops. Then I pushed him all the way over. As the sound of him the bottom echoed through the air, a warmth of pleasure ran through me.

Eventually I found some cleaning products in this building which I used to clean up what I could of the blood, and threw the gun in the well. The blood I couldn't clean up I used excess hay. Now was the part I had to plan out my escape. I looked around, there were bars on the only window in this place so that escape route was out of the question, instead I approached the door and tried the handle—as suspected it was locked. Shaking the keys out of my overalls, there was so many keys on the key chain I didn't know which one would let me out of this place, but I tried every single one until the door let me.

As I ran across the field towards the black SUV which brought me here, I now had to figure out how to discard the car where nobody would look. Then get the taste of the guard out of my mouth, I shuddered thinking back to what he did to me.

* * *

Everybody was staring at me as I walked down Main an hour later. I had already brushed my mouth so many times but nothing could get rid of the fish and tobacco taste, it took everything not to throw up again. My head was still pounding, and there was ringing in my ears. I glanced behind my shoulder in case anybody was watching, when I turned back around the one person I didn't want to see right now stepped out of a nearby store—my brother, Michael.

"Joseph," he said with a smile of relief at first, then it faded. "What happened?"

Both of us looked almost the same, in terms of our our chiselled facial structure and slightly upturned nose. However he inherited mums brown hair, and was lanky whilst looking more child like.

"Guards," was all I could muster up the courage to say.

Michael continued to scan me up and down, I avoided his burning stare by looking across the street at people completing Task 90.

"Where's Carlos?" I finally asked, just to change the subject.

"Oh. He was just in the canteen," Michael responded, but his voice was delayed. His eyes narrowed afterwards.

"Do I look at him a certain way?" I asked. I kicked myself; I was asking too many questions. Maybe he knew I was homosexual and would turn me in to the guards.

"No, you don't." He scratched the back of his neck. "I have to get back to Task 14 though," Michael answered, then hurried off.

I stayed in the street looking around for guards. Then I remembered I had to complete Task 10. Which was fucking ironic, going to a church within an hour of murdering somebody, but this time, I was going to church to maintain it. Not to confess my sins.

* * *

There were two arm cuffs in the narthex of the church. One said *Task 10* the other said *Task 105*; I sighed as I put my arm through the Task 10 one.

With a flash of green, I entered the church. It smelled musty and staring at me was the giant Jesus on a crucifix. The statue was a beautiful bronze, with two other statues at the base kneeled down in prayer, the story it portrayed was of sorrow. I bowed to the statue due to how badly I screwed up today. *Forgive me Father, for I have sinned.* Then the sound of steel toe boots on wood got louder, when I turned my head a guard was standing next to me.

"ID 498763, welcome," the guard said. His voice echoed around the tranquillity of the church, cutting through the chorus of metal hammers on nails. "The questioning must have gone very well this morning," the guard gave me a menacing smile.

"Yes, sir, they were satisfied with my response," I lied.

"The organ needs polishing," the guard said, pointing to a pile of supplies near a pew. He laughed as he walked away.

I felt delirious, but that was maybe from being beaten up. The guards now scared me more than ever, and I felt like I was walking on thin ice if I breathed wrong, I hoped they never found out I killed one of them.

* * *

From the roof of my apartment block, a dilapidated old warehouse building, I could see the entire town of Newton—Zone 14. The green coniferous trees blended in with the orange, red, and yellows of the deciduous trees. It looked like a maze to neighbourhoods, downtown, and the highway to other towns.

When I heard the rooftop door open, I turned around to Carlos; he ran, and threw his arms around me. I held him tightly, and gripped his white T-shirt and broke down crying, as the familiar strong scent of his aftershave filled the air.

"I'm here," he whispered into my ear. "I got your note."

I squeezed my eyes shut, and choked on tears. Not wanting to let him go. "I had to kill a guard today," I admitted through a whisper.

Admitting it out loud was a huge relief, which made me sigh. Yet, Carlos pulled away from our embrace, his brown eyes with flecks of green glowed in the sunset. He looked stern, and scared.

"You did what?" he asked.

Wiping my eyes with the back of my hand, I winced in pain from the black eye forming. But I nodded, his hands returned to my waist. "I had to, he kept kissing me, and he strangely knew about us."

"Jesus Christ, Joseph," Carlos spat. He let go of me once more, pacing the rooftop with his hands on his hips. I laughed at the religious significance with my name, paired with Jesus Christ. Something I had read about in The Bible during Task 105 as a child. "This isn't funny! You're a dead man walking."

"Not if they find out," I admitted, exhaling a breath.

Carlos looked at me as he sighed heavily, then he squeezed his eyes shut while rubbing the bridge of his nose. I wanted to know what was going through his head, instead he pulled me back into his embrace and held me tightly. I relaxed all over again.

"Well this is something I didn't expect to see."

My eyes widened at the voice, and I turned my head towards it,

Michael stood by the door—leaning against the red brick. Carlos pushed me away quickly and turned toward my brother, his throat bobbed as he swallowed air, I noticed his breathing became heavy.

"How long have you been standing there?" I asked, my voice wavered.

Michael shifted, as he folded his arms. "Long enough." He smiled. "How does being a homosexual work?"

I looked at the sky, then at Carlos as he scoffed and looked at my brother, he ran a hand through his hair out of nervous habit; like he always did above ground.

"Hugging does not equal homosexuality," Carlos reminded him.

My brother looked at us both, his eyes widening with revelation. "I just assumed, because I've only ever seen a hug like that from married couples."

"Keep your nose out of it," Carlos snapped.

Michael changed the subject, and made everything a million times worse when he asked. "So, what did it feel like to kill a guard?"

I had no idea how to possibly answer my brother. Knowing full well that anything outside of Our Leader's regime was foreign to him, he didn't understand the world like me and Carlos did. But now Michael knew what I was, and what I did more than two hours ago, I was even more terrified of him than the guards.

6

Nadine

The large dome structure with the floating walkway, which I had found during my first night in The Rebellion, was something nicknamed The Pit. As I sat to the right of Judas, with Taylor on his left, he looked troubled and beat up as he hung his beer bottle between his index finger and thumb into the abyss below us. The air around us smelling of that weird smell in a kids play centre.

"I had to kill somebody today," Judas finally admitted.

I turned to look at him with a raised eyebrow, even Taylor leaned forward to do the same. Pressing my beer bottle to my mouth, I took a large gulp of the bitter liquid.

"Please tell me you killed a snail while doing one of the tasks," Taylor exclaimed as she picked at the frayed fabric on her ripped jeans.

Judas shook his head. "Nope. One of the guards pissed me off, so I shot him then threw him down a well."

I saw the spray of beer as Taylor spat her drink out, now the room smelled like a weird concoction of a kids play centre and beer—it wasn't a good combo. My stomach tied in knots, and I looked at Judas. Even if I barely knew him, I knew him enough to know this was out of character, if this was truly a part of his personality I'd be wherever

The Educators wanted me.

"Is this a first?" I managed to ask.

"Yep." He looked at his hands, then took a drink.

"The first one's always the hardest," Taylor said. I leaned forward to look at her. "I'm just saying." She threw her arms up defensively.

Judas laughed and looked at Taylor, she smiled at him then leaned back on her hands staring at the night sky around us.

My mind suddenly wandered to all the corridors in The Rebellion which were slowly driving me mad, I sucked in a breath. "What is above ground?"

"Hell," Taylor responded with a smile when I looked at her.

I glanced at Judas when I heard him snort then chuckle silently. Taylor threw her head back and laughed.

"You know, I might tell Carlos I'll do it," I announced stupidly. Then I looked at Judas who's face had turned to stone. "I'm going to get Listed."

* * *

It'd been two days and entire move to Zone 7 since I had decided to become Listed. My heart beat thumped rapidly as I followed an extremely handsome man named Ezekiel through the underground highway—he had told me there were multiple highways like this one which was named Highway 8. The ceiling of Zone 7's Highway 8 was exceptionally beautiful, decorated in an ornate mosaic mermaid with fish and what appeared to be water, each door to each individual tunnel was encased in a marble arch. What caught my attention was at the end of Highway 8 was a giant sheet of metal which blocked off the end of the corridor, there was a line down the middle of it which signified it was some kind of giant door, and even stranger was a normal sized door welded into the interior of the left side.

"What's through there?" I asked Ezekiel, pointing to it.

His crystal blue eyes didn't match his dark complexion, but he pulled them off. Ezekiel sucked in a breath. "Olympia," he responded.

"If I'm that close, why can't I just go home?"

Ezekiel scoffed. "I would love more than anything to allow you through there, but it's guarded by the Importers, you have to gain their trust and have a worthy enough reason to leave." He sucked in a breath. "Though you have a worthy enough reason to leave, they don't trust you."

Well that sucks.

Ezekiel opened a door labelled 7:5, and lights came on.

"Ladies first," he said, holding the door open for me. "To the infirmary."

I stepped forward into the tunnel.

* * *

Right in front of me in the examination room was this arm cuff contraption. It flashed different colours: red, green, and purple. My throat went dry, and I looked at Ezekiel, who leaned against the cupboards. He was in the same overalls and white T-shirt I'd seen all the Listed wear, dreadlocks fell past his shoulders. I sat on the uncomfortable bed, trying to get comfy.

A nurse came into the room wearing a white coat and green scrubs, she had a face mask on and gloves. She was carrying a bag that read *Etonox Pain Relief* on it. My heart skipped a beat. What the fuck was I getting myself into—did I just make a horrible mistake?

"Okay, Nadine Ellis?" she asked, reading from a computer tablet. "After this procedure, your new name will be Bethany Gladstone, ID

005718."

I exhaled a breath as she placed the bag next to me then handed me a pipe hooked up to whatever was inside. I held it in my right hand at first.

"Best to hold it in your left hand," Ezekiel pointed out. I nodded and switched.

The nurse sat behind a computer and typed in information. "When you're ready, insert your arm into the cuff."

I hesitated as I put my arm through the flashing device. With a whoosh, it clamped down on my arm like a Venus fly trap. I sucked in a breath, wincing at the discomfort.

"I'm going to start," the nurse said.

She hit a button on her computer. Then it started.

Instantly, the device became warm against my skin to the point it felt like I had just shoved my arm into an oven at 400 Fahrenheit. The pain was so immense that I was screaming as my heart hammered in my chest, the device whooshed while it worked its *magic* on my arm, tears were rolling down my cheeks. If everybody had to be awake for this procedure, it was an utterly barbaric experience citizens had to endure which textbooks conveniently left out. As I started sucking in the pain relief like my life depended on it, I realised it only took the edge off, throwing it one side I tried to breath through it. Why did I decide to do this? Why didn't I ask how they made people Listed?

"Stop!" I yelled to the nurse. "Please, I can't take it anymore."

The nurse looked up from her computer. "Once the process has begun, it can't be stopped," the nurse informed me.

I arched my back and screamed even louder when the device started making a spurting noise and I lost all the feeling in my hand. The dull feeling of warm liquid being pumped into my very obvious burn made me start trembling, my stomach rolled and I wanted to throw up.

When it released me, I cried out and looked at my arm which was bright red with bits of skin lifted up and there it was the barcode. I curled up on the bed, and held my arm out, while I sobbed. The wound was still burning furiously from the experience.

"That's it, it's over now," Ezekiel announced.

I looked up when the nurse pushed herself away from the computer, she approached me with a green box of something. My eyes felt very heavy, and a dizziness washed over me as my body started to feel like a dead weight. Everything went black.

* * *

That evening I was curled up in bed in my Zone 7 apartment, tears streamed down my face as my arm stilled burned furiously from the Listing process. So far it came in waves of discomfort, and my whole body shook while trying to heal as the pain medication wore off. A knock at the door made me glance up, but I felt too weak to move.

"Nadine, are you in there?" It was Ezekiel, which gave me some comfort that he took it upon himself to check up on me.

"Yeah." My voice came out small and weak. Not loud enough for Ezekiel to hear me.

I tensed up when I heard a key slide into the lock, wondering who was letting themselves into my space. But as the light from the corridor flooded into the apartment, a dark shadow came into view before being plunged into darkness again. Footsteps echoed around my space, and they entered the bathroom, I heard the clink as the pull string hit the tiles then white light cut through the darkness. Ezekiel came into view with flowers.

"How are you feeling?" he asked, looking concerned. I shrugged, as he reached down and placed the back of his hand on my forehead. "You're burning up," Ezekiel pointed out as he sat on the end of my bed. The flowers in his hand were all different shades of pink and purple.

"Put them in the sink with water," I instructed.

Ezekiel stood up, and started filling the kitchenette sink with water. Once he was satisfied with the water level, he placed the flowers in there.

"I think we should get out of this apartment, and cool you off a bit," Ezekiel suddenly proposed as he leaned against the kitchen counter. "Like getting out of The Rebellion, for instance."

My heart instantly started racing when he approached me, and took my hand to help me sit up. "Where are we going?" I questioned.

"It's a surprise," Ezekiel answered with a smile, as he slipped my shoes on my feet for me. What a gentleman.

Ezekiel helped me stand up; I wrapped the beige cardigan tightly around me. It was the warmest thing Taylor had given me before leaving Zone 14. Then I let Ezekiel guide me to the *surprise* location, no matter how nervous I felt. Adriel had told me if Ezekiel was leading me out of The Rebellion for any reason, then it most probably meant he was taking me to my execution. But would Ezekiel do such a thing?

* * *

At the top of the ladder I realised I was on the roof of an abandoned sports facility, which sat on the outskirts of an ancient city. The night air was cold, which made me tighten my cardigan around my body for some warmth. Golden lights were corridors to neighbourhoods which led to a castle on a hill, the town appeared to be sleeping and peaceful in a sadistic way. I instantly recognised this was Zone 7 from the news reports growing up.

"Adriel told me if you led me out of The Rebellion, then you'd kill me," I admitted, looking at my feet.

NADINE

I looked up when Ezekiel started laughing. "Come on," he said as he wrapped an arm around me and guided me to a spot near the edge of the roof where we both sat next to each other. "If you're embarrassed about looking like shit, every Unlisted who's gone through the process has looked just like you afterwards."

"Shouldn't you be in your government house?" I asked as I scoffed out a smile, and looked at my heavily bandaged arm.

"Yeah, but the process messes with your head. I know Hunter wouldn't have the decency to check up on you," Ezekiel explained.

I nodded, and pushed my hair behind my ear; it still smelled like hair dye chemicals from when they dyed my hair brown and gave me a government approved hairstyle. Once my teeth started chattering from the cold, Ezekiel took his jacket off and wrapped it around my shoulders. Eventually he pulled me in close, it felt weird considering I had only known him for two days, but I craved the comfort.

"How do the Zones work?" I asked, feeling his hand lazily stroke my arm.

"They're just to keep track of our ID numbers, and cage us in. Only Zone 7 has differences in tasks with it being the Capital and all," Ezekiel replied with a smile as he looked out at the city.

"There you are," a voice said behind us.

Ezekiel dropped our embrace, and I turned around around to see who it was. Hunter, the co-leader of Zone 7 stood by the hatch which led us back underground. He had waist length white hair with contrasting black roots tied into a messy bun at the base of his neck.

"What do you want?" Ezekiel asked with a smile.

"All preparations for Nadine to transfer to Zone 14 are in order," Hunter announced with a smile.

My stomach rolled, making me feel queasy, I just wanted to recover from being Listed and stay in the safety of Ezekiel, not be carted off to another Zone. My blood started to boil from anger; I just wanted to go home.

*　*　*

The next day, I slammed the book shut and breathed out heavily. The majority of my time in Zone 7 was spent in this classroom, each wall was made of thick white brick with no windows, only a clock on the wall to indicate what time it is. Children's pictures lined some of the walls, on the back wall were storage bins labelled with students names, and coat hangers. But my gaze fell on Ezekiel, who looked very comfy as he leaned back on the teachers chair to inspect his nails. He glanced up at me, and slowly leaned forward with a raised eyebrow.

"This is impossible," I spat.

Ezekiel stood up from the desk, slowly approached me then sat on the desk in front of mine, one of his feet resting on the chair the other resting on the ground by the tip of his toes. He leaned over, and opened the book, the task system glaring at me like it had been for the past hour.

"How do you find out your tasks for the week?" Ezekiel questioned.

I scoffed, and folded my arms over my chest. "You use a CTM. It's also where you find out how many credits—money—you have earned."

He smiled as he nodded, both his hands clasped together in his lap. "Task 90."

"Yard work," I responded.

"Task 1075." Ezekiel smirked.

"Trick question, there is no such thing as Task 1075," I replied with a smile.

Ezekiel laughed, and looked down at the book. My head was pounding from trying to remember so much information in a short space of time I looked down at the bandage which concealed my barcode and sucked in a breath—I couldn't believe I was doing this. "Task 10."

This is where I drew a blank, I tried to remember, it was right there on the tip of my tongue but I couldn't pinpoint what *Task 10* was. I ran a hand through my hair while exhaling a very long breath.

"I don't know, burning non-religious articles?"

Ezekiel threw his head back as he started laughing. "Nice try, it's Church Maintenance." He continued to laugh while speaking, his voice boomed against all four walls.

"I'm never going to remember all these," I groaned, resting my head on my hand. "How everybody remembers all these is beyond me."

Ezekiel faced me directly, looking into my eyes, I averted my gaze to the dry erase board behind his shoulder. I really wasn't cut out for a life in The Republic of Denmé, but I had come too far now to turn back, and I was the idiot with a barcode to prove it. When the school bell rang out I glanced at the closed classroom door, Ezekiel also gave it a quick glance as the sound of children running around the corridor sounded like a clap of thunder alongside playful laughs, chatter, and shouting. I felt bad for the Unlisted children down in The Rebellion, never being allowed to see sunlight unless it was in the weird screens they had.

"When the regime came into existence I was ten, it was difficult for me to remember all these tasks because I had to go to a work camp the following year." Ezekiel stared off into the distance as he spoke, there was a sadness in his eyes. Then he looked at me. "It gets easier over time, and you have remembered a lot."

I swallowed the lump in my throat, and butterflies fluttered in my stomach. "Have I ran out of time to remember all of them?"

Ezekiel looked at me, then at the book. "You leave for Zone 14 on Monday, so in a way, yes. But every single Zone in The Rebellion has tons of copies of these books, we teach this to the Unlisted kids from first grade, so Carlos can hook you up, if you need a refresher." He shifted on the desk.

That information hit me like a wrecking ball.

I only had three more days in Zone 7 to remember this entire book, the fear of being caught out if I forget the task names made me more determined to remember every single one. Within three days my new life in Zone 14 would begin, until they figure out how to get me home. Within three days The Rebellion would be my only safe haven.

7

Nadine

The train journey from Zone 7 was a first-class experience, curled up in a corner among chicken coops that smelled of ass, and surrounded by other Listed people, who were sitting there sobbing. Some of them were whispering, *"I'm sorry Great Leader"* like she gave a shit; I was already infuriated at this country.

Holding my arm, I sat there and focused on the wooden ground, feeling the roughness of the hay that covered the floor, I swayed side to side at random intervals with the train. There had been about thirty people when this train journey started, and now there were five.

Covering my ears as the train came to a screeching halt, the door swung open and a guard stood there with a gun pointing at us, my heart started racing, and I sunk deeper into the corner I was sat in.

"Zone 14—Newton," he said roughly. "ID 005718, ID 156905, ID 020257."

Pushing myself to stand up, I lowered myself out of the train with shaking limbs, I felt warm with fear. Directly in front of me was another guard with a device in his hands.

"Come on, new ones. Check in!" this guard screamed.

I hesitated as I approached him. "Bethany Gladstone—ID 005718,"

I said confidently, extending my right arm out.

The guard punched me square in the mouth, my head snapped back painfully, a yelp escaped my lips as I fell backward. Curling on the floor, I pressed a hand to my mouth, and there was a streak of blood on my skin. Feeling a boot drive into my stomach, I fell on my side, and I could feel tears stinging my eyes. I let out a cough and was frozen in place. The guard roughly grabbed hold of my right arm and scanned my barcode.

"ID 005718. You're a pathetic bitch, understand?" I remained silent. "How dare you anger Our Leader. Behave in this Zone, you may be redeemed."

Hearing the guard snort, I felt liquid rain down into my face. My stomach churned and I wanted to be sick until a hard fist drove into my cheek. That was it, my body shook as I started crying, why did I choose to get Listed?

"We have a cry baby," the guard called out with a laugh, dragging me to stand up. "Was going to give you a tour of East Block, but you've pissed me off. Find your own way to Apartment 37A."

I groaned as he grabbed me, then gave me a knee to the stomach.

* * *

This must have been Main Street, shops lined the street like a corridor. I was still sobbing and was hiding my face from other people, feeling their eyes burn into my skin like they had X-ray vision. Still not knowing where the hell my apartment was, I decided to sit on the sidewalk and curl up, I quickly broke down sobbing; the pain in my stomach made me want to yell out.

Hearing footsteps approach me, there was a thud, and I jumped.

"Sometimes I feel like sitting on a sidewalk and crying too," a male voice which sounded like Judas announced. "Too bad I can't because, well, you know the tasks, yawn."

Lifting my head up, I saw this guy looked like a younger version of Judas, yet his hair was lighter not jet black. He was smiling, looking around the street we were on, waiting for me to respond, then his gaze fell on me.

"Are you sure you want to be sitting next to a Zone transfer?" I grumbled.

"So that's why you're crying, and lemme guess, guards gave you those injuries," the Judas-looking guy pointed out; I nodded.

"How did you guess that?" I asked him. My gaze fixated on watching people on the other side of the street pick up trash—*Task 50 or 15.*

"I used to be the same, thinking Our Leader was the one protecting us. But once I started doing tasks, and after my dad was executed, it became obvious she's only protecting herself." He looked at his hands as he spoke in a hushed voice.

"Sorry to hear that," I replied.

"It's okay." He let out a small laugh. "My name's Michael, ID 498765."

"My name is Na—" I stopped myself. "Bethany, ID 005718."

"Ah, Zone 7, is it nice there?"

"Wait, how do you know I'm from Zone 7?" I asked. Michael was mysterious but sounded extremely clever.

"Everybody knows the first two digits of your ID number is your Zone. Forty-nine is Zone 14. Zero-zero is Zone 7," he responded. "I'll show you around, come on, let's go," Michael said, taking my hands then helped me stand up.

I didn't want to ask him if he was Judas's brother, but if he wasn't, I would be shocked. There were so many similarities between them both, and it didn't make sense otherwise.

But I reluctantly followed him as he made his way down Main, as he walked, he picked up trash and threw it in nearby trash cans. I jogged to catch up to him, the pain in my stomach twinged in protest, eventually we were walking side by side.

On every single building, there were giant posters of President Sanchez, and these were more terrifying to see in person than on the news.

"Nothing really special happens on Main, you'll see the posters of Our Leader." He looked at me with a cheeky smile. "They're questionable."

I laughed, despite Michael being mysterious, he had a good sense of humour. Already I could tell we were going to be good friends.

8

Judas

Hot water rained down my body. I closed my eyes and sighed heavily as I let all the thoughts of the past week wash down the drain. It had been exactly a week since I killed the guard, and exactly a week since I had seen Nadine. Despite my best efforts to convince Carlos not to allow her to go through the Listing process, it ultimately failed once we got the email that Ezekiel had already approved it. I was terrified what she would experience above ground. After a while, I rested my head against the cold tile of my apartments shower, focusing on the water, the way it dripped off of my hair. Maybe it was easier to do as Samhain suggested and get her killed—that thought was equally as terrifying as allowing her to be Listed and out of the question, she had to go home. Just, my relatively dormant life had been turned upside down since she came to Newton, Zone 14.

***

Exiting the bathroom, I ran a towel through my wet hair, and I froze when my apartment's front door opened. My sister walked in with grocery bags, she smiled at me as she went into my kitchen, throwing them on the counter.

This section of my apartment was an open plan kitchen and living area, with the bathroom next to the front door. Behind my sofa was a four person dining table. My sofa was a green colour which faced the large windows, and to the right of it was my bedroom.

"What are you doing here?" I asked, walking towards the dining table.

Gabrielle pulled out groceries and opened my fridge.

"I just dropped off groceries for Michael, now I'm doing the same for you," Gabrielle announced as she stocked up my fridge.

"Shouldn't I be the one doing that for you?" I asked. "I am the oldest, after all. We can't repay you for this; credits don't work that way."

"Being the middle child, I should be allowed to treat my siblings to groceries," Gabrielle protested and started filling my cupboards. "Besides, if I didn't do this, Michael would end up dead in a ditch; he doesn't understand how to live alone yet."

She was only sixteen, she didn't understand how to be a little selfish yet.

"Fine, but tell me before you do this in the future."

Gabrielle waved her hand and then wiped it on her overalls. I couldn't believe my siblings sometimes.

* * *

Driving down the highway towards the next town over called Ellenwood, I could see the corridor of red, yellow, and orange trees all blowing fall leaves into the road. The only sound in the car was Godfrey McRitchie's wheezing; he hated the radio on in the car, so it was an awkward silence.

Resting my head on my hand, I controlled the wheel with the other, feeling the cold leather material on my skin. This was the type of vehicle I had driven back to Newton in when I killed the guard—it made me shudder. Or was it the cold air that was coming through the back window because Godfrey also insisted it had to be down.

"Both hands on the wheel, boy," he wheezed out.

"Yes sir," I said, following his instructions.

Glancing in the rear view to see him glaring at me, we had to get him a belt extender to secure him into the car, and his three hairs waved around in the air. Having two hands on the wheel was uncomfortable, it reminded me of passing my test at thirteen years old in the work camps, but I sucked it up.

"How's your sister, boy?" Godfrey asked. I glanced at him and then focused on the road.

"She's fine," I replied.

"Good, she's very beautiful, isn't she."

I bit the inside of my cheek and sighed. "I haven't given it much thought," I admitted.

My gaze shifted to the rear view mirror when I heard the sound of a zip coming down, and suddenly felt not only sick, but furious. My grip on the steering wheel tightened when I saw him touching himself over the thought of my sister.

"Those big beautiful eyes, the raven hair," Godfrey growled.

He wheezed whenever he moaned, and I didn't want to think of him in bed with his wife. Godfrey sounded like two balloons being rubbed together to create that ear-splitting squeak.

"How's the wife and kids?" I asked quickly, anything in the hopes of getting him to stop.

The wheezing sound did actually stop, thankfully. I even relaxed when I heard his zip come up, and when I glanced in the rear view he was back to glaring at me.

"You ruined the mood, boy," he spat.

"Sorry, sir," I lied.

Since I had rescued Nadine, the more everybody who was associated with Denmé's government were getting on my nerves, and testing my patience. I wanted them all gone.

* * *

Back in Newton, I walked up the stairs of Apartment Block West. I checked the clipboard of Task 11's chores to complete. The first was a mysterious smell coming from Apartment 05D. I breathed heavily as I climbed to the first floor and picked up the set of keys in the tool box.

I was familiar with this scent that resonated out of the door, the smell of death. Sighing, I didn't even bother knocking on the person's door, just unlocked it, pushed the door open, saw a foot, then went to find a guard.

There was a guard leaning on the railing to the stairs leading to the second floor

"Suicide in Apartment 05D," I said quietly. The guard looked at me.

"Are you sure, ID 498763?" he asked.

"Either that or they've learned to levitate." Now was not the time for jokes, but if the guard was going to be a moron about it.

He sucked in a breath and pushed himself away from the railing. "We'll see to it, thanks for the information."

I made my way up the stairs to the second floor, passing the guard on the way up. I had to sort out a leak on floor three which was reported.

Sadly, I was becoming numb to these events. People were waking up to the torture we had to endure in the regime and that it was complete bullshit, I didn't blame them. I was in the same position myself five years ago, after the regime murdered my father.

JUDAS

* * *

It was 6 p.m. looking up from my book as Michael burst into my apartment with a woman behind him. She looked familiar, but I couldn't pinpoint where I had seen her before; she had chin-length brown hair, hazel eyes, and wore the government uniform. My gaze fell to her split lip and cut on her cheek.

"This right here is my smelly brother, Joseph, ID 498763." The girl laughed at him, even that laugh sounded familiar. "Joseph, meet Bethany, ID 005718."

"Hello, Bethany, your number indicates you've transferred from Zone 7." I turned to Michael. "Also, that was rude especially to an acquaintance."

"It's nice to meet you Joseph, yes my ID number is going to change in twenty-four hours." Like a light bulb, it clicked. That was Nadine, and I gave her a smile. "Also, I don't mind Michael's comment, I have an older brother I know what they're like."

Michael pointed at me. "I'm giving her a tour of Newton, want to join?"

I looked at my watch, then looked at him. "Curfew's coming up."

He stopped, and checked his watch. "Well, that concludes our tour of Newton, I guess," he groaned. Then he proceeded to sit on my floor with his arms folded, pouting his lips like a toddler.

"What happened to your face?" I asked Nadine.

She gently touched her face, and winced a little as she sucked in a breath.

"Guards," she said with a forced smile. "I'll be fine."

Today was Nadine's first day within the Denmé regime and guards had put their bastard hands on her. If I had any authority in The Rebellion, I would have made Ezekiel revoke his decision, telling him that making her Listed was out of the question. She was the safest down there, not out here. My grip on my book tightened, and I did everything not to show my obvious anger.

9

Judas

Down in The Rebellion, myself, Nadine and Carlos shared a large cheese pizza in the centre of the table in Crusty Boys. Rather questionable name, but the pizza was amazing. Carlos held my hand under the table and ran his thumb against my knuckles.

"How's life above ground?" Carlos asked her, putting a slice in his mouth.

"It's going great," Nadine replied with full-on sarcasm. I noticed she ate pizza with a knife and fork.

"That's blasphemous," I commented, taking a bite out of my own slice. Nadine furrowed her brow, then looked at what I was staring at and started laughing.

"It stops your hands being greasy," Nadine replied.

A hand came out of nowhere and took a slice of pizza. "Hey!" I started then noticed it was Taylor, who sat next to me eating the pizza she stole.

Taylor was wearing a black playsuit, with her bright green hair in a braid. She smoothed out her clothes and then moved her hair over her shoulder.

"Freeloader much," Carlos commented with laughter.

"Yep, can't beat free pizza," Taylor said. "What happened to your face, baby girl?"

"Guards beat me for being a Zone transfer," Nadine replied.

Taylor sucked in a breath and helped herself to more pizza. "Fuckers, should have remained Unlisted, living the good life with free pizza."

"I'm going to send you a bill," Carlos joked while eating.

"Send me a bill, and I'll send you my knuckles." They both laughed; Carlos and Taylor acted like siblings most of the time.

Feeling Carlos kiss my cheek, I asked. "Have the importers said anything yet?"

"They think Nadine's a government spy," Carlos announced.

Taylor burst out laughing, even I did, Nadine's eyes narrowed as she ate pizza. My head rested on Carlos's shoulder, and I rubbed his arm.

"You know as well I do, Our Leader would not keep an Unlisted around until she's twenty-one years old, then let her loose in Zone 14, of all places," Taylor spat out.

"Give me a lie detector if you have to. I'm struggling to remember all these tasks," Nadine snapped defensively.

"Another indicator she's not a spy, if you're from here, you know the Task system like the back of your hand," Taylor said.

"Do you know the task system?" Nadine asked. Taylor nodded and smiled.

"I may be Unlisted, but all Unlisted down here know it. We even know every Zone ID code," she replied with a smile.

That was a good point. Everybody from Denmé knew the Task system, and Nadine just had to go through a week's training to understand it all.

* * *

Thirty minutes later, I walked back to my apartment block with Nadine on my right and Carlos to my left. I noticed there was a large crowd forming outside the apartment block. Nadine slowed down, whilst I continued walking at normal speed.

"What's happening?" Nadine asked.

Carlos shrugged and nervously ran his hands through his hair. He looked around for guards like he always did, another reason I wanted freedom. As we approached the crowd, I noticed there were two half-naked males in the centre, bound together with zip ties. People were throwing rocks at them while laughing and cheering whenever they cried out in pain, I winced at their misfortune.

"Homosexuals," I whispered to Nadine. She gasped and covered her mouth.

I saw my brother and sister on the other side of the crowd, and tapped Carlos's shoulder whilst pointing to them, he nodded so we made our way over. We pushed through the crowd, and stopped in front of my siblings—Michael looked stern with his arms folded whereas Gabrielle joined in with the action.

"They were caught having sex," Michael informed me.

My heart skipped a beat, and glanced at Carlos as he sat on the steps, then stared at his feet. He was always too uncomfortable to watch when these events happened, which was often enough to make me uncomfortable. Over the past three years, I had taught myself not to think of us in this position.

"Our Leader has always said their life style is wrong, they have defied her rules to keep us safe," Gabrielle spat as she threw a rock. The crowd erupted in cheers as the rock she threw hit one of their foreheads, spraying blood everywhere.

"You can't help human nature," Nadine interjected, wincing at another onslaught of rocks. Michael nodded in agreement.

I commended my brother for keeping my deepest secret. Since he had found out, he had treated Carlos and I like he didn't find out anything, despite Michael being brought up with the same beliefs as Gabrielle. Realistically he should be hating us both right now.

Military vehicles turned down the driveway towards the crowd, all of us ducked as a gun shot echoed around the drive way. A guard was hanging out of the sunroof of one of the vehicles, a gun in his hand.

"Everybody, stand up! Except for the homosexual hostiles," the guard bellowed.

We all stood up, the two guys in the middle had both passed out from the assault, so they couldn't stand up even if they wanted to. But I looked at the gun in the guards hands, and put my hands up; Nadine, and Michael copied. When I glanced behind my shoulder, Carlos had done the same.

"Go back to your apartments!" the guard demanded.

To my shock and horror, nobody moved. They all stood there motionless. From the corner of my eye, I saw one guy kneel down, pick up a rock, just as he was about to throw it, the guard shot him directly in the chest.

Michael took a small step backward. I copied him.

Nobody else moved.

Another small step.

A gunshot filled the air. I heard Michael scream out then the sound of him falling made me turn my head around.

"Michael!" I screamed.

10

Judas

I ran alongside the gurney surrounded by several nurses. Michael had tears streaming down his face, clutching my hand so tight I was losing the feeling. He was screaming and crying; his blood soaked the material underneath him even with a tourniquet.

"I want my mum!" He sobbed and yelled out in pain.

"Mum's coming," I said reassuringly.

Doctors wheeled him through a set of doors, and I got pushed back, forcing us to be separated. Forcing Michael to let go of my hand, watching him reach out for some kind of comfort broke my heart.

"No!" I screamed, trying with all my strength to get to my brother as he screamed my name and struggled against doctors pushing him into the gurney.

Tears blurred my vision, and the sound of steel-toe boots on linoleum came closer, a painful grip on my upper arms jerked me back forcibly.

All of a sudden, I felt a prick, then liquid shoot into my neck.

I felt dizzy almost instantly, then everything went black.

* * *

Jerking awake, I looked around. My head was pounding, I didn't know where I was, but I saw rows of chairs. Feeling something warm running against my hand, I turned to look at where it was coming from. It was Gabrielle, who was knelt beside me scrubbing the blood off my hands, there was a cup next to her that was full of rust coloured water. She sniffled and wiped her nose with the back of her hand, pushing her hair behind her ear.

"What happened?" I groaned out

"You freaked out. Guards had to sedate you," Gabrielle snapped. She looked at me, her brown eyes filled with tears. "Michael had to get surgery."

Pressing my hand to my face, I just cried. Even though my head pounded, I just couldn't imagine life without Michael. He'll be fine, I told myself over and over.

"What do you mean, they shot my child by accident!" I heard a shrill voice erupt in the room. I lifted my head up while wincing. It was Mum talking to the receptionist behind a desk. "These children are the only thing I have left!" Mum shouted.

Mum was in government uniform but had a beige cardigan wrapped around her. I gasped as she covered her mouth to stop from sobbing loudly, when I saw mum fall to the ground and broke down crying, I knew I had to take action. Prying my hand away from Gabrielle's soft grasp, I ran over to Mum.

Crouching down beside her, I held her close. Mum clutched my arm and let out a sob which resembled a shout, I ran my hands through her wavy dark brown hair like Michael's and just let her get all her emotions out.

* * *

Michael sat up in his hospital bed. It was this wooden thing that couldn't be reclined like the ones we had in The Rebellion, in his arm was a single IV drip to some clear liquid, the sound of the heart monitor pumping out paper was loud. My brother happily ate ice cream while smiling, high on whatever drug they gave him, his injured leg elevated by a string on the ceiling. Gabrielle was asleep in a nearby armchair, and I leaned against the wall next to the sink.

Our mum ran her hands through Michael's hair and smiled.

"Do you have a permit to visit me, Mother?" Michael asked, handing the spoon to her.

Once you were fourteen in The Republic of Denmé you were legally an adult, and had to live alone. Completely cut off from your parents unless you obtained a permit, it would have been better if these permits weren't so rare to get.

"No, but the guards are letting me see you," Mum replied, pushing the spoon away with a smile.

"Mum," Michael said through giggles. "I got shot."

I didn't know how Michael could laugh in this situation, just how could he laugh? Michael should be furious at the guards for shooting him, he was innocently doing as they told us to do but they shot him anyway. None of this entire situation was right.

11

Nadine

Gospel music blared out of the speakers in the grocery store, I was holding the handle of a shopping cart filled with inventory while it was pulled by Judas's sister, Gabrielle. Her long black hair fell in a straight line down her left shoulder, and her muscular arms peeked through her uniform. It smelled like baked goods and cardboard boxes in here, such a weird smell. My mind kept wandering to Michael, if he was okay in the hospital—thinking of my family back home in Olympia. Then she stopped at the tinned food section, looking at the clipboard again then at me.

"Alright, we need a tray of tinned tomatoes," Gabrielle instructed.

I nodded, going to the shopping cart and heaving up the whole packet of tomatoes still in their crate, my arms felt like they were going to snap with the weight, burning with over exertion as I heaved it into place. Taking out a knife, I cut the plastic and peeled it off in one quick motion.

"How is your brother?" I asked. Gabrielle scratched her cheek as she read the list.

"Ten tins of carrots," Gabrielle instructed. "Which brother?"

"Michael," I replied, thinking she would figure that out on her own.

NADINE

I picked up as many tins of carrots as I could handle and placed them on the shelf.

"Thankfully, it's nothing substantial." Gabrielle smiled, stepping forward and taking one of the tins I had placed on the shelf, it had a dent in the side. "Please be more diligent with your work," Gabrielle spat, as she threw it into a plastic bag filled with trash tied to the cart.

"Sorry," I responded, picking another tin.

Hearing steel-toe boots on the linoleum, I turned around to see a guard, and my heart skipped a beat.

"Is ID 495718 doing a good job?" the guard asked. I looked at Gabrielle.

"Yes sir, we are just slightly distracted this morning due to a family incident yesterday," Gabrielle responded calmly then went back to the clipboard.

Without warning, a hard fist drove into my cheek. I slammed into the shopping cart and fell on the floor. Tears stung my eyes and I coughed, tasting the metallic flavour of blood. The guard grabbed a fistful of my hair and pulled me back, I groaned out loudly.

"You're walking on thin ice, ID 495718," he growled into my ear.

"Get off her!" Gabrielle shouted.

The guard let me go, and I fell forward and hit my head on the floor; I let out another groan and touched my head. I winced when I heard the sound of a slap, followed by the clicking of a belt being undone. My mind raced with possibilities of what that meant.

With a crack, his belt pelted me across my back, I screamed out in agony and started sobbing loudly, curling up into the fetal position. I screamed again as another crack of his belt hit my back, my spine burned from the impact. By the time his reign of terror was over, I was a trembling mess on the floor.

* * *

An hour later, I had never driven a car so expensive before, the leather steering wheel was comfortable, and so were the leather seats—despite occasionally having to adjust to stop my back stinging from earlier. Wooden embellishments lined the dash and interior of the doors, I loved it, one piece of technology clearly not banned was a GPS mounted to the windshield which showed where I was heading. A town called Stapleforth, Zone 14. Everything should have felt relatively back to normal; I was above ground and driving down a highway. But it wasn't normal in the slightest, for 12 p.m. on a Friday, the highway was far too quiet with only one car heading in the opposite direction, and I was driving a stranger to a town I didn't know to complete Task 21.

A wheezing sound came from the guy in the back. Godfrey McRitchie, I had been told his name was, I felt sorry for his grotesque size, knowing he was gorging himself on food while other people in this godforsaken country were starving.

"Miss," he wheezed out. I glanced at him in the rear view.

"Yes, sir?" I questioned, focusing on the road, drumming my thumb on the steering wheel—it felt unnatural to hold the steering wheel with both hands.

"Tell me, how you got those cuts on your beautiful face?" Godfrey wheezed out.

Calling my face beautiful made me shudder, knowing he was way, way older than me. I swallowed and shifted in my seat. "As you are aware, I am a Zone transfer. I made a mistake during Task 5."

In the rear view, I watched Godfrey nod. Then he looked at me. "Zone 7, beautiful Zone that one. They make beautiful women too."

Biting the inside of my cheek, I nodded with a forced smile, my eyebrows raised when I heard his zip coming down. *Oh my god.* "Erm, sir. What is your meeting about today?"

He moved his hand from his crotch. "That is none of your concern,

Miss," Godfrey snapped. "Interrupt me again, and we can add to those cuts."

Swallowing air, tears stung my eyes, and I nodded. "Sorry, sir, I was just making small talk." My voice was small and timid. I noticed my hands were trembling.

Godfrey made me feel extremely uncomfortable and unsafe, I didn't know him well enough to talk about anything else. I just had to listen to him moaning.

* * *

Later, after a shower, I found myself walking through Apartment Block East's halls looking for anybody to talk to. Walking up to the third floor where I knew Carlos and Michael resided, I was mostly wanting to communicate to Carlos, knowing Michael wouldn't be home and Judas lived on the fourth floor. Passing through the wooden doors, I stopped briefly when I saw a figure coming out of Michael's apartment, only relaxing with the reality it was Gabrielle. Michael had told me she lived in West Block, so I felt puzzled on her presence here after curfew, but I continued walking and knocked on Carlos's apartment door.

"How's your face?" Gabrielle asked with a smile as she approached me.

"It hurts like a bitch, but it's fine," I admitted, wincing as I tried to smile back. Gabrielle's smile dropped, and she looked at me sternly.

Gabrielle let out a nervous laugh, massaging the back of her neck and looking around the corridor. She tilted her head toward me. "Where did you learn to speak like that?"

Thinking back to what I had said, I metaphorically kicked myself for not being careful with my language. Ezekiel had told me swearing was illegal. "Ignore that. What are you doing out on East Block after curfew?"

"Our Leader gracefully granted me a permit to help clean Michael's apartment," Gabrielle replied, then checked her watch. "I have fifteen minutes remaining."

I forced a smile and nodded. "Our Leader is kind like that." *Pass me a fucking bucket.*

"Also, I have been selected to be a Zone transfer myself," Gabrielle announced.

My eyes widened, and I looked around the corridor. "What crime did you commit?" I hissed.

"No crime. As a thank you for being a great advocate for Our Leader's cause for a safe society, they want me to transfer to Zone 7 to learn how to be a Zone Director," Gabrielle explained with a big excited smile. "Don't tell my siblings, they won't let me go."

Sucking in a breath, I nodded with a smile, Gabrielle turned and walked away. She waved as she left the corridor.

Knocking on the door to Carlos's apartment again, I waited and checked my watch, the door swung open, and my eyes widened to see Judas. He was breathing heavily while looking flustered with his black hair and uniform a mess, behind his shoulder, I could see Carlos emerge out of his bedroom looking the same way while clipping his overall straps into place. He was also breathless.

Putting a hand to my mouth to suppress an awkward laugh, I breathed out and said. "Sorry to disturb you, but I need to talk to somebody. Can we go to my place?"

Judas looked behind his shoulder at Carlos. "Alright, yeah we can do that," he replied breathlessly as he grabbed his boots.

Knowing how dangerous it was for their relationship above ground, I double checked if Gabrielle was still around, thankfully she was gone. I also didn't know the guard's patrol schedules yet, so hopefully none of those were around.

Hearing the thud as Carlos finished getting his boots on, we all left his apartment, and made our way to the second floor where my apartment was.

12

Judas

Nadine handed me a herbal tea then wiped her hands along her overalls, sitting down at her dining table next to Carlos. Her apartment was identical to mine, only difference was she had a yellow sofa. I wondered what she needed to talk about so urgently.

"I asked Gabrielle this earlier, but how is Michael?" Nadine asked.

"He'll fine thankfully," I replied and sipped the contents. "But, Mum's taking it pretty hard. They've not granted my permit to see her yet."

Nadine nodded as she drank the tea. I noticed she had more cuts on her face, but I didn't want to question it—I even caught Carlos looking at them. She looked around the apartment, and we stayed in silence for a little while.

"What is up with Godfrey McRitchie by the way?" Nadine asked and laughed a little.

"Oh, you met him today?" I asked. She nodded, Carlos rolled his eyes as he drank from his own mug.

"I had Task 21, and he sounded like a squeaky toy," she explained through a cringe, and I laughed. "Then he jerked off in the back seat while thinking of me."

"He did that to you too? He did it with me over my sixteen year old sister." I heard Carlos start choking on his drink, coughing loudly. As I tapped his back, he relaxed and looked disgusted.

"What a creep," Nadine spat while looking at Carlos. "Guards hit me before that, then after."

"I noticed," I said while continuing to rub Carlos's back, trying not to laugh at his misfortune of choking on his drink. Nadine's eyes glazed over, and she blinked back tears, exhaling a breath.

Suddenly, Carlos stood up. "Come on, let's go."

Nadine looked up at him, then at me. "Where are we going?"

"We all need an escape, so let's go," Carlos replied.

I knew exactly what he meant, a night in The Rebellion would be amazing after the shit storm over the past couple of days.

* * *

It was late, around midnight, and Nadine was passed out and curled up on Carlos's sofa in his underground apartment. I put a blanket over her and moved her hair away from her face, then I turned towards Carlos.

Carlos was dressed in a black T-shirt and grey joggers, lying on the bed. As I approached, he crawled up to me. Grabbing me by the waist and pulling me close, our lips met, and his mouth tasted like toothpaste. With one quick motion, I was on my back, staring up at Carlos; we both laughed, and I sucked in a breath as our lips met again—just being near him was all I needed lately. I laughed even louder when he kissed me haphazardly around my face, and I clapped a hand over my mouth to quieten down so I didn't wake Nadine.

"You're so weird," I commented.

Carlos looked at me with a smile. "I'm just in a good mood," he replied before kissing me again.

Our kissing abruptly stopped when I heard clapping in the apartment. Carlos turned to look at the person clapping, even Nadine sat up and rubbed sleep out of her eye. Ezekiel stood there, dressed in the government uniform.

"You two are gross. Nadine's right there," Ezekiel commented.

"We're allowed to kiss," I grumbled, feeling frustrated that I couldn't have any free time with Carlos alone lately.

"What happened?" Nadine rubbed her eyes, she squinted at us then Ezekiel.

"Ezekiel, can't you just act normal and use the front door instead of The Tunnels?" Carlos questioned. I ran my fingers through his hair, craving another kiss like he was a drug.

"Tunnels are more fun. I'm a mole who comes bearing news."

Carlos rolled off me and sat up straight. Even though I was frustrated, I also sat up and waited like Nadine was doing.

"The Importers are satisfied, so they will take Nadine home in a week's time," Ezekiel announced. I glanced at Nadine, who started smiling.

Since Nadine had chosen to be Listed, the guards had put their bastard hands all over her which infuriated me. I couldn't even imagine how bad her mental health was right now, and because of this, I didn't want to wait a week for her to go home. I wanted her out of Denmé as soon as possible.

13

Judas

Two days later, I threw a boulder on top of a mound of dirt, Nadine patted it down to secure it in place. She sighed heavily as I heaved another boulder and put it down next to the one I had just placed. We were working in perfect harmony together.

A guard was behind us with a gun in his hand. I swear if they touch Nadine during today's task, I was going to lose it.

"Do you want to start lifting the boulders?" I asked.

"I'm a chicken, I will actually snap," she replied. "But okay." I laughed.

Switching positions, she bent down to try and pick up a boulder, but her arms strained. I approached her and tried seeing where she was going wrong.

"Lift with your legs, right now you're putting all your strength in your arms," I instructed. "Watch me, so you know what to do."

I squatted down, lifting a heavy boulder then heaved to stand up, putting it next to our already straight line. I watched Nadine copy my movements. Despite heaving and her face going bright red from exertion in the process, she managed to lift the boulder and set it down. After giving each other a high five, we both laughed.

"Oh my god, thank you," she said.

"You've never had Task 16 in Zone 7 or something?" I asked. I noticed the guard looking at her, noting her inexperience of moving a boulder.

"No, I was always on Task 17," she lied while sounding out of breath.

"Explains a lot," I replied.

Task 17 was a permanent task of Teacher, an easy lie to make her lack of knowledge viable. I patted down some soil around the boulders we had just set down, and waited for her next one to come over.

* * *

A while later, sitting on the steps to my apartment block, I watched people do Task 50 on the spot that still contained Michael's blood from where the bastards shot him. I stiffened at the sight of a military vehicle travelling down the apartment's driveway and stopped at the entrance, I was thinking they were after me again, and I didn't know why that was my first thought.

The door opened, and a guard jumped out, holding two wooden crutches, he opened the back, and somebody hopped out. When the vehicle's door closed, I realised it was Michael who was holding a paper bag, smiling at the driver. The thump of his crutches sounded out as he made his way over to me.

"ID 498765," the guard said. Michael looked behind his shoulder. "Do you have somebody to help you to the elevator?"

"Yes, my brother, ID 498763," Michael replied. "Thank you."

I stood up as the guard got back in his vehicle. Michael looked uncomfortable on the crutches and was wearing government-approved nightwear, grey sweat pants and white T-shirt. The pants leg rolled up where his injured leg was, so his white plaster cast was on display.

"Ready to go?" I asked.

Michael nodded, handed me his crutches then stuck his tongue out while trying to hop up the stairs to our apartment block. He held my arm for support, and once he got to the top, I handed him his crutches back as we made our way to the elevator. He was the lucky one who had the key to it, whereas everybody else had to walk up the stairs.

* * *

Inside Michael's apartment, I looked at Michael with his leg stuck up on the backrest of the brown sofa as I cut a ham sandwich into triangles in the kitchen. Michael looked sleepy, despite this I walked up to him and placed the plate on his chest.

"Why, thank you, Joseph Wells." He started laughing.

I laughed too and shook my head. "Are you comfortable?" I asked.

"Sometimes I get shooting pains up my leg, but I'll be fine," Michael replied, then bit into his sandwich with a smile. I loved his enthusiasm about this entire situation.

Jumping at the sound of his front door opening, I looked, and two men in black suits walked into the room. One guy had grey hair with a scar across his left eye which he appeared to be blind in, and the other guy had black hair.

"Is this the residence of Judas Wells?" the grey-haired one asked. I stiffened at hearing my birth name above ground.

"No, but I'm here," I responded. "This is my brother's apartment."

They started whispering to each other and checking a computer tablet. I glanced at Michael, who had one of his eyebrows raised, then he frowned.

"We are unaware that Mrs Samantha Wells had more than one child," the grey-haired one responded.

"She has three," I responded coldly. "What is this about?" I asked, feeling uncomfortable by their presence.

"We are ORS—Olympia Relief Service. Your aunt Hannah Johnson has been trying for seventeen years to get you to safety in the comfort of Olympia. We have only just infiltrated the border," the black-haired guy explained. I heard a thud as Michael dropped his sandwich.

The two men produced ID cards and showed them off. I saw the hidden seal in the light to show its legitimacy but didn't bother looking at their names.

"Wait, there are actually other places outside of The Republic of Denmé?" Michael asked; he sounded excited. "Also, what is that weird box in your hands?"

"Yes, there's a lot of other places. Now that we know she has two other children, I'm sure that will extend to all of you." The black-haired one shifted on his feet, ignoring the second question.

"So, you're saying, Michael, Gabrielle, and I can come with you to Olympia?" I asked out of shock and confusion. The two men nodded.

"We have tried locating your father, Eric Wells, but we don't know his location."

I bit the inside of my cheek. "Well, it's obvious you can't find somebody who's been dead for five years." The two men looked shocked and put the information into their computer tablets.

"*Joseph,*" Michael hissed. "If we choose to go with you to Olympia, how do we get in touch? I want to explore a new town."

I glared at Michael for even asking. I didn't even trust these people, and he's there being handed a freaking business card with their information on it. This wasn't right. Mum has always told us that she was an only child.

"We should get going, it's been nice speaking to you, Judas, Michael," the black-haired one said, then left the apartment.

"Why do they keep calling you Judas?" Michael asked, looking at the business card in his hand.

"It's my birth name before Our Leader saved us," I replied. I plucked the business card from his hand and read it.

JUDAS

* * *

A frantic but rough shove on my shoulder woke me up from my slumber, and my eyes flew open to see Nadine looking at me with terror in her eyes.

My bedroom was almost in complete darkness, if it wasn't for my living room light which flooded into my room. Carlos stood in my bedroom doorway, holding a gun towards the front door. I sat up dazed and confused.

"They've found out, Joseph," Nadine announced, terror in her voice.

"Found out what?" I was still confused.

"They know I'm Nadine Ellis."

I was instantly awake, the sudden realisation hit me. Throwing the covers off me, I got out of bed, hearing the distance sound of apartments being destroyed downstairs.

"How do you know they found out?" I questioned as I left my bedroom.

Nadine looked extremely pale as she and Carlos followed me towards my front door.

"I was having a chat with Carlos, and they just came barging in. I didn't know Carlos was packing until he shot the lot of them and we got our asses out of there."

After opening my front door, I stopped and looked at Nadine, not understanding most of what she just said; it was like she just spoke in an entirely different language. Shaking my head, I didn't even bother getting my shoes on as I jogged out of my apartment—knowing my boots would take too long to lace up in such circumstances.

Carlos appeared at the side of me, taking my arm as he guided me to the end of the corridor which housed a door to a janitors closet. I trusted this man with my entire life, but I didn't think going into a closet to hide from guards would help.

***

The cold floor tile of the janitor's closet made me feel cold—colder than I already did. Or was it because I was so tired. Carlos carefully moved an empty shelving unit, revealing a hidden door frame. *Why hadn't I noticed there was a door there?* It didn't have a handle. He grabbed a nearby screwdriver and rammed it into the keyhole with all his strength, the door came free as he pulled and musty air hit us instantaneously.

Gunshots from the hallway sounded like bubble wrap being popped, my heart raced as more sounded outside.

"This leads to the basement where we need to go," Carlos explained in a hushed voice.

As we all stepped through the door it led to an abandoned staircase. Only the moon outside illuminated the stairs from a window. Wooden boards were strewn around the stairs, and it was dusty filled with cobwebs.

Carlos dragged the shelving unit back, then shut the door behind us. My heart skipped a beat, I could hear the janitor closet door starting to rattle through the secret door. Looking around, I saw a large boulder nearby and ran towards it, lifting it up, and carrying it over to the door, wedging it in place, so they couldn't open it.

"It won't hold, let's go," Nadine said quickly as the sound of breaking wood filled the air. We ran down the stairs as quickly as possible.

The sound of Nadine and Carlos's boots echoed out while my bare feet just made smacking sounds on the concrete.

We were almost at the bottom, then I felt something sharp enter my foot. I yelled out and fell the rest of the way down the stairs. I coughed and sputtered, my entire body was in a wave of pain, especially my foot.

"Joseph!" I heard Carlos and Nadine shout in unison. Carlos grabbed me and pulled me up.

I looked at my foot in a patch of moonlight, seeing a rusty nail embedded into my skin. Feeling Carlos scoop me up, he knew as well as I did, I couldn't run like this. Wrapping my arms around his neck, I let him carry me into the dark confines of the basement.

The sound of steel-toe boots coming down the stairs and Carlos's breathing were the only thing I could hear through the darkness. Until the sound of something metal moving caught my attention. Feeling cold air, I was lowered down into somewhere even darker.

* * *

We had made it to Tunnel 14:10, the infirmary where Carlos lifted up a panel and hit a red button. Instantly an alarm sounded, followed by what sounded like metal scraping against rock, I hadn't heard this before in The Rebellion.

I was leaning against the wall with my foot elevated, the nail in there was starting to feel like it had been a part of me forever.

"What is that?" Nadine asked.

"Zone 14's tunnels are closed except parking garages," Carlos announced.

"Woah, what?" She opened the door we had just run through, and sure enough, there was a sheet of metal blocking the way to Highway 8.

"The guards could know where an entrance to a tunnel is, so can't take any chances," Carlos said. Picking me up and carrying me through the tunnel we were in.

His breathing was still heavy from running. I looked behind his shoulder at Nadine, who was following behind us and hugging herself. Then I helped Carlos open a door at the end of the tunnel; my only comfort to this entire situation was seeing the fluorescent white light of the infirmary.

* * *

I sat with my foot up on a gurney. There was a doctor working on fixing it, thankfully he had numbed it enough to the point it felt like a dull moving sensation on my skin. Inside the infirmary it smelled like strong disinfectant, and the sound of heart monitors echoed around.

Nadine was sitting in a chair, resting her head on her hand. Carlos stood next to me, holding my hand for comfort. I could see the gun in his pocket.

Ezekiel came out of nowhere and looked at Carlos sternly.

"How did you get here so fast?" Carlos asked. He sounded slightly anxious as he dropped my hand.

"I was driving to Zone 15 to see Lake when the alarm went off. What the fuck happened?" Ezekiel asked sternly.

"Guards found out my real identity," Nadine admitted without looking at him.

The doctor stood up and went somewhere, but Ezekiel looked at Nadine with a face of stone, looked at my foot, then at me. The fluorescent lights made his eyes look more on the grey side.

"We ran down an abandoned stairway, where I got a nail in my foot," I admitted.

"Nadine. Get up," Ezekiel snapped. I had never seen him so angry before.

She reluctantly stood up, looking small. When she winced, it looked as though she was preparing for him to beat her like the guards did whenever she messed up. However, Ezekiel kept his distance, and folded his arms over his chest.

"Say your goodbyes, we're leaving," Ezekiel said sternly.

Nadine breathed a sigh of relief, but asked. "Where are we going?" She looked at Carlos and I for reassurance.

"Olympia," Ezekiel spat out like it was poison in his mouth.

"What? It's not time. Importers won't let me go home," Nadine was on the verge of shouting but Ezekiel shifted on his feet.

"I'm personally going to drive you myself. Where's your address?" I froze to hear Ezekiel admit he's personally going to drive into Olympia. What if he never returns to Denmé? Nadine looked at us, and then at Ezekiel in hesitation.

"576 Lakewin Drive, Gratisland," she responded quietly.

Ezekiel nodded in satisfaction. "We leave in twenty minutes, tell Carlos to escort you to Tunnel 14:107."

He disappeared behind the curtain, leaving Nadine to stand there, looking shocked and relieved.

14

Nadine

A week had passed since I had to forcibly leave The Republic of Denmé. My hand lightly touched the wall as I walked down the white corridor of my house. Whilst walking my mind kept wandering to Judas, Carlos, Michael and Ezekiel. Police hadn't caught who threw me into Denmé yet, but I was now headline news and reporters were in abundance.

Opening my brother's bedroom door, Wyatt was hunched over his desk filled with books—he was scribbling things in a notebook, wearing a grey hoodie and jeans. Our only similarities were the fact we both had hazel eyes. Wyatt looked mostly like our mum with her blond hair, and chubby face. I looked mostly like dad.

"Mum's got breakfast downstairs," I told him.

"Okay, give me a few moments," he replied.

My gaze fell to a piece of crumpled-up paper near my foot. I bent down and picked it up. I unravelled it, glancing up at my brother to see if he noticed. He was too invested in his work to bother looking at me. It was a printed-out copy of an email:

Thank you for using The Educators, we will carry out the necessary instructions within five working days.

Wyatt had scribbled the email address out. My hands were trembling as I stared at the email then at Wyatt. I saw red and dropped the note. Two quick steps, then I used all my strength to punch him square in the jaw; my knuckles burned from the impact. Wyatt shouted out as I threw another punch into his nose that erupted like a volcano, and then his stomach. I kept throwing punches and kicks at him until he was curled into a ball, covering his head and face while sobbing. Blood covered my hands and his already stained clothes.

I felt strong hands under my armpits, dragging me back

"You're a fucking coward!" I screamed at Wyatt, who was still sobbing in his little corner.

"What is this about?" It was Dad, his brown hair messed up from struggling against my strength to pull me back.

"That fucking email!" I shouted, pointing to it on the floor.

Mum picked it up, her straight blonde hair covered her pink silk robe, and her hands trembled while reading it.

"Henry, call the police," Mum said to Dad.

I breathed heavily as Dad let me go reluctantly, he had grown pale. Tears stung my eyes as I exited the room, shoving past mum in the process. How dare my own brother do this to me.

* * *

The cops had taken Wyatt away an hour ago. I wiped my eyes while I sat at Dad's desk, I glanced at my knuckles which had already formed bruises. I couldn't believe my own family betrayed me, and gave me memories so painful I hadn't told Judas and Carlos half of it. The only person I told was Michael. I did feel guilty about exploiting his naivety about the outside world. But he was easy to talk to, and the fact he looked like Judas made it easier.

Scrolling through the computer, I found myself researching Denmé and the fall of St. Herculia. I had been doing this way too much for a place that held such painful memories for me, but it was my only connection to all the friends I had met there. Ezekiel made it clear there was no going back for me, at least.

Then a thought quickly occurred to me. If I could send out some sort of message to get people to listen, then it's one step to help Denmé citizens regain freedom. Opening the paper drawer of Dad's printer, I laid out a sheet of paper on the desk in front of me. I took a marker out of the pen holder, and wrote down:

The Republic of Denmé needs freedom

Satisfied with my work, I looked out of the window at all the reporters who had set up camp outside my house since I returned; they looked bored holding microphones, and cameras. If I could get a message out to anybody, it would be them. This was it. I had a plan.

* * *

The chime of the front door telling the rest of the house that it was open was the first sound I heard. Then it sounded like a rain storm of camera shutters. Flashes looked like lightning, but there were so many. Even though my eyes stung, I held the sign above my head with pride, all attention was on me, and I was thriving.

"Do you think that will work?" a familiar voice asked.

Lowering the sign slowly, I looked through the flashes of the cameras to see a dark silhouette emerge from the light. My eyes widened in sudden realisation. Rubbing my burning eyes out of pain and shock, this was a dream, it had to be.

"Michael, what the fuck are you doing here?" I exclaimed in shock.

He looked healthier, not as thin, and seeing him out of the blue overalls was so weird. The cast on his leg was replaced with a black plastic splint, the uncomfortable wooden crutches replaced with sturdy metal and comfy supports. Michael wore black skinny jeans, a black T-shirt, and a grey trench coat. Seeing him was like the cameras melted away.

"Is that how you greet people in this country?" He raised an eyebrow.

"What the fuck—means hello?" Michael looked like he made a mental note.

"When we're in shock, yes," I responded quickly. "How did you find out where I live?"

"ORS told me," Michael said with a smile as he used the crutches to move towards me, he didn't stick his tongue out anymore when doing so.

"Well, now you know who I really am," I said with a smile. "My dad works for ORS."

"It was kind of a shock to see you while in the facility, but it's okay," Michael replied, I raised an eyebrow. "Can I come in? My arms are getting tired."

"Yes, definitely, come in." I turned to the front door and made my way back.

I could hear the click of Michael's crutches on the concrete as he made his way up the path to my front door. This was bad; he was in Olympia, not Denmé. He was suddenly in my world.

* * *

I was in my kitchen with Michael sitting opposite me, he was staring at my mum's blender like it was some kind of alien contraption. At first I thought it was weird, but then remembered they don't have blenders in Denmé—above ground that is.

"What is this?" Michael asked. Just as I was about to tell him, he pushed the button. His eyes widened in terror at the noise it made, and I quickly unplugged it so Michael couldn't try again. Michael started laughing.

"You pooped your pants," he said through laughter.

"More like you did," I exclaimed. "If you don't know what it is, don't touch it."

Michael started smiling. "There's a lot of things I touch, but don't know what it is."

I let out a laugh, thinking of all the possibilities of what that statement actually meant. "I'm not even going to ask."

Since meeting Michael, I had grown to find out he had such a cheeky personality. I looked to the kitchen entrance as dad walked in clutching a laptop to his chest.

"Hello, Michael," Dad said, opening the fridge.

"So you told Michael to come here for a friend?" I asked. Dad nodded with a smile.

"After you survived a trip to Denmé, I thought an insider would help, I hope you get acquainted together," Dad said calmly.

"We're already acquainted," Michael pointed out. "I knew her as Bethany, ID 005718 back home."

Dad looked surprised at us both. Running my hands through my hair, I breathed out heavily, completely not understanding what the fuck was going on. I knew Michael had doubts about the regime, but to find out he went out of his way to move to Olympia—and how did he even know ORS existed. Either way I forced a smile at both my father and Michael, knowing it was now my responsibility to keep Michael safe in this new environment. Just like Judas did for me.

15

Nadine

I always loved the smell of new books. The entire scent was indescribable. But as I looked through the children's section with a basket in hand, I checked the list Hannah, Michael's aunt, gave me for the list of school books we had to buy. While shopping for his books, it became clear to me that Denmé children graduated school at the age of ten. So, Michael was there, fourteen years old with a fifth grade education. It angered me more than it should.

However, Michael seemed just about right for his age. He was smart and clever, maybe his mum taught him behind the guards's back before he had to move out; that was plausible, this also explained why Judas and his sister were clever too. Maybe not his sister, she did agree to stoning people.

"Do you know your own reading level?" I asked Michael, thinking he was behind me.

When he didn't respond, I turned around, but he was nowhere to be seen. My heart skipped a beat as I looked around the children's section for him, but it was only myself in here.

Exiting this section, I looked around at everybody, seeing nothing but unfamiliar faces looking through the shelves, some in their seats reading books or looking at board games. I was clutching the basket of books so tightly my hand hurt. Adrenaline pumped through my veins wondering where he could have gone, my mind raced with possibilities, oh my god I would have to tell Hannah I lost her nephew. I would never be allowed to look after Michael again if I truly lost him somewhere in Olympia, or if he ended up hurt or worse.

Moving to another section where the cafe was situated, the strong smell of coffee lingered in the air as I scanned everybody's faces. Swallowing the lump in my throat, then exhaling a long breath, I had to stay calm it was the only way I was going to find him—if Michael was still in the bookstore at all.

Finally, I breathed a sigh of relief to see him curled up in a corner of the cafe, sitting in an armchair by a window with his nose stuck in a book. My panic replaced by irritation at him for not telling me where he was going, I wouldn't be bothered if he knew how to live like an Olympian citizen; which he didn't. Everything was new to Michael in this environment.

Wiping my sweaty palm on my green jacket, I sucked in a breath and started to approach him quickly, then slowed down when I noticed he was crying. As I closed the gap between us, I placed the basket on the floor, looking down at Michael as he wiped a tear away with the heel of his hand.

"You okay?" I asked.

Michael looked up to me. "Is this book true?" he asked.

In his hands was a hardback book, the cover was blue with a familiar symbol on it—a gold circle with a trident through it. Pushing the cover up to see the title, I froze, and my eyes widened—*The Rise and Fall of St. Herculia*. I took my eyes away from Michael for five minutes, and he had already found the book I never wanted him to read. *Smartass*.

Slowly, I nodded at him, making my mouth into a straight line and sucked in a breath, realising he had found out the truth.

"The whole thing about the apocalypse was a lie?" he asked.

I crouched down next to him and placed a hand on his wrist. "Yeah, it was. She wanted to control you guys."

I grabbed the book as he let it go and cried into his hands. My hand on his wrist moved to his back, Michael was crying so loud people started looking at us, to be honest I would be crying too if I had just found out my home country was a lie.

"Is everything okay here?" a concerned book clerk asked as she came over; she had a green apron on.

"Yes, he's from Denmé. He found this book," I replied, holding up the book for her to see.

"Why didn't Joseph tell me?" he cried out.

"To protect you." Was all I could muster as a response.

In the two short weeks I had known Judas, he had probably tried to tell his siblings about the regime being bullshit in the past. But they were so brainwashed at the time that it would just be a bunch of lies to them. However, Michael now knew the truth. Just like a sandcastle at the mercy of the ocean, the illusion set up by President Sanchez had easily fallen.

* * *

Sitting in Michael's aunt's pink bathroom, I was watching Michael massage blue hair dye into a section of his hair from his aunt's toilet, the lid cover was oddly comfy. The dye smelled like roses dipped in chemicals, and the only sound was the crinkling of his gloves whenever he moved. To be perfectly honest, I should not have encouraged this, but when you've gone through a traumatic event, you're going to want to change something about yourself.

"So, this shampoo is going to turn my hair blue?" he asked, looking at me.

"It's not shampoo," I reminded him. "It's hair dye."

Michael nodded; I looked at his cast which he was standing steadily on, wrapped over his black jeans. Otherwise, he was shirtless. I hoped Michael wasn't in pain standing like that, he didn't look like he was in pain, despite the obvious leaning against the cabinet for support.

"What the hell is this?" His aunt appeared in the bathroom doorway. She looked like an older version of Michael's Mum with blonde streaks in her brown hair.

I only saw his mum one time, when Carlos went to his mums house to tell her Michael got shot. Her screams still haunted me.

"Art project?" Michael said. It sounded suggestive, like a question.

Hannah's eyes widened, and she raised an eyebrow shaking her head, then she looked at me in disapproval. After I had told Michael what hair dye was, he was the one who had ultimately decided he wanted to do it, I was just feeling rebellious enough to encourage it; regardless if Hannah approved.

* * *

Evidently, Hannah did not approve of Michael dying his hair and kicked me out of her house. So two hours later, I was now at home, curled up on the sofa. I watched a horror movie while eating popcorn, my heart racing as the serial killer entered a home, knife in hand, and the music intensified. I shoved more popcorn in my mouth and chewed as the homeowner looked past a corner. This was terrifying. Out of nowhere, the serial killer burst through a wall and started slashing everything. I jumped, choking on popcorn in the process, smacking my chest as I coughed until my throat burned and tears blurred my vision, I reached over for my glass of water and took a much needed drink.

After a while I was midway through putting another scoop of popcorn in my mouth, when the doorbell rang, I slowly turned my head towards the front door. It rang again after a few short intervals, as I put the popcorn back in the bowl I moved it to the empty seat next to me, put the TV on mute and stood up as it rang again.

My cold feet smacked on the white tile of my home's flooring as I approached the front door, looking through the peephole. I relaxed to see my best friend, Payton.

The door sang out to signal its opening, and I smiled at her; she had pastel-pink hair and a fluffy white jacket on, a red dress that barely covered her boobs or ass, and in her hands, she had bottles of alcohol.

"Girl, we're drinking!" She let herself into my house. "While I've been on vacation, I've heard you were kidnapped and sent to Denmé, tell me the deets!"

I suddenly felt self-conscious of Dad's stained green sweater and my own black sweatpants I had changed into, but now Payton was in my living room, helping herself to popcorn.

* * *

Taking a big gulp from the bottle of beer I was holding, I hugged my knees to my chest and sighed. In The Rebellion, I only had watered down alcohol that tasted bitter, but the laughter I shared around it with Taylor was a fond memory of mine.

"Did you get a boyfriend while in Denmé? Are the boys cute?" Payton questioned.

"No boyfriend. Cute? Yes, just some of them had boyfriends." I responded.

"Darn it, why are all the cute ones taken," she responded with a pout. "Did you get any of their numbers? Who was the hottest?"

I scoffed and drank alcohol. "Technology is banned remember, so no phone numbers, sadly." Payton nodded. "But, Ezekiel was pretty hot, he had these beautiful blue eyes. Then there's Hunter, he's okay but I didn't like him; he seriously needed his roots re-touched."

As I drank more alcohol, Payton looked around my house as she also drank from her own bottle, then she smiled. "I'm glad you're back."

"They need freedom. One of the guys I met, Michael, he moved here using my dad's secret service; he's only been here a week and so much healthier. Today we went to a bookstore together, and he found that *Rise and Fall of St. Herculia* book we're given in school. It literally broke him," I admitted.

Suddenly Payton's eyes lit up, then she held my wrist, I looked at her. "This may be the alcohol talking, but I know a way to get freedom," she announced quickly. "Get your dad's secret service to put a shit load of those books all over Denmé. Start a war, even better send in the video of the actual election."

I stiffened and looked at her. "Maybe the video is going too far, you saw people getting killed during the earthquake. But, with the book, you're onto something there."

Payton nodded with a smile as she drank alcohol. This plan may just be a stupid drunken plan, but it was a plan nonetheless. All I had to do now was convince my dad to implement it, and I hoped he agreed.

16

Judas

It had been a week and two days since Nadine had returned home. Carlos and I knew this was a dumb idea, but we were above ground in Apartment Block West, where Carlos's mother and Gabrielle resided. I intended to say goodbye to my sister, then Michael, and this was the best way to do it. Then tomorrow I would start my new life underground like an Unlisted. Perfect plan.

I knocked on apartment 28E, Gabrielle's place. I heard the scraping of a chain pull away from the door, and then the click of a lock releasing its grasp to keep unwanted personnel out.

Odd. Guards made it a rule that we were not allowed to lock our apartment doors.

Gabrielle's head peaked out of the door, her eyes red from crying, my heart skipped a beat and I raised an eyebrow at her. Was she safe? I didn't know.

"Hello," I said to her with a smile.

"Hello, what are you doing here?" she said with a false smile.

"I came to say goodbye. I have to go somewhere for a long time." Saying it out loud made tears sting my eyes, she looked at me with innocent eyes.

"Okay."

I just told her I was leaving for a long time, and all she could say was *okay*. Something wasn't right. My suspicions were confirmed when the door swung open, and I froze. Six armed guards were standing behind her, pointing guns at me. I felt like I was on an elevator that lurched to its destination. This couldn't be happening.

One guard squeezed the trigger.

Pain went through my chest, and the world spun at a delirious angle for a moment, and then, darkness.

* * *

I awoke with a gasp, and pain numbed my entire body. I could only open my right eye. Stone and other dirt dug into my skin, and I winced as I sat up. I was on the floor of some place without windows or furniture. Only a single candle filled the room with a warm glow.

Quickly I realised I didn't have any clothes on, just some dirty underwear that hung loosely on my body, I groaned. Curling up, I started crying, mostly out of disbelief that my own sister would work with the guards to get me arrested. But I knew it wasn't her fault, she was probably coerced into it.

Hearing a metallic click, I turned my head to the metal door that swung open, then a plate rattled into the room followed by a metal cup.

"Bottoms up, prick," the sender said before slamming my door shut. The door locked again with a loud click, followed by the sound of keys.

What did he just call me? I didn't care, hunger made my stomach growl so much.

Crawling up to the plate of food, I sighed to see a rotten apple core, stale bread that literally turned to dust when I smacked it against the plate, and a mouldy yogurt.

Was I really hungry enough to contemplate eating this shit? No.

Picking up the cup, it looked like water in the candle light, the smell questionable. Taking a sip, the taste instantly burned my tongue—it was salty and tasted like ass. I spat it across the room and cringed.

What was this?

Looking at the cup, I was more thirsty than hungry. Curling up in the corner by the metal door, I pinched my nose and forced myself to chug down this mysterious liquid.

My stomach made the most disgusting gurgling noises. Like a boat in a rough sea, I felt a wave of bile that found its way up my throat. Running to a corner near the room, I instantly threw up.

Tremors ran through my body immediately after, and I instantly felt cold.

What the hell did I just drink?

I didn't care as I heaved again and again. Even though I tried my hardest not to, it was like my body was on autopilot to get this substance out of me. The place smelled even worse than it already did, farm animals, rotten food, and now this.

* * *

I didn't even know how much time had passed since we arrived in this place. Every day was the same; forced awake by guards, dragged to a brick room with one window, beaten until I passed out, then dragged back to this room.

Was Carlos in this place? I hoped not. It was horrible by so many means.

As I curled up from the throbbing pain in my stomach, I cried, feeling my tears sting the cuts on my face and mixing in with the blood pouring from my nose. I just wanted this over with, to stop being beaten, and just wait for that sweet release of the end. That would be better than beaten senseless in strange rooms by strange people.

When I opened my eyes, somebody was in the room with me, I didn't hear the door open though; how were they here? It didn't matter.

The person was a male in a government-issued uniform. He had black hair with flecks of grey, brown eyes, and a chiselled jawline—he looked just like me, but older, thin wrinkles lined their face, and they had a glow around them.

"Hello, son." His voice was echoey. Angelic.

"Dad?" my voice croaked out.

"You got this."

Dad never came closer to me. I wanted him to. Oh, I wanted him to hold me just one last time; it had been too long.

"I don't think I got this," I choked out as I started crying all over again.

Dad crouched down. "It's bedtime, son," he said.

"I'm not tired."

* * *

The room and my dad melted away. I was standing on the wrong side of a bridge, staring down into a raging river; the wind tore through my government uniform and pushed my hair into my face.

Leaning forward into the abyss whilst holding onto the railing, I sucked in a breath. I felt the heavy weight of dried tears which painted my cheeks, with new tears replacing them. Pulling myself back in again, I stuck a foot out. Just one step, I thought to myself.

Did I want to go out like this? The rocks rose up out of the fast flowing river like mountains, yet from this angle they looked like arrow heads ready

to tear my body to shreds once the water sucked me in.
Either way, I did it. I took that one step.

Falling just enough to stop myself, I grabbed onto the handrail, dangling dangerously over the river, just one slip of my finger, and I was gone. My heart raced. It wasn't my time.

A groan escaped my lips, trying to pull myself back up just made me fall back towards the water, I was losing my strength. I cried out as I tried again to pull myself up, as tears rained down my cheeks.

Feeling two strong hands grip hold of my wrist, I looked up to see Carlos. He looked younger, like when I first met him, with a shaved head, in government issued uniform.

In fact, this was how I met him. Exactly this. Moments away from ending it all on my own terms, right after the news my father had been executed for a crime he didn't commit.

"I've got you!" he shouted over the sound of the river. Carlos grunted, struggling against my weight. "Work with me, come on!" He started pulling me up.

As he pulled, I grabbed the hand rail until I found myself back on the wrong side of the bridge. Carlos held my arms

"I can't be here," I sobbed out. I rubbed my eyes with the heel of my hand, and felt so empty as soon as I wasn't in danger.

"Look at me," Carlos said, his grip tightened, I looked into his eyes. "You are amazing and strong, and you will get through whatever you're dealing with." His words were soft in my ears. "Come on, all it takes is getting over this barrier," he ushered.

I let him guide me back over the barrier, to the safety of solid ground. My legs gave way underneath me, and I fell on the ground.

Carlos wrapped his arms around me. "Take it one day at a time."

I was now convinced that this was a flashback of the time I met my soulmate. Carlos's embrace wasn't the one I had grown to crave whenever I needed comfort, it was awkward, and I could feel how tense he was at showing me any affection—out here in the open. Even worse, he didn't smell like cologne, just fresh linen from Task Three.

"They murdered my dad," I sobbed out into his shoulder.

"I've got a place you can go to escape it all; you can be yourself," he said in a hushed voice, it was like music to my ears.

I liked that idea. A place to escape, not fear being murdered for breathing, just being safe was what I needed.

Suddenly my dad appeared near us. I stared up at him.

"We're going to be in a mess," Dad said.

Dad only said that one time when Our Leader was elected. He crouched down near me and smiled at me.

"It's time for bed, son."

* * *

The sound of humming pulled me out of it. My eyes drifted open, and I was facing the cracked concrete wall of the room I was in, the dusty floor was still uncomfortable as a bed, the stones digging into my skin, the smell of dirt and sweat strong in the air. Except it now had elements of the smell of sage.

Wincing as I rolled over to see where the humming was coming from, the iron clamp feeling around my stomach made it difficult to move from hours of beatings and lack of food. My eyes widened at the source of the sound; six people stood around me, holding candles and wearing cloaks with goat skulls concealing their faces. Despite the pain, I sat up and pressed into the wall, trying to make myself as small as possible; my heart hammered in my chest.

One of the cloaked figures was crouched down to my level, I couldn't see their face, but I breathed heavily, the cold air showing my breath.

Whatever they were, they handed me a brown paper parcel.

"Is it time?" I croaked out, knowing my execution was scheduled soon.

"Yes, Joseph Wells, it is time," the crouched one said while the rest carried on humming. It was a voice I recognised from somewhere. I started crying, I didn't know why. Maybe relief knowing the beatings were going to end, and I would join my father. Over the humming, I could make out shouting then screams—what was happening?

"It's time to bust you out of jail," the crouched one said after a few moments of silence.

Confusion washed over me as I watched them remove their goat skull mask. I felt relief when I realised it was Samhain. Now I was crying for a whole other reason.

He pushed the parcel towards me and smiled.

"What is this?" I asked, my voice was scratchy, I picked it up, the parcel was warm in my hands.

"Food and drink," he said. "The bread, don't eat it all at once, you'll get a stomach ache."

Opening the parcel, it was as he said it was, and the bread had been sliced. Hearing the squeaking of wheels, I turned my head to see a wooden wheelchair roll in, pushed by another person wearing a goat mask—what is it with the goat masks?

"How are you above ground?" I asked. "How is Carlos?"

Two more goat mask people came in, picking me up from my armpits and ankles, their leather gloves cold against my bare skin, and placed me in the wheelchair.

"Carlos has already been saved. He's fine," Samhain informed me.

Relief washed over me, then I was on the move. But was Carlos here with me this whole time? I hoped not.

LISTED

* * *

From the extermination camp to wherever this place was, I must have passed out. This place was covered in symbols and wooden voodoo dolls hung from the ceiling, I was so confused. Humming was coming out of somewhere, but I was so tired it took all my concentration just to focus on eating the bread.

I wondered where we were going and where this place was, it felt electrifying in here, or maybe it was the result of the things on the walls and ceilings. My entire body hurt, but it was better than the place I just left, the smell of incense growing stronger with each passing moment.

I got wheeled through into a makeshift hospital. It looked like an abandoned theatre, wooden beds were lined up with makeshift dividers where the theatre seats were supposed to be, and a grand stage on the back wall had a few beds on it. Along with the smell of incense, it also smelled like mould and disinfectant. Trying to turn my head to see who was pushing me just made me dizzy, and my eyes widened as I tried stopping the room spinning

"What is this place?" I asked.

"Zone 13's Rebellion theatre. We just rescued 100 people from extermination camps, and the infirmary is full," an unfamiliar woman's voice said. My first time in Zone 13 and it was when I could barely stand from malnourishment and beatings.

"Thank you," I said.

We turned right towards a more secluded section of the theatre, towards a back corner in the dark.

"I think you will be comfortable here. Samhain has requested this personally," the woman said.

I was facing a double bed, somebody looking extremely frail led there—grey even—an IV drip was in their arm. They were asleep peacefully, a thick blanket covering them, then I realised who it was—Carlos. Despite all the pain I felt, I tried pushing myself up out of the chair to hold him, but my legs were too weak. With a groan, I fell back down.

Somebody in a goat mask came and picked me up, I was thankful they lowered me down next to him. I couldn't help but start crying, his cheeks were sunken in and dark circles surrounded his eyes. Reaching my hand out, I moved his hair from his face. He stirred but quickly relaxed, staying asleep.

"I love you," I whispered to him.

Wrapping my arm around him and pulling him close, I just cried out of relief he was alive, and Samhain out of all people had saved him.

* * *

The next day, warm water from the shower washed over my body; it was amazing to get clean, even if the hot water sent shooting pains through me as it hit the bruises painting my body. I pressed my forehead on the white tile and just sighed; tears stung my eyes, and I just couldn't believe I made it out of an extermination camp alive.

"Your brother's in Olympia, by the way," Samhain said.

Turning around, I jumped to see him in the shower with me, sitting on the edge of the bathtub. Wearing black skinny jeans and a black T-shirt which were getting wet, I covered my crotch with my hands and looked at him.

"Get out," I hissed at him.

"Well, it's important information you should know," Samhain replied.

"Not when I'm naked and in the shower!" I shouted back at him.

I hadn't been naked in front of a guy I wasn't involved with before, and I certainly wasn't involved with Samhain. Now it occurred to me he didn't have his goat skull on his head, he had a buzzcut that displayed a marble looking scar starting from his right ear to his neck. Everybody knew he had horror stories of his time in an extermination camp, hidden away in his brain somewhere, he never spoke about them.

Samhain nodded, he had his legs crossed, hands held together, he looked around the bathroom in deep thought. He could have easily spoken to me after my shower. But, this was Samhain we were dealing with, half his actions were unexplainable, or they were down right weird beyond measure

"Anyway, ORS is going to help us get freedom soon," Samhain informed me. I stiffened when I heard ORS, but my cheeks were burning from embarrassment. *Couldn't he just leave?*

"How do you know about ORS?" I asked.

"I know a lot of things. Enjoy your shower," he said.

Samhain pushed himself off the edge of the bathtub, and then I heard the bathroom door shut.

17

Judas

Samhain's words still ran through my mind two days later. He had a history of being a pathological liar, so I barely believed him. But I wasn't allowed above ground, so I couldn't verify if this was a fact.

Currently, Taylor was changing Carlos's IV in his underground apartment, he still wasn't fully recovered, but as I sat on the end of the bed, Carlos smiled at me. I could see the bunny sweater I bought him for our second-year anniversary. Taylor was wearing grey fitness leggings with a matching sports bra, and her green hair was tied up, she didn't look like somebody to perform medical treatment at all, but she insisted.

"How did you guys end up in the extermination camp?" Taylor asked, joining me by sitting on the end of the bed, checking for Carlos's feet before sitting down.

"I wanted to say goodbye to my mum," Carlos admitted, looking at his hands.

Taylor nodded, her shoulders dropped, and her eyes glazed over. I wanted to know what she's thinking, she was like my older sister at times too. She shook her head, then smiled.

"Now, you're both stuck with me forever," Taylor exclaimed. "Or until we get freedom."

I nodded with a smile. "Samhain said Michael's in Olympia. Do you know if it's true?" I asked her.

"You know Samhain is a pathological liar," Taylor responded.

"Well, not everything is a lie," I admitted defensively. "He knows things I've not even told Carlos." My gaze fell to Carlos, who's eyebrows were raised. He looked at me inquisitively like he wanted me to explain.

So I told them both about ORS wanting me to move in with my aunt who resides in Olympia and how creepily Samhain knew about it, and his weird prediction about ORS helping us with gaining freedom—which linked to his other weird prediction about a war that is going to ensue when Nadine returned home.

Both their faces looked like stone when I finished explaining everything, clearly they were both in shock and trying to figure out how he knew these details.

"Seeing as I'm Zone 14's co-leader, I can find out," Taylor said, finally breaking the silence that had ensued between us.

"Please do," Carlos said quickly. His voice sounded tired.

Taylor smacked her thighs and got off the bed with a determined smile and looked over at us both.

"Time to do some digging," Taylor responded with a sadistic smile, drumming her fingers together.

I watched her walk out of the apartment; when the door shut, I looked at Carlos, who was smiling at me. Carlos held his hand out, but I led next to him instead, feeling his strong arm around me, smelling his aftershave as we cuddled.

* * *

From the frying pan that was still sizzling, I filled up two plates with chicken curry. Carlos's apartment smelled heavenly of spices; right now, as I looked at him from the counter, I had a bird's-eye view of his apartment. The bed facing the kitchen, to my left was his living space. Underneath my feet was the door to The Tunnels, then the fake windows looking to a city. I had to face reality—this was my home now too, I had successfully moved in with my boyfriend and not by choice, which I would have liked to.

Picking up two spoons, I grabbed both the plates and made my way over to Carlos, who smiled at me as he collected one of the plates from my hand. Giving him a kiss, I then climbed over his legs and sat in the space to his left, thankful the sheets were black.

I looked at his IV drip, trying to help his body recover from whatever the extermination camp did to him. A wave of relaxation washed over me to see him tuck into the plate of food.

"If it's true Michael is in Olympia, he'll be safe," Carlos reassured me.

Heat rose in my body, and my stomach twisted from anxiety. But I nodded as I put a spoonful of food into my mouth.

"I don't believe ORS, or trust them. Why has Mum never mentioned she has a sibling? That's something significant about my family," I responded.

"Yeah, that is odd," Carlos said. "They clearly had a strong relationship if she's willing for you to go to Olympia."

"Exactly, that's what's weirder." I pushed rice onto my spoon. "As far as I'm concerned Michael's in Denmé going about doing his tasks like he's been brought up to do."

Carlos put another spoonful into his mouth. "Yeah, it's out of character for Michael to just abandon his love for Our Leader; he even kisses that creepy statue in the park."

I nodded while chewing a piece of chicken. The spices were like fireworks on my taste buds and it was probably the best meal I've ever cooked for myself.

Yes, Michael was still in Denmé, and Samhain was lying like he does most of the time. My brother was too brainwashed to give it all up, his whole life has revolved around the regime, he doesn't know anything different. It would be too out of character for him to just up and go with an organisation like ORS, then move countries when he loves Our Leader so much.

* * *

It was around midnight, and I was sitting in Taylor's apartment, it was a small studio in the shape of an L with plum-coloured walls, a small white kitchenette, and a sofa bed. She was offered a large apartment when she got promoted as co-leader, but she insisted this was her space. Every Rebellion Zone had co-leaders, these were mostly the Unlisted who ran the place while the actual leaders were outside with the exception of Zones 13, 1, and 4. Those Zones had Unlisted Leaders, so they didn't need the added security of co-leaders yet they still had them.

There was a shopping cart full of boxes near Taylor's kitchenette that she was looking through, pushing her hair behind her ear then wrapping her fluffy purple robe around her slim figure, I could only just make out her pj's had stars on them from her pants.

"Okay, so one of the Listed has gone to both your apartments and picked up your possessions, which are in these boxes," Taylor said, pointing to the cart. She held the handle then scratched her cheek. "Yeah, they have your apartment numbers on it. But it won't matter now, will it?"

"No, it won't," I responded, seeing her look at me.

"I don't know how to tell you something," she admitted.

My heart skipped a beat, and I felt like bad news was coming as she approached me and took my hands in hers. Taylor's hands felt cold, yet they were soft and delicate.

"Several of the Listed have told me Michael's been missing for over a week," Taylor admitted, her voice wavered as she told me, probably to hold back tears..

It felt like my world had just shattered—after spending the past couple of days convincing myself that Samhain had told me a lie, now finding out it could be true. I exhaled a breath.

"How are Mum and Gabrielle taking it?" I asked.

"I don't know," Taylor admitted. "But it's likely ORS took him somewhere."

My mind raced with all the possibilities of where my brother could be located. I didn't think it would be Olympia. Taking his injury into account, it would be dangerous to travel, especially with a broken leg from a bullet wound, what had Michael gotten himself into? The bigger question, where could he have gone to?

18

Nadine

Sitting inside a secluded section of a cafe in Downtown Gratisland, Michael was sitting on the leather sofa with his injured leg propped up, scribbling notes onto his homework. It was weird seeing him out of black clothes; today he was wearing a white hoodie with blue jeans. Payton and I were sitting in matching leather bucket chairs with two steaming cups of coffee on the table between us.

A bannister separated us from the coffee bar, where three staff members hurried about making all kinds of drinks, the sound of the milk steamer screeching and constant chatter livened up the place. The smell of coffee beans and pastries lingered in the air.

"Have you spoken to your dad about sending that book and the footage into Denmé?" Payton asked as she picked up her coffee, leaning back as she took a sip. She was wearing a green crop top with mom jeans, and her pink hair was formed into waves.

"Yes, he said he'll try getting the book into Denmé, but no promises," I replied.

"That's the dumbest fucking plan I have heard."

I turned my head, my eyes widened in shock that Michael just swore. He rarely did due to the years of suppression, the longer he stayed in Olympia, the more he sounded like one of us, and the fact he was losing the personality Denmé constructed for him scared me.

"Why's it dumb?" Payton asked as she put her coffee down.

"Guards will find out, ORS will get found out." He didn't look at us as he scribbled down more notes. Then he finally looked at us, his eyes clouded with worry. "You'll both have blood on your hands, if you go through with this."

A cold chill ran down my spine, I ran my hands down my face and groaned, Payton was silent as she stared at her feet. Either way, Michael had a point. It suddenly became evidently clear that there was a possibility where I couldn't help bring down the regime from the outside; but giving up on Judas and The Rebellion was something I just couldn't bring myself to do.

* * *

A few hours later, I was in my room, curled up on my bed. Just staring into the darkness of night not listening to anything, I didn't care what time it was, the discussion today had shaken me. My nerves felt well and truly shot. The last thing I wanted to do was give up on my friends, I had to reunite Michael with his family in some way. But was it just easier to give up?

That thought scared me more than anything.

Sometimes I wondered what Judas was doing right now, or what anybody I met in Denmé was doing without me there. Even though experiencing it was the worst experience of my life, everyday I found I missed being in The Rebellion, laughing around a table with some good food and friends; my only good memories of being there.

Hearing a glass on my nightstand rattle pulled me out of my thoughts. In fact, my entire room shook, and as quickly as it started, it was over.

Sitting up, I looked around my room, my curtains were still swaying gently and so was the string lights around my vanity. I looked at my clock; it was 12:50 a.m.

"Dad?" I called out, my heart suddenly racing.

My bedroom door opened, light from the corridor flooded into my room and my dad appeared in the doorway with his brow furrowed. I closed my eyes as he turned my bedroom light on, once I opened them again I looked at my pastel purple walls with various posters on them. Dad made his way over to my window and looked out of it, we were used to earthquakes, but this didn't feel like one. Usually, I could hear the ground rumbling and the shaking was more violent; this felt like a little push from the ground.

"We didn't get an alert on our phone that there's been an earthquake," Dad told me, checking his phone while scratching his cheek. He was wearing checked pants and a black T-shirt covered with a blue robe; Dad's brown hair was messed up. Mum walked into the room wearing a silky black sleep suit, and her hair tied up with hair rollers.

"Was it an earthquake?" she asked.

I reached over, checking my phone but still no alerts.

"Still no alerts. Go back to sleep," Dad grumbled.

Mum nodded and exited the room; Dad followed after and shut the light off. Then I was back in darkness and silence, with more questions than I had answers to. I sighed as I laid down on my pillow and just hoped we didn't get any aftershocks, that is, if it even was an earthquake.

* * *

The next morning, there were still no alerts for the mysterious shaking last night. Putting my slippers on, I left my bedroom, walked down the corridor, and made my way down the stairs, using the hand rail to support myself.

I made my way into the kitchen; Mum and Dad were sitting in the breakfast nook surrounded by a laptop which was showing live news footage of a burning building I faintly recognised. The building itself was beautiful, made of marble and surrounded by these ornate statues holding globes of pure jade crystal above their heads. It made the destruction seem peaceful in an odd way; this shouldn't be peaceful, I could hear screaming and sirens.

Picking up a pitcher of juice off the kitchen island and pouring myself a glass, I joined my mum and dad. As I sat down it was evident something was wrong, both my parents looked stern and there was a hint of fear in their eyes.

"What is it?" I asked, setting my glass down and grabbing some toast.

"There's been an explosion at Denmé's capital building," Mum said, her voice wavered with some emotion I couldn't decipher. My eyes widened at the news, the building I was seeing was secret footage from inside Denmé.

"Holy shit, when?" I spat out.

"Around 1 a.m. last night, they can't contain the fire," Dad said.

"Could that be the shaking we felt last night?"

Both my parents shrugged, I tried biting into some toast but a sickness filled my stomach, I breathed out, thinking of Ezekiel and everybody in Zone 7. Gratisland was exactly five hours from the border of Denmé's Zone 7, grabbing two slices of toast, I jumped up and grabbed my car keys.

"Where are you going, sweetie?" Mum asked.

I shrugged my jacket on. "Denmé."

"You aren't going back there," Dad said sternly.

"Not inside, I'm going to the border," I replied with the same stern tone as Dad.

LISTED

* * *

Michael sat in my car's passenger seat; he had the window down and was pretending his hand was a bird. Sometimes he was so weird, but I didn't care. Michael wore his usual grey trench coat that had a black turtleneck peeking out from the edges.

"So, you didn't feel any tremor last night?" I asked.

"No tremor," Michael responded. "So, there's been an explosion at Our Leader's courthouse?"

I sucked in a breath and chewed on my thumb nail while driving, ignoring his question. He now lived an hour West of Gratisland, his town wouldn't feel the after effects of an explosion.

We were ten minutes away from the border, and we probably wouldn't see anything, but I just needed to check.

It was ingrained in my memory the route Ezekiel took to get me home safely, well to my town's hospital. The night I got found out was a night I would never forget, it had taken two days to get back to Gratisland, Olympia.

Turning down a dead-end dirt road, I could hear my car's tires crunching on rocks.

Putting my car in park near a large gate with fading positive messages tied to it and barbed wire on the top, I turned off the ignition and unclipped my seatbelt. Michael did the same.

Getting out of my car, I could smell smoke already, the scent that was crisp and burned your nose. Michael hopped out of my car and took his crutches from the back seat.

"This feels weird," Michael said.

"Tell me about it," I responded, then sucked in a breath.

"What's that over there?" Michael asked, pointing to something.

Looking at what he was pointing at, I gasped. The ground dipped down into a hill just east of the large gate, secluded by a dozen trees and brambles. I could make out it was a road leading to a large tunnel that went underground; it looked big enough to fit trucks in there. No lights were on, and I had to squint to see it. But what made it obvious it was there, was the fact people were piling out of it.

Some injured people were carrying things on their backs. Some people were on the ground, clearly dead.

My heart raced, then I started running towards the people, seeing if I could be of help in any way.

"Nadine!" I heard Michael shout after me, but I was already committed.

The people saw me as I approached, I never looked at their faces, but their clothes were dirty, wet and tattered. My mouth was dry, and I felt a lump in my throat.

"Meet over with my friend," I told each of them as I passed.

These were clearly Denmé citizens, I saw some barcodes.

Even though I told Dad I wouldn't go back to Denmé, seeing these people made me feel compelled to do so. I knelt down next to somebody on the ground, pressed my fingers to their wrist—no pulse as I suspected.

At the sudden realisation I had to go back to Denmé, my heart felt like it could have leapt out of my chest.

19

Nadine

As I ran down the tunnel, I stopped when I felt too sick, leaning forward putting my hands on my thighs and tried to control my breathing. I could hear people coming out of the darkness towards me, their footsteps echoed around the dark tunnel but something that unnerved me was the sound of running water. The smell of burning was so strong now that I had to pull my sweater over my mouth and nose to stop from coughing; even though my throat burned as I suppressed a cough.

With my trembling free hand, I used my cellphone to turn the flashlight on, waving it around the tunnel. As I suspected people were in fact running towards me, like the tail end of a stampede. Then my eyes widened to see water and thick smoke spilling out of the metal door which separated Denmé and Olympia. The door had been wedged open by something heavy and metallic which peaked out of the gushing water. Pointing the light down at my feet, they were already submerged in shallow pool.

Sucking in a breath, I continued walking, occasionally looking behind my shoulder to see if anybody was following me—a stupid thought in this situation. I stopped to allow myself to cough into my sweater; not being able to hold back any longer. My eyes stinging as the smoke hit me. Then I jumped as somebody grabbed me, turning around it was an old man with an unconscious child on his back, he had a large cut on his forehead and clearly in his underwear aside from a stained white tank top.

"Turn back ma'am, you don't want to go in there," he warned.

I noticed he was Unlisted. Sucking in a breath I asked. "Is Ezekiel okay?"

The man continued walking towards Olympia. "Turn back, save yourself!" his voice boomed around the tunnel.

Turning back to the entrance, I took a step forward and hesitated. What was I doing? Everything was telling me to follow the mans advice, but he didn't give me any answers about Ezekiel.

Pushing my fears aside, I put my phone in my mouth, grabbed hold of the door to Highway 8 and climbed over the metal object which kept it open. As I hit the water, I took my phone out of my mouth and gasped loudly as freezing cold water hit my ankles.

* * *

Inside the tunnel, it was a mess. The mosaic mermaid on the ceiling of Highway 8 was now floating in the water, and nearby a large water pipe protruded out of it, spraying everything in its path like a fire hose. I noticed the water was much higher up ahead, but I didn't know if it was an optical illusion. Shielding my head as the overhead lights exploded, spraying sparks like fireworks into the water. Once I uncovered my head I noticed cars floated into barriers and other debris, their alarms blaring with the hazard lights flashing to the beat. Looking around, the marble pillars which encased the doors to each tunnel were cracked from the loose ceiling, making it more apparent I had to move quickly.

Wading my way through the water, I grabbed hold of a twisted piece of handrail and forced myself up the stairs which were now a cascading waterfall. Once I was on the walkway my jeans felt like they were made of lead. From up here I could see the true scale of the destruction, I had to quickly remember which one led to the apartments, running a hand through my hair as I tried to remember; I decided to look at each sign above the marble arches. *Tunnel 7:8.* Yes, that was the apartments; the only place I knew Ezekiel could be.

As I jogged through the water, the smell of burning mixed with sulphur made my stomach churn but I pushed through. I screamed, and fell back into the wall as a large swell of water smashed a car through the barrier into the walkway, narrowly missing me by inches. My entire body was now soaked as water splashed over me, and my hair stuck to my face, I pushed my hair away quickly whilst breathing heavily. I used the cars wheel to stand myself up. Climbing over the hood and dropping down, I started running at full speed, water splashing up to my arms.

Only skidding to a stop at Tunnel 7:8.

My lungs burned and I leaned against the warped barrier to catch my breath, when I looked into the highway I yelped to see a person holding possessions swimming past me, they oddly seemed peaceful in such a chaotic situation. Swallowing the lump in my throat, I turned towards the door of Tunnel 7:8 and exhaled a breath as I wrapped my hand around the handle.

Pulling the handle towards myself, I felt relieved as the door gave way, but then I noticed water start to gush out. Holy crap, no. Not now. As the metal door started to creak, I mentally prepared myself and pressed into the marble pillar. Placing my fingers into a large crack to get some grip on the slippery material. I squeezed my eyes shut as the metal door burst out into Highway 8.

The force of the water sounded like I was underneath a waterfall, and I felt water come up to my knees, spraying more of my arms and face. Now the smell of sulphur and burning had rapidly increased to the point I could taste it, I coughed into my arm as I let go of the pillar, wading through the now knee-high water. The sooner I finished what I set out to do, the better.

* * *

As I ran through the apartments , the water had receded back to my ankles, my only light source was my phones flashlight. The wooden doors strewn about the corridor made a loud cracking noise as I ran over them, the sound of water splashing echoed around me, even as I had to slow down so I didn't lose my footing when hurrying over people's possessions. It felt horrible when I had to climb over a bookcase full of water logged books and children's toys.

Stumbling into the wall to catch my breath, I realised I had coincidentally stopped outside of apartment 19B, the apartment I resided in during my short time in Zone 7. Pushing the door open, I shined my flashlight into the area, it was completely empty now with the furniture bobbing about with the water. Pressing my head to the door frame, I broke down crying, there was so much destruction.

Only when I heard the groan did I raise my head, wiping away my tears quickly. I used the wall to support myself, as I moved my flashlight to shine down the corridor. Nobody. Looking in the opposite direction, I swallowed the lump in my throat—a bad feeling crept up my spine, snapping back to the other end of the corridor when the groan sounded out again.

"Ezekiel?" I called out.

Pushing myself away from the wall, I started jogging down the corridor when I heard another groan. Water sloshed around my feet. My lungs burning in protest from how much I ran against the heaviness of the water, but something wasn't right. Suddenly a loud scream echoed around the corridor.

"Ezekiel! If that's you, hit something so I know where you are!" I shouted more frantically whilst running.

Only stopping briefly to look around the corridor when I heard the creaking. Looking up, cracks had spider webbed their way throughout the ceiling and onto some of the walls, Jesus Christ this was bad. However, I was instantly on the move when a metal banging replaced the mysterious creaking.

The sound was coming from something behind a green door at the end of the corridor, thankfully it was split in two, looking into the apartment I could see a figure on the floor with pieces of furniture on top of them. There was no denying who it was.

Shoving my cellphone in my pocket, I held onto the door frame and kicked as hard as I could. It didn't budge. After trying multiple times with all my strength, the door finally gave way, I felt weak and slightly light headed from using what little energy I had left.

Running into the apartment, I approached Ezekiel, and crouched down to next him—I felt lost on what to do when I realised a book case had fallen on him, along with a ventilation pipe. His breathing was heavy as he grimaced.

"I'm going to get this off of you, just hold still," I explained.

With a loud groan, I pushed the ventilation pipe off of him first, my arms burned from how heavy that thing was. It made a loud metallic bang on the floor. Getting the bookcase off of him was a much easier experience, I breathed heavily and my heart raced as I partially collapsed next to Ezekiel, pushing my soaking wet hair out of my face.

"Nadine, what the fuck are you doing back in Denmé?" Ezekiel choked out through coughs, and he shielded his eyes from my flashlight as I shined it around the apartment.

Sucking in a breath I decided to say the truth to him. "I heard there had been an explosion and people were piling out of the import tunnel, knowing you'd be in here I had to make sure you were safe."

Ezekiel slowly sat up, clutching his left side, my eyes widened once I noticed there was a wooden stick protruding out of his body.

"Holy shit!" I exclaimed, taking my jacket off quickly and holding it against the wound, Ezekiel groaned out and sucked in a breath.

"I need to get to the other Zones," he breathed out, grimacing as he looked down at his injury.

"Highway 8, 9, and 10 are completely submerged in water; it's impassable by car," I explained.

Ezekiel ran his hands through his dreadlocks, consequently breaking down crying like I did a few moments ago. "Fuck!" he shouted.

"We need to move, the water's only going to get higher."

I let Ezekiel wrap an arm around my shoulders, then I helped him stand up. He cried out as he straightened his body, the movement clearly made his injury much worse as warm blood soaked through my jacket and onto my hand. Nobody was going to come and rescue us in here, so moving him was the only way.

Ezekiel breathed heavily. "Nadine, help me write a note to tell people where I'm going." He groaned loudly out of pain.

"Are you sure? It might get swept away."

"Just do it." he instructed, pointing to the kitchen island where a notebook sat.

I guided Ezekiel over to it, where he leaned against a stool as I grabbed the notebook, and scribbled *I've had to go to Olympia*' after showing him the message, he nodded in approval and then he wrapped his arm across my shoulder.

Both of us started walking out of his Rebellion apartment, and back towards The Tunnels.

LISTED

***

As we both walked up the import tunnel, my jeans were now soaked up to my knees, and my hair was stuck to my face from going underneath a heavy stream of water as a result of a burst pipe. I shivered from the cold water inside my shirt, feeling exhausted from half dragging Ezekiel through the labyrinth that was The Rebellion. Whenever he moved Ezekiel winced, his breathing was heavy like mine. I squinted my eyes as I saw saw sunlight for the first time in, I didn't know how long it had been. On the horizon I saw the red flashing lights of several ambulances. Holy shit, did I just cause a big mess? I was so delirious and high on an adrenaline rush at this point

Two people ran up to me and took Ezekiel off my hands. Then I felt arms wrap around me and hold me close.

"How could you be so stupid? Who are these people?" I recognised my dads voice instantly. His embrace was so tight I thought I would snap.

Shaking out of his embrace, I could see that there were roughly a dozen people in ambulances getting attended to by paramedics, Michael was still here sitting on the hood of my car.

"They're part of Denmé's Rebellion," I admitted.

My dad gripped me by the arm and half dragged me back to my car, his face was stern and I was slightly terrified of how angry he appeared. "You told me you wouldn't go back to Denmé and you did anyway! Never do something like that again!" He shouted at me as he let go. Disappearing into the crowed of people.

Once he let me go, I rubbed my arm wincing at how numb it felt. I glanced at Michael, he looked like he had been crying, his hair was so messed up that it covered the blue streak he had put in there.

"I'm sorry for calling your dad, I knew he'd be angry," he said quickly, his voice shaking with obvious worry.

"I'm not mad," I admitted with a forced smile. "Thank you, these people can get help now."

Seeing Michael relax, made me feel slightly more relaxed than I felt. Deep within me, everything was telling me to be on high alert for danger. But I looked at Ezekiel, once I noticed he was approaching from the corner of my eye, he held out my jacket to me with a smile.

"I believe this is yours," he said.

"Thanks," I replied as I took it out of his grasp. Trying my hardest to ignore the blood which stained the green material.

Ezekiel did a double take when he saw Michael, then his eyes widened. Then he looked at me. "So it's true, Michael is actually in Olympia."

"Do I know you?" Michael asked with a furrowed brow.

"Zone 7 Rebellion Leader, your brother has been asking about you," Ezekiel breathed out, then covered his mouth as he started coughing. My heart skipped a beat when I noticed his hand came away covered in blood.

"Wait, all these people are from something called The Rebellion?" Michael asked. His eyes were wide. "And you're saying my brother's part of this?"

Ezekiel nodded he started coughing more, I only felt relief when a group of paramedics came over and took him away. When I looked at Michael, he looked at his hands then at my face.

The shock in his eyes was replaced by something I hadn't seen since he lived in Denmé. Fear.

* * *

An hour later Michael and I were sitting in my kitchen waiting for answers from my dad and Hannah. Currently both of them were in his office discussing the future of rescuing Judas and the rest of Michael's family, but apparently because we were "kids" we weren't allowed to know. I wasn't the one who needed protecting, especially at twenty-one years old.

Michael was happily scrolling through his phone and on occasion scratched his cheek, his injured leg dangling away from the bar stool he was sitting on. I leaned against the counter.

"Are you okay?" I asked.

"Kind of, it's weird to know my brother was living a double life." Michael admitted as he looked at me. "It also explains a lot, like how you managed to get Listed." He went back to looking through this phone, moving his hair out of his eye. I noticed he was watching news coverage of the explosion in Denmé.

I picked an apple from the fruit bowl and played with the stem. As I scratched my head which was wrapped in a towel from a much needed shower, I replied to him. "The Rebellion really was the only place Judas could be free you know, Denmé could be free too if they figure out how to get freedom."

Michael contemplated this for a moment while looking at his phone. But as he slowly looked at me, I sighed, blinking back the inevitable tears that I had been holding since rescuing Ezekiel. But it was no use, tears rolled down my cheeks anyway and I quickly pushed them away.

"Why are you crying?" Michael's face was clouded with concern.

"Today," I admitted. "Everything in Denmé is going to shit, and I just feel useless. I can't help your brother, and I can only sit and watch as more madness unfolds." I sobbed while wiping my eyes; eventually burying my head in my hands and breaking down properly.

Feeling Michael wrap his hand around my wrist and gently pull my arm down, I looked at him as he held my hand for comfort. This felt weird, considering I knew Michael wasn't the type of person to randomly hold somebody's hand, and the fact I saw him like a little brother. Regardless, I smiled at him.

"When Denmé gets freedom, I think The Rebellion can become a museum." Michael proposed.

I scoffed out a laugh and looked at him. "Do you even know what a museum is?"

"No, but I read about them at school. They're old places people look at for fun."

As I wiped my eyes, we both laughed at this proposal; however, it was definitely a possibility down the line.

A cough came from the kitchen door, and I saw Hannah standing there, she was wearing scrubs, and her hair pulled back into a bun. Judging by the paw prints on her leg, I guessed she was a veterinarian. Hannah didn't look pleased with the hand holding.

"You know I'm holding her hand in comfort right," Michael said and rolled his eyes.

"I know," she said somehow managing to flash a smile. "Your father has decided not to assist anymore with helping my family, from today forward it is too dangerous to try and get Judas and the others out."

"What!" I shouted. Pushing myself away from the counter, I started to walk towards my dad's office, but Hannah grabbed my arm to stop me. "Get off me!"

Pushing open the office door angrily, I saw Dad was sitting at his desk, and ran his fingers along the bridge of his nose, he looked exhausted.

"Nadine, it is too dangerous," my dad warned and looked at me when he put his glasses on.

"You promised you would help them!" I shouted.

Dad swivelled in his chair, fixing his tie and glasses. With a sigh, he looked at me shaking his head. "They know where The Rebellion is now, sweetie; they are already starting to target it. Already they are searching Zone 7's Rebellion. Judas and Gabrielle have to be on their own from here on out."

Tears stung my eyes, and I thought of Michael in the kitchen, hearing the news that his brother won't get help—even after my dad promised to help Judas get to freedom, and my blood boiled from anger.

"All of them need help. Just please let me warn Judas or Carlos," I pleaded, tears rolling down my cheeks, and my dad slammed a hand on his desk. Dad growled and looked at me with anger, but I didn't mind him being angry at me as long as I could help The Rebellion from the outside.

"We don't know where to find Zone 14's Rebellion, it's not going to work," Dad hissed and crumpled up paper in his hand.

"I do. Please, please just give them enough warning!" I begged.

"Fine. But that is the extent of our help, we can't bring him to Olympia when it is this dangerous," Dad snapped.

"Thank you," I choked out, wiping my tears away.

20

Judas

Looking through the basement keyhole of my mum's house, I saw her working in the kitchen. The kitchen had yellow tiles and brown cabinets, steam rose from the pans she was cooking with, a guard stood outside her back door.

I opened the basement door ajar, and Mum looked at the movement.

"Mum," I said, waving my hand for her to come forward.

I watched Mum wipe her hands on her uniform, turn the heat down on the hob, checked behind her shoulder, then walked towards me.

Mum shut the basement door behind her, and followed me hurriedly down the stairs. I jogged over to the dryer and turned it on. The fact there were still personal laundry facilities in this house showed its age, since Task 3 was introduced there was no need for such things. It's a miracle the dryer still worked after seventeen years.

"Where have you been?" Mum asked, her cheeks were becoming a blush pink as she exhaled a breath, she placed a hand on her forehead, the other on her hip. "When people told me two of my kids are missing, I was secretly trying to find you guys."

"I've been safe, but I can't be here long."

Mum placed both her hands on her hips, and nodded pacing slightly in front of me. She looked tired, dark circles under her eyes. It was evident, since finding out Michael and I had been missing, that she hadn't been sleeping.

"What do you need to talk to me about?" she asked. Finally mum stepped up to me, tugging on my white hoodie and glancing at my black skinny jeans. "Why are you dressed like this? Where's your uniform?"

"Doesn't matter. But there are rumours that Michael's in Olympia with your sister," I admitted. Feeling like a part of me was missing as soon as I said it.

Mum stiffened, looking behind her shoulder towards the stairs, clearly paranoid of the guards noticing she was missing from the kitchen. Then looked at me.

"How do you know you have an aunt?"

I sighed, looking through the basement window when I saw movement out the corner of my eye. "An organisation called ORS paid us a visit and told us. Why were we never told of this?"

Mum shifted on her feet, looking at the ground. "I immigrated here to be with your father, before we lost freedom, I was actually born in Olympia." She sucked in a breath and looked at the ceiling. "Once we lost freedom, I knew I could never go home, so your father and I agreed to pretend she didn't exist. To protect you guys."

Clearly from years of exposure to the Zone 14 accent, her Olympian one had more or less diminished. Yet, I could understand why she lied to us.

Hearing footsteps above us, I looked up as my heart skipped a beat, even mum shifted uncomfortably when I looked at her. Crap.

"I've got to go," I said quickly.

Mum nodded, wiping tears from her eyes as she pulled me into her embrace. I held her tightly, feeling her rub my back out of comfort, until she pushed me away and headed up the stairs. When she extended her hand out to me, I held it tightly until she had no choice but to let go as she returned to her cooking.

For a couple moments, I stayed alone in the basement, the only sound was the droning of the dryer and the muffled voices above me. But there was no point sticking around, so I slipped out of the window before guards could find me.

* * *

Back in The Rebellion twenty minutes later, I could hear shouting coming from the jail. Slowing down to a stop as I got to the door, peaking inside Taylor was standing there with her arms folded over her chest. I had never seen her look so formal, today she was wearing a white dress with a grey blazer, her hair pin straight down her back. In front of her was Adriel and Archie, then my gaze fell on Carlos he was breathing heavily and looking furious as he spoke to a surprising guest. Samhain. He was leaning back in the chair he was sat on, looking very smug.

"You blew up the capital building" Carlos shouted. "Do you have any idea what you have just fucking done!"

My breath caught in my throat, and the world spun at a delirious angle to the point I had to hold onto the door frame. Either way, I wanted to be involved in this discussion, so I pushed myself to join everybody. Carlos was the first to glance up at me, I knew it was something serious when he didn't look happy at my presence being here, then his gaze fell on Taylor. A silent communication between them both.

Taylor turned to me, and gently pushed me out of the jail, looking around the corridor to see if anybody else was around before speaking.

"What's going on? I could hear shouting from the entrance."

She sucked in a breath. "I don't know how much you heard but

Zone 7 Rebellion no longer exists."

I blinked a couple times . "What?" I exclaimed. "I heard something about Samhain blowing up the capital building but how? What?"

Taylor's eyes glazed over and she blinked back tears as she returned to having her arms folded. "Yeah well, that explosion was to send Our Leader a message. But it was so powerful that it burst several water pipes, the entire Zone 7 area is flooded. Even Zone 4 and 8 have minor damage."

"What about Ezekiel?" I breathed out.

"That's the scary thing," Taylor admitted. Scratching behind her ear. "We have no idea where he is, we have called all seventeen Zone's, he's not in any of them. Even dive teams haven't found him."

I exhaled a breath, glancing into the jail, feeling a cold chill run down my spine to see Samhain staring directly at myself and Taylor; ignoring Carlos's shouting. But after five years of being in The Rebellion, I knew Samhain well enough to know he did this. At the start of this week he was the person who saved mine and Carlos's life; now, I didn't recognise him. Samhain had officially doomed us all.

* * *

Ten minutes later, I shut the door to my apartment. As I slid down the door, my hands were trembling and my heart raced. I brought my knees up to my chest, and gripped a handful of my hair as I tried to calm myself down. Tears stung my eyes, this was all too much in a short amount of time. As I let go of my hair, I looked up to the ceilings ventilation pipes, and sucked in a sharp intake of breath with a groan.

Not being able to hold back, I broke down crying.

With everything from the extermination camp to losing my brother, then to find out the person who saved mine and my boyfriends life had just put us in all danger; it was all too much for myself to handle. Then there was the added fact of The Rebellion, even when I was allowed above ground this always felt like home, but as I was adjusting to life down here, it was becoming suffocating.

These past two weeks had been a whirl wind, and now all of my built up emotions poured out of me like a tsunami. I sobbed loudly as I let myself curl up on the apartments floor, staring at the back of the large corner sofa. With Carlos recovering from whatever the extermination camp did to him, and the added stress of the current situation, I couldn't bring myself to confide in him. I hated him worrying about me with these circumstances at play.

A knock at the door pulled me out of my thoughts.

"Carlos are you okay? I can hear you," a woman's voice said.

Wiping my eyes with the heel of my hand, and sniffling. "It's Judas," I groaned out, choking on tears.

"Would you like me to find Carlos?"

Sucking a breathing, I wiped my eyes again and responded quietly. "Please."

The sound of footsteps retreating made me feel relieved, even though it made me start crying all over again.

* * *

A few hours after my breakdown, I found myself in a boat with Carlos and Xander, Zone 4 Rebellion Leader, who steered us into Zone 7. Leaving behind the cracked mosaic titles on Zone 4's ceiling of Highway 9 which were in the shape of constellations, and then we entered utter chaos.

Cars floated around in waist-deep water, on occasion these hit the already warped barriers of the walk way. Our only light source was from the large flashlight Xander was holding as he swept the light around the tunnel. There were fragments of a mosaic ceiling floating around in the water, when I looked up it looked exactly like Zone 14's ceiling—concrete dirt. A large pipe protruded out of the ceiling at the bottom. Light fixtures, hung dangerously near the water, spraying sparks around with loud hissing noises. The marble pillars which encased the doors to each individual tunnel were cracked, some completely destroyed with potential to trap any possible survivors inside.

Within the water, I saw a few corpses floating around, sadly you could have mistaken them for being asleep if it wasn't for their skins bluish colour. My stomach lurched, I couldn't help but grip the side of the boat and throw up. Instantly I felt a hand on my back, feeling relieved to see it was Carlos.

"Are you okay?" he asked as he moved my hair out of my face. I nodded, wiping my mouth with the back of my hand. "Where are we going?"

I looked at Xander, he had shoulder length brown hair with one side shaved and streaked purple. He wore black skinny jeans, and a loose fitting tank top, showing off a dragon tattoo which painted the majority of his chest.

"Tunnel 7:8, we're going to look in Ezekiel's apartment again," Xander responded.

I watched as Carlos sat back on his side of the boat, I still felt queasy from seeing the bodies even as I reached over and held Carlos's hand. "Has anybody thought to check on his above ground apartment?"

Slowly Xander nodded, his eyes glazed over. "We've already checked, he hasn't checked in for any tasks today either."

The scraping noise which came from the boat as it bobbed over debris made my heart skip a beat, we were well on our way to Tunnel 7:8, I noticed a sign above the door saying 7:15. Suddenly the boat lurched forward as Xander put it into a higher gear. I didn't know why I agreed to go on this excursion, maybe it was because life underground became boring after a while.

I closed my eyes, trying to think of a happier place to be than be inside what was practically a tomb at this point. Only opening my eyes when the boat stopped.

When Xander stood up, the boat rocked violently. I couldn't believe how tall and slender he was, what was even stranger was seeing the barcode tattoo on his right arm; just like mine and Carlos's except it was crossed out with red ink. Everybody knew Xander was an Unlisted, so why did he have it? Was it irony?

At the end of the tunnel there was a thick metal door, held open by something fully submerged. Beyond it was ominous darkness with the slight hint of light.

"What's down there?" I asked.

Carlos shrugged. Xander stood on the edge of the boat, causing it to lean uncomfortably to one side, I thought we were going to capsize—but as he gripped onto the handrail and hauled himself over to the walkway, the boat swayed as it righted itself. I couldn't help but notice the water was up to his knees.

"That's Olympia," Xander replied.

"If Olympia's that close, why don't all the Unlisted leave?" I asked. "It seems easy to go through."

Xander sighed heavily, running a hand through his hair. "Would you leave if you didn't know what was waiting on the other side?"

The question was clearly rhetorical. In my head I had already answered an obvious *no*. Carlos was the next to stand up, I gripped hold of the sides as the boat once again leaned heavily to one side, as he hauled himself up to the walkway.

I was the last to haul myself over.

***

My jeans were also soaked up to my knees by the time we got to the apartments. It was evident from the drastic difference in the amount of water, that most of it had found its way into The Tunnels, I was thankful we didn't have to wade through knee high water all the way through. Doors were broken and strewn into the corridor, they crunched as Xander, Carlos and I stepped on them. It was deathly quiet, aside from the sound of running water, and an alarm blaring from an unknown location. I held onto Carlos's hand as he guided me over large pieces of furniture which had found themselves blocking our path.

By the end of the obstacle course of furniture, I was breathing heavily and felt utterly exhausted. Only stopping briefly when we got to an apartment at the end of the corridor, in the doorway a green front door was split into two pieces on the floor.

"This is Ezekiel's apartment," Carlos informed me.

Xander scanned his large flashlight around the room before stepping inside, Carlos took my hand and guided me into the apartment. The first thing I noticed was how strange and foreboding it looked when the false windows of The Rebellion were turned off. From the light of the flashlight I noticed there was a large crack in one of them.

However, this apartment was a very grand place indeed. The windows were encased in marble, with some obvious cracks in the material from the force of the impact. His bedroom was to the left with marble textured windows looking into the rest of the space, even if his bed had been pushed into the doorway by the force of water. Next to that was the large kitchen and a bathroom nearby.

When I saw the broken bookshelf on the floor, I approached it and crouched down, my eyes widening in revelation to see a large red mark on the floor.

"Hey guys, what's this?" I asked pointing to it.

Xander approached me, got down on all fours then licked the floor. It took all of my effort not to retch, I pressed a hand to my stomach as it gurgled.

"It's blood," Xander confirmed.

"That's obvious, but did you have to lick it?" I hissed. He smiled and winked at me as he knelt down on the ground. "Clearly it means he's injured."

Looking at Carlos who was in the kitchen, he turned around holding up a notebook, there was a page torn out of it and I noticed blood covering the edges. "Who's been in here before us?"

Xander shrugged, due to not being a Leader I wasn't allowed to know that information so I had no idea either. Something did seem fishy, the tear was sloppy, Ezekiel was a perfectionist, and wouldn't tear a page out like that; even if he was as injured. Carlos only sucked in a breath, placing the notebook down.

"If he's injured—" I began.

"Or dead," Xander interrupted.

"Well, let's not jump to conclusions. He clearly left a note to give us a message." I pushed myself off of the floor, and approached Carlos, looking at the notebook.

Carlos drummed his fingers on the counter. "And somebody has clearly gotten into this apartment and torn this entire page out to make us not get it."

This entire situation didn't seem right, who would disrespect Ezekiel enough to try and make us think he's dead? Everybody trusted Ezekiel and you could sense his calming presence when he walked into a room, he had no enemies aside from Our Leader, and the only time I saw him truly angry was when he was taking Nadine home. An even bigger mystery right now was Ezekiel's location.

"We need to get out of here, I have an uneasy feeling about this," I announced after a few moments.

Nobody disagreed.

* * *

Back on Highway 8, Xander climbed over the barrier of the walkway, jumping back into the boat. It swayed back and forth as it adjusted to his weight, he sat down. Carlos climbed over next, and I followed, sitting back in my original position.

"Ready?" Xander asked.

Both of us nodded, I watched Xander pull the chord, and with sputtering sound, the engine started. He moved the stick that controlled the movements and before I knew it, we were heading back in the direction of Zone 4. Back to relative safety.

None of us spoke as we cruised through Zone 7, I tried my best to avoid looking at the water and the corpses floating about. I exhaled a breath heavily. My mind racing with what the mysterious note would have said, and why would somebody tear it out. Somebody in The Rebellion clearly knew his whereabouts, and wasn't telling anybody.

Only being pulled out of my own thoughts when the tunnel rumbled angrily around us, the force of the vibrations splashed water into the boat. I looked around as my heart rate increased as the creaking sound started.

Then I tensed as Carlos gasped loudly, following his gaze, the entire tunnel around us was coming down like a landslide, absorbing everything in its path of destruction.

Holy shit.

One minute, Xander was shouting as he tried to increase the boats speed.

The next, the compact dirt of the tunnel caught up to us, it felt like hail as it rained down. Yet it crashed into our boat with such force, we capsized and I cried out as I was plunged into the icy depths of the water below.

21

Judas

I sucked in a huge breath with a wheeze, coughing and spluttering as I emerged out of the water. Looking around there was just a large mound of compact dirt where the tunnel had collapsed, I breathed heavily and looked around frantically for Carlos as I started treading the water which was now so deep I couldn't touch the bottom. My heart hammered so hard against my ribs, I thought they might break.

"Carlos! Xander!" I shouted out. My voice sounded weak.

All of a sudden, a head popped up and gasped for air. I instantly felt relief to recognise Carlos. Immediately swimming up to him, I grabbed him and held him close. After giving him a kiss, I breathed heavily, trying not to cry out of relief.

"Where's Xander?" Carlos asked. He was breathless while he scanned the water.

"I don't know," I said, looking around. "Are you okay?"

Then I heard the familiar sound of a boat scraping against debris, it was followed by a spotlight which shone upon myself and Carlos, shielding my eyes as I turned towards the source of the light. Feeling relieved at the fact it was another boat, on the front was a silhouette of a person, when she finally came into view it was Abrianna Martin,

Leader of Zone 6—blonde hair rained down to her waist and she was wearing government uniform. There was six others in the boat with her, including Zone 2 Leader Oluchi Adorette. My gaze fell to the gun Oluchi was holding, I knew it was only a precaution as to why she had it.

"We heard the collapse from Zone 4," Oluchi exclaimed as she stood up.

Abrianna nodded, looking behind her shoulder then back at us both. "Get in the boat, both of you."

I swam up to them both. "Xander's missing," I announced as I gripped the side of the boat, using Oluchi's help to pull me inside.

"All of you find him," Abriana instructed to the others in the boat.

One by one the other people in the boat dived in on a mission to save Xander. I leaned over the side of the boat and pulled Carlos inside, even though I was shivering from how drastically different the temperature was outside of the water.

Carlos's brown hair clung to his face, and he was breathing heavily as he got comfy, I noticed he had a large cut above his eyebrow which ran blood down his face. We needed a doctor, and fast. Despite this, all that was left to do now was wait, we couldn't lose another Zone leader to this explosion.

* * *

An hour later, Carlos paced in front of me in the Zone 4's infirmary waiting room, blood still ran down the right side of his face, but it wasn't a significant injury. The walls of the waiting room were porridge beige, and the chairs were green, it was unappealing to look at. I had a thermal blanket wrapped around me, and I could feel cold water droplets coming off my hair.

They had found Xander at the bottom of the tunnel pinned down by a four-by-four wood panel, he had already inhaled a lot of water.

Abrianna stood close by, staring at nothing. Oluchi was sitting by one of the windows; watching the virtual world go by, her dark brown braided hair tied into a pony tail.

"Are you okay?" Carlos asked Abrianna.

"More like, are you? You both should go back to Zone 14, you both need showers," she said.

Turning her nose up at both mine and Carlos's newly applied cologne, *Eau de Sewage* the unique collection from The Tunnels. Now's not the time to joke, I did agree with her, but we had to find out if Xander was going to live first before any plans of showering could commence. I looked at Carlos, his wet T-shirt showing his bare chest, my gaze dared to travel lower. Quickly shaking the thought of shower sex out of my head, I exhaled a breath as I continued waiting for Xander.

Carlos looked at me and smiled, he reached out and held my hand. I rubbed my thumb against his knuckles, like he did whenever he comforted me. He seemed to appreciate it, I saw his shoulders drop as he relaxed.

"Is Xander a Listed?" I burst out. "He has a barcode tattoo."

Abrianna and Oluchi looked at me, both of them started laughing as if it was an inside joke. Did I just ask a stupid question? No this seemed to be a fond memory for both Oluchi and Abrianna

Abrianna laughed and looked at me. "Oluchi and I dared him to get that when we got drunk one night. It was hilarious."

We all laughed at the thought of him getting a barcode tattoo. He obviously never went through the actual Listing process, every Listed person's barcode was a permanent scar, not even a tattoo remover could get off. They burned it into your skin then added the ink.

The waiting room went silent when the reality hit us, just the fact our friend could no longer be here, and we had no idea. None of this would have happened if that explosion hadn't gone off.

*　*　*

The ride back to Zone 14 was in silence, Xander would live, which was a good thing. There still no update on Ezekiel which was driving me insane, so much had happened in the past twelve hours that my head hurt. My greatest fear was that The Rebellion had been discovered by the government as a result of the explosion, this was the only place I could live right now and be free.

"Is Hunter fine with taking Ezekiel's position?" I eventually asked Carlos, leaning into the passenger door.

Carlos nodded and chewed on his thumb nail as he drove, I glanced at his other hand on the steering wheel; we both had various cuts on our bodies from having an entire tunnel collapse on us. But nothing as serious as Xander.

"He's got to be fine with it, he's the back up Leader for 7," Carlos's voice sounded like he did above ground. Small, filled with fear and anxiety.

The strangest thought suddenly occurred to me that I just burst out and asked Carlos about it. "Do you think he's the one who got rid of the note?" I responded.

Carlos shifted in his seat. "I honestly don't know what to think at this point." He sighed heavily. "But accusing the new leader of The Rebellion isn't going to go down well if he finds out, you know he has a bad temper."

I nodded and looked around Zone 18's tunnels. The ceiling was painted like the sky. I could admit to myself that I did miss seeing the real sky; did all the Unlisted feel this way? I thought about speaking to Taylor about these feelings. Hopefully, she could sympathise with me.

As we left Zone 18, I knew we were back in Zone 14 with the tunnels now just a bare concrete dirt nothing special.

"Why did we never paint our ceiling?" I asked. Such a dumb question.

Carlos pressed his head into the headrest and looked thoughtful.

"Hendrix hated it. Said we were warriors against the regime so it wasn't necessary because it's a temporary home." He looked sad speaking about Hendrix. The old Rebellion Leader for Zone 14 before Carlos—I'm told he got caught rescuing Unlisted and was executed on the spot.

Somebody on the walkway frantically waved the car down, it was a blond guy who looked like a deer in headlights with panic. I heard Carlos turn his blinker on, and he pulled onto the side of the road. I rolled my window down.

The blond guy was breathless. "There are people from outside requesting to speak to you."

"Sorry, what?" Carlos spat. "Why did you let them in? They could be from the government or anything."

"They're ORS," the guy said.

My stomach lurched at the sound of that organisation.

"What do they want?" I asked.

"I don't know. Taylor's speaking to them in Meeting Room Three of the jail." The blond guy looked around.

"Tell Taylor we'll be there as soon as possible," Carlos snapped.

* * *

Walking into the jail, with Carlos holding my hand after we both had a much needed shower. My hair was still wet, but I was happy to finally be in dry clothes—Carlos's black hoodie and some grey sweatpants. Being the leader he was, Carlos got changed into a grey business suit.

JUDAS

Carlos knocked on the door to Meeting Room Three then walked in, I followed. This room looked the same as Meeting Room Two, just smaller. The same guys who spoke to Michael and I were sitting there, computer tablet in the hands of the guy with black hair. I bit the inside of my cheek as I looked at them. My gaze caught Taylor, who looked at me, forcing herself to give me a smile.

"Judas, hello," the grey-haired guy said.

Carlos's brow furrowed, and he looked at me, I gave a small smile in return, it still unnerved me they knew my birth name. Both Carlos and I sat in the seats opposite ORS, then I exhaled a breath.

"So, you must be Carlos, Judas's boyfriend and leader of The Rebellion for Zone 14."

Carlos's eyes widened, and he looked at the guys. Then at Taylor, who shrugged at how they got this information, ORS knew too much, and they just seemed like this was perfectly okay. It wasn't okay.

"How did you get this information?" Carlos asked sternly. I saw his jaw tense.

"Michael told us," the black-haired guy informed us. Carlos relaxed.

"Michael?" I asked, leaning forward on the seat.

"He's adjusting very well in Olympia, driving your aunt up the wall," the grey-haired guy said. I narrowed my eyes, not sure what *driving up the wall* meant, but I'll take it. "How has life been above ground? Your apartments are empty."

"Carlos and I have been forced to move down here permanently after ending up in an extermination camp," I admitted, looking at Carlos for reassurance, he nodded in approval and held my hand. "The Rebellion Leader from 13 rescued us."

Why did I feel like I could tell them this information? Well, they did give me updates on Michael, so we were now even.

The guys stiffened, and they looked at us both in shock.

"Can I see some ID?" Carlos requested, letting go of my hand.

The men nodded quickly and each pulled their ID badges off which were clipped onto their black blazers, Carlos took both quickly and inspected them.

"I've already checked their ID—" Taylor started, but Carlos held up a hand to stop her speaking and squinted.

"Mr Daniels?" The black haired guy nodded. "Mr Kalovski?" The grey haired guy nodded. Carlos handed their IDs back.

"What is the purpose of your visit today?" Taylor asked. "How did you know how to find us down here?"

Yes, that's what I wanted to know too.

"Nadine Ellis told us the location of this place," Mr Kalovski started. My eyes widened, and my stomach twisted. Nadine was with ORS? "You may have heard The Rebellion in Zone 7 collapsed around an hour ago."

"We were in it when it collapsed," Carlos grumbled.

The two ORS agents stiffened, shifting in their seats to sit up taller, Mr Kalovski linked his hands together. But I was shocked when Mr Daniels started smiling.

"Explains the bandage on your head," Mr Daniels replied.

Mr Kalovski exhaled. "That was an explosion from President Sanchez. She knows the Rebellion exists and where it is, guards are looking for entrances in all eighteen Zones—that is why the explosion was set off. Nadine and Michael insisted that we tell you."

"Sorry?" Carlos said, his eyes widened.

Both guys nodded. Taylor gasped, terror in her eyes, and she covered her mouth, evidently trying not to scream. Even my heart skipped a beat out of fear.

Carlos pushed himself away from the table and ran out of the room, I looked behind my shoulder, not sure what he was doing. The two men looked confused.

"I can't go back into an extermination camp." Taylor started sobbing into her hands.

When the alarms started blaring around us, it was as if the whole world had stopped turning. It was official, The Rebellion was no longer our safe haven.

22

Nadine

I held the strap of my purse as I walked down the hospital corridor, the click of my sneakers on the floor could be heard as well as the beeping of machines and the smell of disinfectant.

Fixing my baggy shirt that had risen up, wiping lint off my black leggings, I looked around as nurses hurried into rooms to check on patients, stopping at Room Five. Smoothing my hair down, I knocked on the door.

"Come in," a voice choked out.

Pushing down on the handle and opening the door, I smiled at Ezekiel, who was in a hospital bed. He looked extremely tired, with tubes coming out of his nose, his hand on his stomach. I glanced at his heart monitor which beeped away.

"Hey," I said smiling at him. "I forgot to get you some flowers."

"Darn it, now I have nothing pretty to look at. Just four depressing walls," Ezekiel responded, flashing a weak smile.

I laughed as I sat on a plastic chair next to his bed. It was true, flowers could really turn this room into something less depressing, all the walls were white and there was an empty space in the corner where a bed should have been.

NADINE

"How are you holding up?" I asked, adjusting in my seat.

Ezekiel sighed, looking around the room, he coughed then groaned as he grimaced. "As great as I can with two broken ribs."

I nodded, tapping my feet and looked at my hands. Pushing my hair behind my ear. There was an awkward silence around us which I didn't like. But eventually I sucked in a breath and said. "So, what's happening when you get discharged?"

"Last time I spoke to somebody about it, they're going to assignment me to an apartment and start rehabilitation counselling." Ezekiel scoffed and smiled as he looked at his hand with tubes coming out of it. "Like I need that."

I furrowed my brow and looked at him. "Why do you say that?"

"The Rebellion is kind of the same way with their laws, I'm used to it."

Shifting in my seat, I looked around the room. To know he was moving to Olympia was a strange concept, but maybe it could be a missing puzzle piece in helping test the regime to its limits from the outside.

After my meeting with Ezekiel, Payton and I were in my room. Payton was on the bed, throwing a ball of socks up in the air and catching it in her hands.

I leaned against my bed frame, wondering how a crack got in my chest of drawers; it wasn't there yesterday. Opening a bottle of water, I took a drink.

"Have you ever wondered if a guy fucks you just to masturbate?" Payton asked.

Spitting the water out, I turned around to look at her. Payton seemed unfazed.

"No, what the fuck is that question?"

I watched her catch the socks, then roll onto her side with a deep in thought smile. "Think about it, instead of doing yourself, just do somebody else."

I scoffed then shook my head at her. Feeling something hit my head, the ball of socks rolled out onto my hardwood floors. With a laugh, I crawled on the floor to grab them. Feeling hands grab my ribs, a scream escaped my throat, falling on the floor in a fit of giggles as I curled up. Payton also laughed.

"You're such a bitch," I said, covering my mouth as I laughed.

"I hope your friends in Denmé can get out before that bitch succeeds," Payton exclaimed suddenly. Her voice sounded heavy.

Gradually I stopped laughing and looked at her. With a heavy sigh, I sat up, holding the ball of socks then rolled it along the floor.

"I hope I gave them enough notice."

"Yeah. If your friends are anything as cool as Crutches, then I'm excited to meet them."

Michael had earned his nickname as Crutches because of his leg. He liked it. I was excited for my friends to meet Payton too; she could see who saved my life, I owed them everything.

"Hopefully, you meet them. Dad's not helping get Judas's family out anymore."

"Word of the day: optimism." Payton's mouth curled into a smile.

Yes, optimism, but when there were over a thousand lives at stake, I didn't feel optimistic.

At dinner, I spun spaghetti on my fork, sighing as the news droned on in the background, it showed that bitch President Sanchez. She was standing outside the beautiful ornate building that had exploded. Smoke still came out of the gaping hole in the roof. President Sanchez had her black hair tied tightly back in a bun, a burgundy beret on her stupid head and wore aviator glasses—and infamous military outfit.

"I have kept this country safe for seventeen years, and to know people are threatening that safety underground is blasphemous," she spat to the reporter.

Scratching the side of my eye, I put a loaded fork in my mouth and sighed. Nobody was safe in Denmé, not even those in The Rebellion, as far as President Sanchez was concerned. I just wished I could do more to get Judas, Carlos, and Gabrielle to real safety; not the false ideology President Sanchez set up.

I looked at my arm, the barcode peaking out of my mint green turtleneck, the permanent scar on my body. There were some days I could still feel the pain of the Listing process, the sound of my skin burning, even the smell. With a shudder, I suddenly lost my appetite, as I pushed my plate away I focused on the TV.

"Do you think your laws are strict?" the reporter asked. He sounded foreign.

"Absolutely not. My people love this country, and I love them," Sanchez answered back quickly, I couldn't help but scoff. "We will find those who threaten the safety of Denmé, and I will show no mercy on their utter defiance to this great nation."

I couldn't believe how insane President Sanchez was sometimes, a life full of oppression wasn't safe, and denying people of personalities wasn't safe either. I felt powerless knowing I could do nothing more to save those in The Rebellion from this monster.

The sound of my phone ringing woke me up. Rubbing sleep out of my eye, I checked my phone. Squinting at its brightness, running my thumb along the screen to accept the call, I pressed it to my ear and led on my back.

"Hello," I said, rubbing my eyes a bit more, putting my hand on my forehead. My voice sounded scratchy like a broken record.

"Come and pick me up," the person on the other side said. Their voice sounded shaky and masculine.

"Who's this?" I asked, then yawned.

"Michael."

Sitting up, I checked the time. It read out three in the morning.

"It's three in the morning. Where are you?" I asked.

"I'll text you the address, just pick me up."

"Okay, I'll be there," I said.

Feeling groggy, I left the warm confines of my duvet and got out of bed. I contemplated if I should get into some everyday clothes. But there wasn't any point knowing full well I would get back into them once home.

Grabbing my jacket, I opened my bedroom door and made my way downstairs.

Turning down a street to an abandoned warehouse on the outskirts of town, Michael was leaning against a wall, his crutches hanging from his arms. He was dressed all in black, blending in with the shadows. I beeped my horn as I pulled up, honestly, I felt like I had been hit by a truck, I shouldn't be driving.

Michael's face lit up when he saw me and made his way over to me, he opened my car's passenger door, cold air filtered in making me shiver. I could hear music playing from inside the warehouse, I furrowed my brow and ran a hand through my hair as he got into my car. The smell of alcohol hit my nose as I heard the click of his crutches being put in the back, then he shut the car door, and got belted up. As I looked around the abandoned street, I heard him laugh.

"What?" I asked, looking at him. His face was flushed. "Have you been drinking?"

"Nice outfit." Michael smiled as he spoke.

I looked at my bunny P.J. bottoms and glared at him.

"You didn't answer my question." After I noticed he was safe, I pushed my blinker up and turned into the road then made my way down the street. The blinker turned itself off with a thud.

"Okay, yes, please don't tell my aunt. I'm meant to be at something called a sleepover with my friends, and they led me here. Then they started snorting this weird powder that made them laugh, and I didn't feel safe anymore."

I felt relieved he thought to ring me than do that.

"Thank you for ringing me," I said. "But no more drinking. You're fourteen. It's not safe, you could have got seriously injured."

The yellow street lights lit up the car at random intervals, the headlights also assisting with the drive home. Michael laughed, which caused me to look at him and raise my eyebrow.

"Is this the kind of thing either Judas or Gabrielle would do if I grew up in a normal country?" he asked. I forced myself to focus on the road.

"Yes, exactly that. I'm doing the work of both your siblings right now," I said, trying to force anger into my voice, so he knew I was angry. I bit the nail on my thumb. "You're injured enough without getting shit-faced and causing your leg to be more damaged."

Michael laughed. "What's shit-faced mean?"

"Means so drunk you aren't aware of yourself," I said back sternly.

He laughed and clapped his hands together. Pushing tears away from my face, I don't know why I was crying, maybe through tiredness and worry about Michael.

***

In my bedroom, I put a duvet on the floor while holding another duvet in my arms. Michael was on my bed, his crutches and coat on the floor, he was already asleep even with the bedside lamp still turned on.

Putting the duvet down, I reached over and turned the lamp off.

I wriggled my way into my makeshift bed on the floor, thankfully we had underfloor heating, so despite the discomfort, it was at least warm.

Hearing Michael whimper something about a guard in his sleep broke my heart, no child should be having nightmares like that, no children anywhere should be treated as cruelly as the Denmé regime treated people.

I sighed whilst I pulled the second duvet over my body and closed my eyes, still hearing Michael mumble in his sleep, and I was just thankful sleep came very quickly.

* * *

I yawned as I walked into the kitchen the next morning at exactly 10 a.m., rubbing sleep out of my eyes as I approached the kitchen island where the coffee machine was placed. Today was a good day for coffee. Once I refilled the water and placed a cup in its rightful location, I looked through our coffee pod holder. Grabbing the *Morning Joe* I placed it into the coffee machine, and hit the start button.

"Nobody told me Michael was staying the night." I jumped at the sound of my mums voice, and looked at her as she entered the kitchen.

She was wearing a figure hugging grey pencil dress with a black belt around her hips, ready to begin a days work. Her hair tied into a tight bun at the back of her head, in her hand was a mug of coffee and a magazine. Mums heels clicked as she approached the dining table, I only just noticed Michael was sitting there eating breakfast, I felt horrible not acknowledging him.

"Last minute decision," I grumbled. "Morning, Michael."

The smell of coffee was strong in the air, I wanted to drink my cup of coffee right now but it was still pouring.

Mum looked through her magazine as she sipped her own coffee. "Well, I'm glad Michael is safe."

That was when Michael decided to stand up from the table and limp over to me, I was worried about him inflicting more injury on his leg by walking unassisted. Anyway he wrapped his arms around me, I laughed from how awkward it felt.

"Mrs Ellis, your daughter is officially my sister from another mister," Michael beamed as he spoke.

Seeing him go to kiss my cheek, I flinched away and shouted. "No! Too far!"

We both laughed as we pulled away from each other, I could hear mum laughing along with us. I shook my head, being thankful my coffee was finally ready. Just as I was about to reach for it I jumped at the front door slamming as it sang out twice.

Turning my head toward the kitchen entrance, hurried footsteps echoed throughout the house, and suddenly dad came into the room breathless. Dad had a panic in this eyes, his brown hair was a mess and he looked exhausted; his suits top button was undone and I had no idea where his tie was.

"They've found Rebellion entrance to Zone 2!" Dad wheezed out as he leaned against the counter.

I stiffened at the news, looking at Michael then at mum. Both of them had gone very pale at the news. Leaning against the counter, I exhaled a breath and pressed a hand to my stomach which felt like a zillion butterflies were in there.

"Did everybody get out?" I asked, my voice wavering.

Dad nodded, still trying to catch his breath. "Thankfully we gave them enough warning, Carlos managed to email everybody in time."

Relief washed over me, this was like a game of cat and mouse with an entire country. Where else could people in the Rebellion hide once President Sanchez got to the very last Zone? Shaking that thought out of my head, I swallowed thin air.

"Nadine," Michael said quietly. I looked at him. "Is my brother going to be safe with Our Leader finding The Rebellion?"

"I hope so," I responded.

23

Judas

I stood next to Carlos and Taylor in The Pit. With the help of Adriel, who sat underneath us, he rigged these images to depict the ocean instead of the night sky. Currently almost everybody from Zone 14 sat in here, and those who couldn't fit were listening from the corridors to our left and right.

"That's two Zones now who have been ransacked by guards. Luckily, we were given enough warning," Carlos started. I watched everybody nod. "This only means one thing. We must declare a war between The Rebellion and Our Leader. We need rights, we need freedom."

The pit erupted in a roar of people shouting, they pumped their fists in the air, and everybody clapped in agreement.

"We have already made agreements for Hunter to send Our Leader this message. Those who want to learn how to shoot, meet me down in The Range in an hour," Taylor spoke up.

Carlos nodded at me. "Okay, filter out," I said to everybody.

Even though I had butterflies in my stomach for what the future held, this was the best decision for the sanity of all The Unlisted. Heat rose up in my body, and it became difficult to breathe.

"Taylor, can I talk to you?" I said quickly, tears stinging my eyes.

She looked at me with worry, but nodded, Carlos didn't look happy but only Taylor could understand this.

* * *

Taylor sat on a newly acquired red beanbag chair in her apartment, where she got it was beyond me. Her apartment smelled like a vanilla-scented candle, but there was no candle in sight, so it confused me. Taylor was wearing high waisted ripped jeans and a loose-fitting black tank top. I sat on her sofa bed with a bottle of beer in my hand, it was flat and tasted like water, but Taylor's eyes burned into me.

"What was it like when you moved down here?" I asked.

"Honestly, it was hell. I didn't understand why I couldn't go outside," she responded. "Why, what are you feeling?"

"I just feel like I am missing so much above ground, like I'm detached from the world," I admitted, taking a drink of the watery alcohol.

Taylor nodded and gave me a smile, she looked deep in thought. My gaze drifted to her window which showed a city landscape outside.

"Yeah, that's normal, it gets easier with time." She smiled.

Taylor pushed herself out of the beanbag chair then wrapped her arms around me, she felt warm, and her soft hair tickled my arms. Taylor smelled sweet, like candy, but I didn't know if this was from perfume. Feeling Taylor pull away, she crouched down and grabbed both my hands.

"Things will get easier, Judas, right now, it's confusing, but trust me you have Carlos, who is going to help you through this."

I smiled at her, really appreciating this time together to get all my feelings out. Knowing that how I'm feeling is totally normal, and I'm not just being weird.

All I needed was time to adjust, it's bound to be a shock to the system. Probably every Unlisted had the same feelings, I was slowly adjusting like they had to, even deal with the trauma that the extermination camp provided.

The Rebellion was one big family at the end of the day. All of us had each other's backs.

* * *

Shutting the door of Carlos's apartment, it was silent. I felt deflated as Carlos wasn't there to greet me, instead it was just a view out of his apartment windows with the large flat screen. The entire space smelled like him, and I physically craved him. Pressing a hand to the wall, I took my shoes off and headed into the kitchen, opening the fridge I took a bottle of water out.

"What is it that you couldn't talk to me about?" I jumped at hearing Carlos's voice, I turned around and looked at him. He looked angry.

"It's nothing," I lied.

"Clearly wasn't nothing, you were crying when you told her you wanted to talk!" He raised his voice. Tears stung my eyes, I hated being yelled at, especially by Carlos.

"Only Taylor would understand," I admitted quietly, wiping tears away.

"What the fuck do you mean only Taylor would understand?" He was now shouting, and I was conscious about the neighbours hearing. I jumped when he slammed his hand on the counter. "Judas, just please fucking talk to me!"

"Fine!" I shouted back. "I'm having a difficult time adjusting to this! I'm used to being here for a day or night, not an entire fucking week!"

When I sucked in a breath, it sounded like a wheeze, and I covered my mouth, leaning against the counter for support as I sobbed loudly, rocking backward and forward. He had every right to be angry because I did keep a lot from him recently, while this entire situation was going on I didn't want to pile more crap on his shoulders.

"Judas." I heard his usual calm voice say.

Squeezing my eyes shut as I sobbed. My throat burned and felt like there was a rubber band wrapped around it.

"Let's go."

I opened my eyes and looked at him. "Where?" I asked.

"I'll have to speak to Thora, but I think we need a date."

A war was about to happen, and he wanted a date in Zone 9. The fuck. But I nodded, wondering what he had in store for us.

* * *

As we drove through the tunnels, it was scary seeing slabs of metal cover every single door to protect against the government, only sections not covered were the parking garages. Several cars drove around Highway 15.

Zone 9's tunnel was painted to look like graffiti, which showed off Thora's fiery personality. I glanced at Carlos, who was dressed in grey business pants and a white button down shirt, he looked especially handsome tonight. As we turned the corner into Parking Garage 9:135, we came to a stop at a yellow barrier which blocked our path, standing by the security booth Thora was there spinning a set of keys on her finger as Carlos wound down the window—slowly she approached the car.

"Tell anybody about this, and I will have to murder you," she warned.

"Noted," Carlos replied as she handed the keys over.

"Turn right at 9:278, follow the road until you arrive at a gate, unlock it with those keys and you'll have arrived," Thora explained.

He nodded with a smile. I wondered where he was taking me, Carlos was keeping it a big secret wherever it was.

***

I stepped out of Carlos's car. We were outside, above ground, this felt wrong. I raised an eyebrow at Carlos and wondered how this was possible. There were no houses to be seen and we were surrounded by the ocean. I could smell the saltiness of the sea, and it clung to my skin; the waves churned, throwing sand like snow.

"Where are we?" I asked, when I turned my head to him he gave me a quick kiss then opened the trunk.

"Crystal Shores, Zone 9," he explained as he placed a bag by his feet, then put the back seats down. "Top secret Rebellion facility because we don't know if the guards patrol this bit. Only Leaders know about it, and now you."

I nodded with a smile, feeling rebellious with this date idea. As I looked around, I had doubts guards would even bother with this place. I leaned against the car, watching Carlos spread out a blanket across the back seats, every so often he glanced up at me. Slowly, I sat in the trunk bed, Carlos laughed as he handed me a bright blue bottle of alcohol from the bag at his feet; I fished around in there for the bottle opener, then popped the cap off.

"It's no wine, but—"

"It's perfect," I ended his sentence, then gave him a kiss with a smile.

Carlos had an identical bottle, and opened it as he sat next to me. I looked at the stars with a smile, soon pointing to a shooting star, I made a wish and for once it was real so it would come true.

"I love you," Carlos said before kissing me.

"Ditto," I replied as I kissed him back.

Eventually I found myself laying down in the trunk, my feet resting on the front seats when I laid out fully, Carlos did the same. Out here, the night sky was so clear it was perfect to stargaze together.

"There's Big Bear." Carlos pointed to a set of stars in the shape of a bear. I gasped. "That brightest star is what you look like to me in a crowded room."

I cringed and laughed. "Could you add anymore cheese to that statement?"

He laughed too as he sat up, then plucked the bottle of alcohol out of my hands and placed both of them in a nearby cup holder. As Carlos laid back down, he wrapped an arm around me, then used my chest as a pillow, I gave him a kiss on the head as I stared up at the stars.

* * *

We had been in each others company just star gazing for a while, feeling the cold sea air travelling around us. Eventually, Carlos sat up, I stayed in the same position waiting for him to return, both my hands on my stomach. My relaxed mood diminished, and I felt deflated as the trunk closed on us.

"Got a bit cold," Carlos told me.

I nodded, then he crawled up to me, giving me a kiss on the lips. He tasted like the alcohol we had been drinking together. As we shared more kisses together, each one grew in intensity, I clutched Carlos's shirt as he unbuttoned mine.

Pulling away, I looked into his eyes while breathing heavy, then I stared at his lips. "I might know a way to warm you up."

Quickly realising we were all alone out here, nobody to disturb us. The thought was more arousing then us kissing. Since Nadine arrived it had been almost impossible to be alone together without getting disturbed, it drove me mad. I pulled Carlos into me, and I kissed him while unbuttoning his shirt.

"You're reading my mind," he gasped through kisses, as we tugged each other's shirts off and threw them to the side.

I moaned, and wrapped my arm across Carlos's shoulder as he

started kissing my neck. Only letting go, and sucking in a breath as he moved to my chest, his hands explored my torso, then he licked all the way down to my V-line where he unbuttoned my jeans. Carlos looked up at me—waiting for my approval.

"Please, do it," I gasped.

Biting my lip as Carlos pulled my pants down, then my underwear came off. My erection out in the open, then I waited for him to make his move. Carlos smiled up at me, then placed his mouth around it, I moaned loudly and buried a hand in his hair—the other hand pressed against the closed trunk cover. The feel of his tongue sent waves of pleasure through me, I moaned and moved my legs behind his back, and arched my own back as I moaned his name. Grateful I finally had Carlos alone.

"Stop," I managed to gasp.

Carlos did as instructed, wiping the side of his mouth with his thumb with a sultry smile. I was breathless.

"Everything okay?" he asked as he looked me up and down.

I sat up and kissed him roughly as I unbuttoned his pants and put my hand down there. The feel of his erection in my hand made him moan enough to move away from my touch, both of us laughed through sloppy kisses when Carlos hit his head on the roof.

"Take them off," I instructed after composing myself; then kissed him roughly again. Carlos had turned me on to the max.

Again, he did as I instructed and we were both naked in the small confines of the car. I didn't know or care how this would work. But he kissed me until I was laid back down, staring up at him. Then he moved away as he reached down for something in the well of the back seat. Hearing the squirt of the bottle, I felt stupid for forgetting lube.

Quickly forgetting about my stupidity as he rubbed his cold, wet fingers against my entrance, I moaned loudly and arched my back. When he stopped, I brought my legs up as far as they would go. Carlos soon got into position, moving me until my ankles were securely under his armpits, feeling him against me.

Finally, he thrust his way inside of me, gently at first as he slid deeper into me, inch by inch. I gasped out pleasure, and gripped hold of the blanket I was led on. A loud moan escaped my lips. I was thankful my body was used to him now, so it was only slightly uncomfortable.

"Fuck," I gasped.

Carlos laughed, as I pushed against his size, he moaned as he pulled back and drove deeper inside of me. I gasped and bit my lip, looking up at him.

"It's about time this happened." He moaned as he continued pulling back, then thrusting into me. "Been thinking about this a lot lately, it's just so difficult to be alone." Carlos bit his lip as he sucked in a breath. I kept moaning, and started moving my hips, despite occasionally hitting my head on the trunk of the car.

"I love you," I gasped out as I moaned.

Carlos then pulled back and thrust into me extremely slow, then stilled inside of me. Moving my hips in silent protest of his abrupt stop. We both moaned as he went deeper inside me, whilst he lowered himself down so we could kiss.

I wrapped my legs around his back, and I pressed a hand to his cheek as I kissed him deeply, tilting my head back and moaning loudly as he placed his hands on my hips and started moving again. The new position was giving my body a whole new sensation, I moved my hands around his shoulders and dug my nails in.

"Are you enjoying this?" he asked as he kissed my neck.

"Harder," I gasped.

He obliged quickly, and this time our movements were faster, and deeper until we were both covered in sweat; with each passing moment the space between us got warmer like a summer heatwave. The pleasure he was giving me was indescribable.

Both of us needed this moment. All of our worries washed away, and suddenly it was us just in the world. Within a world full of ominous darkness, it was just me and Carlos—my light of safety to guide me home.

I squeezed my eyes shut, and started shouting his name. He leaned in, and kissed me deeply to get me to quieten down, his breathing heavy. My fingers found his hair, and I cried out as he pounded me. Around us I could hear the car start to creak as it moved with our motions, but I didn't care. Underneath my hands I could feel his muscles work as he fucked me in all the right ways. I was almost there, but I didn't want to stop. Then I felt Carlos move his hand down to my dick.

"Don't make this stop," I moaned.

"I can't hold on much longer," he managed to gasp, then moaned loudly. While he pounded me, he played with me. I cried out again as I felt release, my muscles tensed up, then I came.

Carlos carried on for a couple more moments, he moaned my name, gradually slowing down as he came inside of me. I laid there, breathless with a feeling of euphoria. We shared another kiss, moaning slightly while he continued to move his hips as he led on my chest. Both of us were covered in sweat, and I ran my hand through his hair. There was one last shooting star which I could see out of the back window, which was full of condensation, so I made yet another wish.

* * *

I slept the entire ride home. Throughout our entire relationship, I had never needed a date more than tonight, and after what just happened I was deeply satisfied.

Back in Zone 14, we walked hand in hand down the corridor to our apartment, making our way to the black door, which was different from every other door. Carlos pressed me against the wall, his hands securely on my hips as he kissed me deeply, I was smiling so much jaw hurt. All we needed was this one night to be allowed to forget everything. Tonight, none of our problems existed.

Alas, that couldn't happen. The illusion nothing was wrong, was ripped away as Taylor emerged out of her apartment looking like she had just see a ghost, her eyes red from crying.

"I'm sorry to ruin date night, but they just found Zone 5!"

My smile quickly faded, and a deep sinking feeling overwhelmed me. I swallowed the lump in my throat, and looked at Carlos whose eyes were glazed with tears. This couldn't be happening.

24

Nadine

It had taken me an entire week to pluck up the courage to visit Wyatt; we were separated by Plexiglas with only a phone to talk to him. The phone was cold against my ear, and I looked at my brother, he looked tired and his eyes were bloodshot.

"Nadine, you need to listen to me," he choked out, not looking me in the eye. Instead Wyatt just stared at the wooden shelf in front of him.

As I leaned forward, I rested my arms on the shelf in front of me as I sighed, trying to see what was on his side of the glass. "Why should I listen to you when you got me thrown into Denmé?" I spat back, trying to throw anger into my voice.

"It's not only me, it's also Dad." Wyatt's voice trembled as he spoke, his hands trembling on his lap.

My blood boiled. "Don't bring Dad into this!" I raised my voice to the point guards started looking at me.

I exhaled a breath trying to calm down, Wyatt raised his head.

"Do you remember that mysterious bruise you woke up to the month before you got taken by them?" He leaned on the hand that held the phone.

"Yes."

"Dad implanted a tracking device in you. We knew you had to be the one to go to Denmé to help us find Judas Wells, the several other times we tried everybody was executed. His boss approved it." Tears rolled down Wyatt's cheeks as he pressed a hand to the glass.

I was frozen in my chair, tears stung my eyes, as I blinked them away my heart raced. All the sounds around me went silent, and everything was a blur. As I put the phone back in the holder, I pushed myself away from Wyatt and grabbed my purse as I stood up. Though I couldn't hear it, I knew he was screaming my name as guards carted him away.

Clutching my purse tightly while I walked out of the visitation room, I cupped a hand to my mouth as I let the tears flow.

Finding out my dad was another person who betrayed me and put me into Denmé, this entire situation just became more messed up than it already was. I felt physically sick and violated. Even worse, I needed to get this thing out of me.

* * *

I didn't remember how I got in my car, or how I ended up on the highway. My mind was still racing at the confession Wyatt gave me earlier, I couldn't even bring myself to turn the radio on in my car, I knew for certain I wasn't fit to drive my hands were shaking too much and my vision was blurred from crying. But that's all I could do in this moment—drive.

Wiping my tears away, I decided to give in and ring Payton, exhaling a heavy breath and adjusting in my seat. Tapping my thumb out of impatience on the steering wheel, biting my lower lip waiting for her to pick up.

"Yo! Wassup, bitch!" Payton called out with a laugh; it was loud on the other end like she was at a party.

"Pay, do you know where I can get an X-ray without going to a doctor?" I questioned, my voice wavered.

Payton was silent for a few moments before she asked. "Why? What happened? You sound terrified."

I adjusted my seat belt which felt like it was constricting me. "Wyatt told me Dad's put a fucking tracker in my arm, I need an X-ray to find out the truth but if I go to a doctor then dad will know."

"Fuck me side ways," Payton exclaimed.

"No thank you," I replied, even though she couldn't see it, I smiled for the first time since I found out this news.

"Dirty bitch," Payton replied, she sighed heavily. "I think my friend Drake can hook you up, he runs a vet clinic and has connections. Your dad is messed up for this."

I sucked in a breath. "Please call him, then give me the details."

"Will do, bye."

When she disconnected the call, I ran my trembling hands through my hair and looked around the street as I pressed my foot to the accelerator to pick up speed. Only now did I realise the Importers suspicions of me being a government spy were correct, just I had no freaking idea. My dad deserved to rot in the same place as Wyatt.

* * *

Payton's friend Drake did actually hook me up with a *no questioned asked* X-Ray in his vet clinic after closing. A few hours later, I sat backwards on a swivel chair waiting for him to come into the room, Payton was sitting on a different chair looking through her phone watching funny videos on it. Then the door opened.

"Well, it's definitely there," Drake announced as he put the X-ray up to a light box and inspected it. He had brown hair with orange flecks in it, wearing scrubs, and he wore a mask under his chin.

"Can you remove it?" I questioned, quickly looking at Payton who

NADINE

finally put her phone away, her eyes widened when she saw the tracking device.

Drake scratched the back of his neck, looking over at us both. "I work with animals, not humans. But judging by the placement, it could be possible to remove it, I'll just have to make a few phone calls," Drake explained to us. "But you should know that you may get muscle or nerve damage by getting it removed."

For the second time today my world shattered, I groaned as I ran both hands down my face and then looked at Payton. That was not what I wanted to hear, all I wanted was this thing out of me. She gave me a nervous smile.

"You know, fuck the repercussions and get this thing out me," I snapped. Looking at Payton who nodded in agreement. "We're close enough to Denmé's border into making Dad believe I went back, after this I'll disown my family. So please do it."

"What about your stuff?" Payton questioned.

I hadn't thought that far ahead. "I'll work it out, but I can't have my dad monitoring me anymore."

Drake looked hesitant but slowly nodded.

"Okay, I'll speak to some friends who can remove it at a cost. Then we need to obtain a brace for your arm," Drake instructed while turning off the light box. He looked around and sighed.

"Deal. Just get it out."

Then he left the room, clearly off to speak to his connections who may or may not help me out of this situation.

25

Judas

At a desk in the deathly-quiet library, I ate a protein bar and took down notes as I read from a large textbook with a thick layer of dust on it. When I looked around there were some people at computers, others chatting around tables, mostly college kids were in here trying to do research for their assignments. All the walls were brick and the false windows really brightened up the place.

Next to this little secluded corner I was in a labyrinth of bookcases, even I could get lost in those. Honestly, it was stupid that I had to teach myself most of what I know now. The Rebellion had a collection of books which were prohibited above ground, to stop us questioning how the world works. But down here it was public knowledge. When I first joined The Rebellion I took some of my notes above ground with me and taught my siblings in secret, when we had some downtime from the tasks.

I jumped when a thick book slammed onto the desk, I sighed heavily to see a huge pen mark now crossing over some of my notes. Just as I was about to shout at the person I realised it was both Adriel and Archie, as they sat opposite me. They were both in government uniform, the only way I could tell either of them apart was Archie's sarcastic smile.

"Fucking hell, you both scared me," I breathed out, finding a clean sheet of paper and switching the page I was on.

"Well shits hitting the fan," both of them said in unison, in that weird way twins usually did.

"Sorry?" I said looking up.

"The Rebellion has just retaliated for the government blowing up Zone 7," Archie responded with a smile.

"During Task 21, Archie here." Adriel thrust a thumb in his brothers direction. "Played the radio and the government broadcast was replaced by news coverage of when the regime was brought into existence, exposing its true nature. Then at the end it said *Property of The Rebellion*," Adriel explained with a large smile.

Hearing this news was like the air around me had all the life sucked out it. Feeling a chill crawl down my spine, I didn't know The Rebellion even had news coverage of when that day happened.

"How did we get the news coverage? I thought Our Leader destroyed it all." I closed the textbook and tapped a pen against the note book.

"Beats me, but I know Hunter's holding an emergency meeting in ten minutes in the auditorium." Archie stretched out across the table.

"We might sneak in there," they both said, again in perfect unison.

Pushing myself away from the desk, I left my textbook behind, and hurried out of the library. Determined to get to the auditorium, if I was allowed in there at all, just to see what the hell was going to happen after The Rebellion had now unveiled the truth.

* * *

When I neared the auditorium, I could already hear the loud and bustling conversations, I wiped my hands on my jeans and pulled the door open. Seeing Hunter leaning on the podium, typing information into a computer, I tried to sneak past him, I didn't know if he was as lenient as Ezekiel with non-leaders being in these meetings. But I wasn't fast enough, he instantly looked up and flashed me a smile. He was a slender man, with waist-length platinum hair and black roots in serious need of a touch up, his eyes were a rich brown.

"Joseph," Hunter exclaimed. "I was hoping you would join us. Do you have any other stowaways we need to know about?"

I stiffened and looked at him. Giving him a nervous laugh to break the ice a little, scratching the back of my head. "No, Nadine was the only one."

"I'm just messing you with you. Carlos and Taylor at the back, we'll begin the meeting shortly."

An uneasy feeling suddenly overwhelmed me as I turned around and started ascending the stairs, glancing behind my shoulder to see if Hunter was still watching me, thankfully he wasn't. Maybe his weird behaviour of calling me Joseph, and asking about Nadine's situation was him trying to make an impression now he was Head of The Rebellion, well he was going the wrong way about it.

I jumped and gasped as Samhain grabbed my wrist, I looked down at him. He was in a row by himself, his feet up on the chair in front and wearing his goat skull like a Jewish Kippah.

"Told you a war was going to happen when she returned home." Samhain's smile was sinister.

"My brother had nothing to do with this, it was all you," I snapped. "If you weren't such a pathological liar, nobody would have thought you were lying about it."

Samhain nodded as he contemplated this information. "I was wrong about that detail." He glanced behind his shoulder. "Carlos is waiting for you."

I was thankful when Samhain let go of my wrist, and I continued my ascent up the stairs. Finally getting to the row where Carlos and

JUDAS

Taylor sat, giving Carlos a quick kiss as I pulled a chair down and sat in the seat next to him. Suddenly the entire auditorium fell silent, and my eyes widened when Xander walked through the door covered in blood.

Cradled in his arms was a hamster cage he held protectively against his chest as he ascended the stairs, his hair had recently been dyed black and now looked a complete mess—it also looked like he had been crying.

As if on queue there was a solitary clap coming from none other than Samhain.

"Nice outfit, bro!" Samhain exclaimed.

"Fuck off," Xander growled.

I didn't know where he was going to sit, but eventually he was on our row and pulled the seat down next to me and got seated, letting out a jagged breath; then he started checking on whatever was in the cage.

Once Hunter coughed, the bustling conversations started again, Carlos leaned forward in shock. So did Taylor.

"Is everything okay?" Carlos questioned.

Xander shook his head, letting out a slight laugh then rubbed his eyes with the heel of his hand. "I was the one to start the broadcast, and then they found Zone 4." Suddenly an orange and white hamster emerged from the depths of the cage, looking like it had only just woken up. Xander's face instantly lit up. "I had to fight people to get Meaty out of there. Even kill some guards."

I gasped and looked at Carlos and Taylor, their eyes clouded with concern. When Carlos held my hand, I rubbed my thumb over his knuckles.

"Is Meaty okay?" Taylor asked.

"You are, aren't you." Xander talked into the cage as Meaty sniffed the air, and got acquainted with his new surroundings.

Then there was a loud clap over the speakers, I looked up to see Hunter holding a microphone in his hand as he walked around the little stage area of the auditorium. He scanned all of us, I had never see the auditorium so full.

"As of today, I become the new Head of The Rebellion, taking over from Ezekiel wherever he may be," Hunter spoke softly but with authority. "With this comes some understandable change. First things first, I would like to promote Judas Wells as a third co-leader of Zone 14."

My heart skipped a beat, and I sucked in a sharp breath. Even though I knew everybody was cheering and clapping, clearly happy about this change, it sounded like everything was under water. What was happening? Why did I get promoted? Would I even be a good Rebellion leader? I was terrified of what this meant for me.

Looking at Carlos, both he and Taylor were beaming out of pride. There was no swaying Hunter's decision, I knew that much. So it was evidently clear as of today, I had a right to be in this seat and not just invited because I was dating Carlos.

"Furthermore, I request all Zone Rebellion Leaders who are willing to come to Tunnel 7:14 to assist with those who have lost their homes, and to push forward with retaliation efforts to hopefully take down Our Leader," Hunter announced to the crowd. "Participation in this is strictly voluntary."

I knew Carlos would want to go to Zone 7 to help out, but I had a bad feeling about it. The one place guards would be sniffing around like flies around shit would be there, I didn't know what Hunter was thinking either when proposing this ridiculous idea.

26

Judas

Zone 7 had something called a hotel, I had never seen one in 14 but from what I gathered it was a place of rest. Due to the explosion there was no electricity yet, as a substitute we all had been given candles or battery powered lamps. I was grateful the water was still running, supplied by Zone 4.

As I led on the bed, I stared at the television which waited to be watched, its grey facade staring at me. In this particular room it smelled like cheap air freshener and damp. The only sound was the water from the shower hitting the basin, then it squeaked as it stopped.

Carlos emerged out of the bathroom a few moments later, he patted his hair dry with a towel, I looked him up and down. The only thing he was wearing was grey sweatpants, water droplets clung to his defined torso.

"Good morning," I said, turning to look at him.

He dropped his towel then climbed onto the bed, sliding into the gap between my legs. I let out a laugh as he held my wrists down then kissed me deeply. The cheap air freshener scent being masked by the hotels musty 3-in-1 shampoo, conditioner and body wash which emanated off of Carlos's body. Only when he let go of my wrists and moved them onto my hips did I wrap my arms around him, pulling Carlos down so I could continue kissing him, running my hand through his still wet hair. His hands moved up my shirt, I laughed as I pulled away to glance down, then I looked at his face.

"Do we have a few moments before briefing?" Carlos questioned, before kissing me.

I kissed him back then checked my watch over his shoulder. "Hunter said eight sharp, we got around two minutes."

Carlos pouted as he laid down fully on me, rubbing my chest. "But the mood lighting is so perfect." He kissed my neck then looked at me.

I didn't care about the time, instead I rolled him onto his back, and placed my hand on his cheek as I kissed him passionately.

Only stopping, and glancing behind my shoulder when I heard a knock on the wall, I sighed heavily to see Samhain standing there with his arms folded, he looked bored. Then my gaze fell onto Thora who was accompanying him, she covered her eyes and turned away.

"The meeting's about to start, Hunter told us to fetch you both." Samhain's mouth curled into a smile. "I can easily tell him you need a few more moments to freshen up, let you finish off."

I sat up, breathing heavily and looked at Carlos who also sat up, fixing his wet hair. An awkward silence settled on the room, I didn't know how to respond.

"That won't be necessary, we aren't having sex," Carlos replied. "As you can see we're both pretty much more or less dressed."

"You know, some people like the sex with clothes on thing." Samhain shrugged.

I could feel my cheeks burning, and I covered my mouth to stifle a laugh, glancing at Carlos who had his face buried in his hands evidently embarrassed.

Thora smacked Samhain on the arm, he jumped and held it protectively. "You're disgusting!" She looked at us both. "I'm sorry I told Samhain to knock, and not just come in."

Her blonde dreadlocks fell to her elbow, and she wore cargo pants with a black tank top, showing off a concealed tattoo of a dragon on her back. Which was strange, it oddly resembled the same one Xander had. I wouldn't question it though. Samhain took her by the arm and tugged her towards the door.

"Don't keep Mr. Tauscher waiting," Samhain called into the room as he left.

An hour later, I was above ground in a small group led by Zone 16's Leader Alana; she was a feisty woman with bright-orange curly hair. The others in our group were Carlos, Xander, and Thora. Currently we were hidden down an alleyway which over looked Zone 7's Main Street. It was magnificent strip of road, filled with cobblestone paths with a row of palm trees down the middle, and the white brick storefronts all said different things. However, my blood boiled when I saw their various array of clothing stores—I had never seen this above ground. It was clear that Zone 7 was being treated differently, and that wearing non-government issued uniform outside of tasks was not only allowed but encouraged; in other Zone's like 14, this usually would lead to a trip to an extermination camp.

On the street I could see people going about doing their daily tasks, oddly enough there were no guards that I could see. With a wave of her hand, Alana led us out onto the street where we jogged over to the other side and slipped down a narrow side street.

My breathing instantly became heavy, having admittedly been a bit lazier than normal while adjusting to life in The Rebellion, I had even forgotten how uncomfortably itchy the uniform was.

As we walked quickly down this street, I was amazed at the white brick buildings which looked pristine and ancient, all of them had wrought-iron balconies. I could smell the various flowers from some of these balconies which had been turned into gardens, and I was surprised to see laundry hanging from a couple of them. Did they do their own laundry in Zone 7 too? Life was strange here.

At a T-junction I almost walked into Thora as she came to a sudden and abrupt halt. She was looking at the sky, her eyes wide and shrouded with fear. I followed her gaze and my heart skipped a beat to see a huge fireball hurtling towards us.

"Erm," Thora squeaked out.

"Get down!" Xander shouted.

Carlos instantly threw me to the ground and shielded me from the the imminent impact. I shielded my head and squeezed my eyes shut.

I didn't know how much time had passed, but all I could focus on was the weight of Carlos on top of me.

There was a thunderous roar above my head, the ground beneath me shook violently, and my hearing suddenly sounded like I was being held underwater. All I could think of was Zone 7's Highway 9 collapsing in on me as debris rained down over Carlos and I; it felt like sand being thrown at me.

Only feeling release when the weight of Carlos lifted. Slowly looking up, I gasped and covered my mouth to see a huge gaping hole in one of the buildings, exposing bathroom tile, and the pink wallpaper of a child's room. Water sprayed out into the street, soaking children's toys, and various pieces of what used to be the building which now littered the street below. The smell of burning was so strong I couldn't help but cough. Even though my hearing still failed me I could hear a warped alarm.

Slowly looking around, everybody was dusting themselves off and looking around, from what I could see nobody was injured apart from some minor cuts and scrapes. Carlos turned me around, and I looked at him.

"Are you okay?" Carlos asked. I was also thankful my hearing came back at that moment. The sound of the alarm blared out, and my heart skipped a beat when I heard people screaming.

"Yeah, what was that?"

Carlos shrugged as he pulled out a tissue from his overall pockets and dabbed my head with it. My eyes widening to see the tissue come out a dark red with blood, oh god where else was I hurt? After a couple moments he kissed me. For once I didn't feel absolutely petrified of him doing that above ground.

"Alright let's keep moving," Alana instructed in her distinct southern drawl as she fixed her overalls.

Carlos helped me stand up, and after brushing myself off, I watched Alana nod as she started moving quickly up another street.

Honestly, I felt like giving up after the fireball. Our assignment was to patrol an apparent safe route to the castle where Our Leader resided, Hunter had stated it was so safe that we didn't need weapons. But I was more terrified of being weaponless than anything right about now.

The road we were currently walking on rose into a hill, it was so steep my breathing became heavy and it was like climbing a mountain, yet I found myself focusing on Alana who led the way. She walked slowly with her hand behind her, ready to signal for us to do something.

My eyes widened at the top of the hill and I came to a complete stop, holding my hand out to stop Carlos walking any further, in our path were six guards blocking our way holding guns aimed directly at us. I glanced at Alana, her face had turned a deathly shade of white. I swallowed thin air.

"All of you are coming with us!" the one in the middle bellowed.

"Like hell you are!" Alana shouted back.

One of the guards shifted toward another guard, not taking his gun away from us. "I'm taking out ID 498763! I loved hearing his father plead for forgiveness in his final moments."

"If you're taking ID 498763 out, then I'm taking ID 494011."

My blood boiled and I stepped forward, however, Carlos pulled me back. I noticed his breathing was heavy. We were all completely at a stand still.

I jumped and squeezed my eyes shut when a loud bang reverberated around the street, feeling something warm brush past my face, I only opened my eyes when I heard a loud groan. One of the guards had been shot directly in the heart. Another bang made me jump, and subsequently another guard went down.

It was like watching domino's as one by one the guards went down into a crumpled mess, then there was only one guard left. Exhaling a breath, I turned around to see who the assailant was.

My eyes widened, and my throat instantly constricted to see Gabrielle holding a gun at the final guard.

"Gabrielle, no!" I screamed at the top of my lungs as she squeezed the trigger.

Shaking out of Carlos's grasp, I started running towards her, my heart racing. All thoughts of our assignment out the window, replaced by the need to save her. *Bang.* I stopped suddenly, and my breathing momentarily stopped when I saw her lurch forward—the fear in her eyes was something I would never forget. She pressed a trembling hand to her stomach, blood already staining her overalls.

Gabrielle aimed the gun again, tears were now raining down her cheeks as I started running towards her again, my heart raced as I tried to get to her in time. She squeezed the trigger again. There were two gun shots.

All I saw was the blood spray out of her side, then she collapsed, I cried out as I skidded towards her. I pulled her up onto my lap, holding her like she when she was a baby, pressing a hand to her wounds trying to stem the bleeding. Her eyes fluttered as she tried to remain conscious. I was already sobbing, it was difficult to breath, the smell of blood was everywhere and I heard the sound of running.

Suddenly Carlos was in full view.

"Can we help her?" I pleaded towards him, my lips quivering.

All he did was shake off his jacket, she sucked in a breath and grimaced as he put pressure on her wounds. I noticed a tear roll down Carlos's cheek.

"Did I get him?" she asked weakly. I didn't care, I wiped her tears away with my thumb and breathed out as I gently rocked her.

"I don't know," I choked out, running a hand through her hair. "Why be that stupid?"

"After guards got you" she responded, her speech becoming delayed. "I thought you were mad at me for it."

I broke down even more than I already was. "No, I was never mad at you for that. It's the guards fault not yours."

She gave me a slight smile. It hurt to breathe with the lump in my throat, and I looked at Carlos who was also crying now.

"Joseph," Gabrielle said quietly. "I heard the broadcast."

I sobbed and wiped my eyes so I could see my sisters face. "She lied, didn't she?" I asked Gabrielle, already knowing the truth.

My sister slowly nodded, then she stared into space. "I can see dad."

"No, stay with us, we're getting you help." I choked out, looking at Carlos who turned his head away. "Stay with us for Mum and Michael's sake." I stroked her hair.

"I love you." Her final words were almost inaudible. But I heard.

Then she slipped away, one last smile painted on her face.

Carlos instantly let go of the pressure on her wounds, curled up into a ball, and broke down crying. His trembling hands covered in blood ran through his hair.

She was gone.

My sister was actually gone.

Looking down at my sister, I pressed her against me and rocked backward and forward as I tried to breathe. Gripping hold of her government uniform, I started sobbing loudly. Breaking down even further as I screamed into the air.

27

Nadine

Flashes of lightning lit up the night sky with each clap of thunder. The sound of heavy rain on the flat roof above me sounded like a rhythmic drum. Even as I glanced at the parking lot below me, the rain hit the concrete like tiny bullets.

I groaned as I dragged a suitcase behind me, passing apartments where some curtains were open, revealing people going about with their lives. Some were watching TV, others were oddly asleep with their lamps on—I wondered what they did for a living. I stopped briefly to adjust my coat which was hanging off of my shoulders, it was difficult to put it on correctly when I was in such a hurry running away from home whilst mum and dad were both at work; especially with one functioning arm.

Water droplets from my hair dropped into my shirt, which made me shiver when it mixed with the cold air. I was so cold I could see my breath whenever I breathed out.

As I approached apartment twenty-five, I could see the sliver of light through the closed blinds from the window. I propped my suitcase against the wall and knocked on the door, loud enough to be heard by the occupants inside. I jumped as another clap of thunder rumbled the sky, and tensing up when sharp pains shot up my arm.

I relaxed when the door opened with a click, Ezekiel appeared in the doorway holding his side, which was still clearly painful for him; then his gaze fell onto my suitcase.

"Can I live with you for a bit?" I asked quickly, sighing at how crazy this sounded. "I would stay with Payton, but my parents are looking for me" Another clap of thunder made me jump, I winced at the pain in my arm.

Slowly Ezekiel nodded, stepping further into his apartment and opened the door wider for me to enter. "Sure, come in."

Taking my suitcase, I walked past him and into his space. I gasped out of surprise with how nice his apartment looked. A brown L-shaped sofa was to the left of me facing a flat screen TV, then it opened up into a white kitchen which overlooked the living area in the top left corner. Next to that was a corridor shrouded in darkness, which probably led to a bedroom and a bathroom, but that was anybody's guess.

As I walked deeper into the apartment, I propped my suitcase against the wall near the corridor, and sucked in a breath, my teeth chattering from the drastic temperature change from the outside.

"You look soaked, I'll get you a towel," Ezekiel exclaimed as he shut the door, then walked past me and disappeared into the corridor. He emerged a couple moments later with a towel, which I took and started running it through my hair, then Ezekiel leaned against the wall, his gaze fixated on my arm brace. "What happened to your arm?"

"Long story," I groaned as I walked toward the sofa. "Let's just say, I found out how I ended up in Denmé."

Ezekiel sucked in a breath, and walked toward the kitchen. "Well you're welcome to stay as long as you need, sit and make yourself at home."

I slipped off my dripping wet coat and placed it on the back of a dining chair. Then I collapsed on the sofa, shocking myself as I sank down further than I thought I would. But I let the furniture wrap around me in a comforting embrace.

My eyes became heavy, all the exhaustion over the past couple days as I planned my escape hit me like a ton of bricks. I didn't fight the pull of sleep, I let it take me away into a place of relaxation.

* * *

Waking up with a gasp, I was led fully on the sofa, moving a blanket from my face which wasn't there when I fell asleep. The smell in the apartment had changed, it wasn't a bad smell, it was the smell of food; greasy cheese pizza to be exact.

Using my good arm to help me sit up, I looked around the apartment, the TV was now turned on but was on mute, and there was Ezekiel in the kitchen eating some pizza while pouring some drinks on the counter. Rubbing my eye, I let out a groan.

"How long was I out?" My voice sounded groggy, and I picked my damp hair away from my cheek; my hair felt like it was glued together.

Ezekiel glanced up at me, then he opened the pizza box up and fixed me a plate. "It's been about thirty minutes, I was just about to wake you up; I ordered in pizza."

He picked up the plate, and came into the living space, picking up a side table then placed it in front of me; setting the plate on top of it. I watched Ezekiel disappear back into the kitchen and pick up his own plate along with some drinks.

"Thank you, for letting me stay, and the food," I said as he sat next to me.

"Your country is beautiful," Ezekiel admitted, as he placed his plate next to mine.

I smiled at him. "Michael said that too." I picked up my pizza and took a bite, making a noise from how delicious it was.

Ezekiel smiled, as he reached for his cup he accidentally brushed against my arm. I sucked in a breath as a burning sensation flowed from my shoulder to my fingertips, I closed my eyes waiting for it to subside. When I opened them again, Ezekiel was looking at me with a raised eyebrow.

"Are you okay?" he asked.

I nodded, taking a drink from my own glass to ignore the pain. Ezekiel's gaze on me lingered for a few moments before he took another bite of pizza. Despite how painful my arm was, since taking the tracker out, it was worth it to be off the radar.

Just as I was about to take another bite of pizza, Ezekiel turned to me. "Can I do something that's been on my mind for a while?"

"Erm; sure."

My breath caught in my throat as he leaned into me, he was so close I could feel his breath on my lips. Then he held my waist, and before I knew it we were kissing; it was like fireworks had exploded in my mind. Butterflies filled my stomach. I didn't know what to do with my hand, so I placed it on my lap. Giving in, and kissing him back. I let him start pushing me onto the sofa, then he pulled away quickly. Ezekiel clutched his side, and coughed, grimacing in pain.

Sitting back up, I was breathless, and looked around the apartment. "Are you okay?"

"Yeah, I should have waited to heal more before trying that" he admitted. Then he looked at me. "This isn't going to make living together awkward is it?"

I shook my head, this time I was the one to lean into him, and kissed him on the cheek. He seemed to relax at this gesture. I picked up my pizza, and took a bite.

Since rescuing Ezekiel, I did feel a stronger connection to him. But I didn't know if it would amount to anything quite yet.

NADINE

* * *

Two days later, I was staring at my brother behind the glass. The phone was cold against my ear, and I glanced at Ezekiel who was sitting next to me for support, I had told him everything of what my dad and Wyatt did to me; he was furious.

Wyatt's gaze lingered on Ezekiel for a few moments. "Who is this?"

I watched Ezekiel lean forward, and pick up the second phone. "A friend." Was all he replied.

My brother nodded, still looking at Ezekiel like he was a force to be reckoned with, then he looked at my arm brace. "I wondered why dad was furious when he came to visit yesterday."

"I'm staying with Payton for a while," I lied, Ezekiel remained silent which I was thankful for. "I'm going to report Dad."

Wyatt laughed, and looked between Ezekiel and I. "His boss approved the plan, so that's not going to get you far."

"She didn't consent to it, so Nadine has every right to report the issue to his boss whether he approved it or not. It's unlawful and immoral," Ezekiel spat.

I watched Wyatt's gaze return to Ezekiel, then it fell to his barcode and Wyatt's mouth curled into a smile. "Shut your mouth, you're Denmé scum, you don't know how our laws work."

"I may be Denmé scum, but at least I'm not the scum bag who attempted to murder their own sister," Ezekiel spoke calmly as he leaned back in his seat, looking at Wyatt.

I covered my mouth, trying to suppress a laugh at Ezekiel defending me, even if it was in that scarily calm way before somebody started shouting. Wyatt glared at Ezekiel, leaning back as his jaw tensed then he looked at me.

"You know, The Educators are only one email away. I wouldn't be so quick to abandon our whole entire family," Wyatt snarled.

My eyes widened, and my heart started thumping. "Wyatt, what do you mean?" He put his phone away then he stood up and walked away. "Wyatt!" I shouted. But it was already too late, guards had already let him back through the door.

Yet again Wyatt and made my whole world stop for a brief moment. I stood there, holding the phone in my trembling hand with tears stinging my eyes. I breathed heavily and looked at Ezekiel, he slowly stood up. Smoothed out his ripped jeans, and white T-shirt then grabbed my bag; slipping it over his chest.

"We should go," Ezekiel instructed, taking the phone from my hand and putting it back in the holder.

I nodded, and pushed a tear from my eye. Then he led me away.

* * *

A few hours later myself, Payton, and Ezekiel were tucked away in a corner of our usual cafe spot in Downtown Gratisland. The energy was alive with bustling conversations, with the usual screeching of the coffee machine as baristas steamed milk. Payton was sitting next to Ezekiel, her eyes travelling a line from his head to his feet.

"Nadine was right, you are hot," she said with a smile.

My eyes widened, and instantly my cheeks started to burn "Pay!" I hissed, touching my cheeks hoping Ezekiel couldn't tell I was blushing.

Ezekiel smiled as he looked at me, then at Payton. He laughed as he leaned forward, and picked up his coffee; taking a sip. Just as I was about to get my own coffee, Payton thrust her hips followed by a point in my direction, then Ezekiel's.

"I can see you," Ezekiel pointed out.

Payton started laughing, her cheeks growing a shade pink. She picked up her iced coffee, turning her back to Ezekiel as she took a drink. My cheeks hurt from how much I was trying not to laugh.

NADINE

I shifted on the seat, and cleared my throat. "Michael's getting dropped off by Hannah, he should be here soon."

As if on queue, the click of Michael's crutches filled the air. I turned around and saw him struggling up the stairs, as he tried to juggle his crutches and a cup of coffee on a tray. Just as I got ready to stand up, Ezekiel beat me to it, taking the cup of coffee from Michael's hand.

"You could have called us over to help you carry all this," Ezekiel informed him. Letting Michael hold his arm as he limped up the stairs.

At the top Michael groaned. "I fucking hate this, I just want to be independent."

"Well, when you're better you won't have to rely on help," Ezekiel explained as he helped Michael sit next to Payton, she smiled at him as she flicked her hair behind her shoulder.

I moved up to allow Ezekiel to sit in the empty spot on the sofa next to me, and as he sat down he held my hand. My hand felt small in his, but it felt safe. I looked at Payton who mouthed *I knew it* toward me, my whole body became warm and I cleared my throat for the second time.

"Wyatt said The Educators are only one email away before he walked off," I admitted, taking my hand out of Ezekiel's grasp as I picked up my own coffee.

Michael looked at all of us, propping his leg on the coffee table. "Who are The Educators? Are they like teachers?"

"They're people from Denmé who kidnap outsiders, and take them into the country to show citizens what happens when you go against Our Leader," Ezekiel explained.

I saw Michael stiffen as his eyes widened. "Since last night, there's been a car following me. I thought my aunt had set up security for me or something, but she's clueless."

"What do they look like?" I asked as I took a drink.

Michael shrugged. "The windows are blacked out, they never leave the car."

I noticed Payton shifted uncomfortably in her seat, looking behind my shoulder, I followed her gaze to see a male walking up the stairs.

Even though Downtown Gratisland was a bustling shopping area, with a lot of strange and wonderful visitors daily, this guy seemed out of place. He walked with purpose, like somebody who had been in the military, and despite being inside a coffee shop he didn't have a drink in his hands. The mysterious guy looked at Michael too long to be a coincidence, then he stalked off towards a small corner of the coffee shop which faced our group directly.

Turning back to the group, I let out a jagged breath. "There will be hell to pay for if my dad has set The Educators on Michael," I announced, anger boiling my blood.

Everybody but Michael nodded. Instead Michael's gaze was fixated on the strange guy who was very clearly watching our every move.

28

Judas

The dark void I had been staring at for God knows how long, was suddenly replaced by light. Now staring at me like a smack in the face was a tropical beach. Looking around, the rest of the hotel room was still in darkness, the red light on the TV made it more apparent that they fixed the electricity in Zone 7. Inside this hotel room, it smelled like lit matches from the variety of candles we had burned through. Yet I sank back into the bed I had called my sanctuary, wiping my eyes for the umpteenth time as I sighed heavily; adjusting the pillow.

Hearing the thud as the door hit the rock that kept it open, at first I thought it was Carlos but the atmosphere around the mysterious person didn't feel like him. So I pulled my comforter tighter around me, in anticipation it was just somebody coming around to check the electricity or something, and they'd leave me alone soon.

Instead I heard Thora's voice say. "Hey, how are you feeling?" I felt the bed sink down as she sat on the end of it.

"The usual," I mumbled, feeling myself choke up.

I felt her hand on my leg. "Can I convince you to come with me to Tunnel 7:20? It might make you feel better."

"Where's 7:20?" I questioned, loosening the grip on the comforter.

Thora smiled. "A surprise."

Propping myself up on my elbow, Thora wasn't wearing her dreadlocks, instead her natural brown hair fell to her chin—it was wavy from the various braids which held the dreadlocks in place. She looked different, but in a refreshing way.

"I suppose it couldn't hurt," I admitted, slowly sliding out of bed.

The bitter coldness I had felt inside, since my sister was taken from me, was returning, but I pushed it down as I slid my feet into the sliders at the bottom of the bed. Lately, I had only left my bed to go to the bathroom and to eat. When I glanced at Thora, she smiled at me.

"There we go," she said softly as I stood up. She pushed herself off of the bed, and stood in front of me.

I cringed when I ran my hands through my hair, it felt slimy. But I sighed, wiping away the tears which had started to blur my vision, when I shoved my hands into my pockets I reluctantly followed Thora out of the hotel room.

* * *

Tunnel 7:20 led Thora and I to an abandoned sports facility, when we arrived we used a ladder to climb up to the roof. She sat there, hugging one of her legs she brought up to her chest, and stared out into the entire city of Zone 7. Night had fallen, and the city was lit up in gold, and I realised that without the windows in The Rebellion, nobody would be able to tell if it was night or day down there. Glancing behind my shoulder, I saw a barbed wire fence, then a sheer ominous darkness which led into Zone 8. When I returned to the city, I glanced at the giant white castle on the foothill with its red roofed turrets—it glowed in the night due to the various spotlights surrounding the exterior walls.

It was so cold out here, both of our breaths were visible. Due to only having the hoodie to shield me from the cold, I felt bad I had nothing to offer Thora.

"How does it feel being Zone Leader?" Thora asked with a smile, playing with her laces as she spoke.

I sucked in a breath, then sighed. "Honestly, I feel like I only got it because of Carlos." I hugged my knees to my chest.

Thora let out a laugh, and shook her head. "No, Ezekiel's been wanting to make you Zone leader for a while, but thought it's best to wait until you both got married before promoting you." She leaned back, letting out a breath. "Ezekiel watches, you know, he knows everybody comes to you for help if they can't find Carlos or Taylor."

I furrowed my brow and looked at her. "Well that's nice to know." I shuddered when I had to push my hair out of my face, I really needed a shower. "What have I missed?"

"Not much, we're all in this big argument because some want to retaliate, and some say to just try returning to normal."

I scoffed. "They're hunting down each Zone, the only thing we can do is retaliate, sitting like ducks is out of the question." From the corner of my eye I saw something bright like the sun hurtling through the air. I had to do a double take in case my eyes were deceiving me. "Erm, Thora, what is that?"

The impact boomed across the entire city, and the building beneath us trembled. A fire ball erupted out of the castle, resulting in a landslide which swept down the foothill, filled with debris and other dirt mixed in. I was frozen where I sat as a loud alarm blared across the city to signal danger.

"Samhain, what the fuck," Thora hissed, pushing herself to stand up and ran to the hatch we had climbed through.

After a moments hesitation, I copied her movements, even if Thora was long gone by the time I had started my descent down the ladder. One last glance at the city of Zone 7, I noticed several other fireballs hurtling through the sky.

My legs were trembling by the time I got to the bottom of the ladder, now only lanterns guided me back to The Tunnels. I stopped briefly to catch my breath, in here it smelled musty and old, then I noticed something in the worn-out sports field *St. Herculia Giants* spelled out in red and gold. There it was again *St. Herculia*.

But what did it mean?

* * *

I was breathless by the time I entered the lobby, it was a beautiful ornate space with marble floors and walls; some of the marble encased floor length mirrors. Then I felt relief to see Carlos standing by the reception desk, he looked up and started smiling at me immediately. I jogged up to him, and pulled him into my embrace, gripping hold of his shirt and breaking down crying which I had been holding back since leaving the hotel. Carlos held me closer, I felt him run a hand through my hair.

"What happened?" he questioned, I could feel his voice vibrating through his shirt.

I pulled away, and looked at him, wiping my eyes and breathing out. "I went to 7:20 with Thora, then Samhain blew up some of the castle."

Carlos looked at the door to the restaurant, which we had turned into a meeting space, his gaze clouded with concern. "I wondered why Hunter just called for an emergency meeting." He looked at me. "Samhain's been talking about doing that, never thought he'd actually do it."

"It's Samhain," I pointed out.

Carlos nodded with a slight smile, then held me at arms length. "Well, you Mr. Wells, need to freshen up, you smell like garbage."

I laughed. "Love you too."

"Meet you here in say twenty minutes? I'll tell Hunter to wait 'til then."

I nodded, giving Carlos a kiss before I walked toward the staircase which led to our room. As I pushed the door open, I noticed he was watching me, and there was a deep sadness in his eyes before the door closed.

* * *

Just like the lobby, the dining room was just as grand and encased in marble, except instead of mirrors on some of the walls, these were replaced with windows. Even though this restaurant was now used for Leader meetings, the lingering smell of food indicated that the restaurant was still thriving when we weren't using it.

Carlos, Thora, and I were sitting in a booth, watching from a distance as Hunter shouted at Samhain in front of everybody at the main table. Hunter was loud when he yelled, and every time he did so I jumped—which resulted in me having to hold Carlos's hand for comfort underneath the table, or I would flip out. Even though Hunter looked gentle, his temper was anything but.

"Why the fuck did you not wait for my orders?" Hunter shouted.

Samhain crossed his arms over his chest. "I did what you cowards were taking too long to do!" he shouted back. "You're one of the fuckers who wants to surrender!"

I jumped as Hunter smacked the table, which made a loud metallic sound as cutlery jumped from the vibration. Then he jabbed a finger into Samhain's chest. "I am the head leader of The Rebellion, not you!" Hunter snarled. "You get permission from me!"

"Don't fucking touch me," Samhain growled as he smacked Hunter's hand away, fury in his eyes.

Honestly, I thought they were about to start throwing punches. I glanced at Carlos who seemed calm, but his eyes said something different. When I returned my gaze to Hunter and Samhain, I watched Hunter walk away as he ran his fingers through his half tied up hair. I still wondered how he could fight with it being so long.

"Samhain, everybody knows you have health issues, but it is imperative you get permission from me, before you go off and get us all killed. It's already dangerous being in this hotel," Hunter explained in a more calm manner.

I shifted in my seat as Samhain stood up. "Did Joseph need permission, before you got his sister killed? You're the one who sent them out without weapons." I gasped and covered my mouth, Hunter suddenly became pale and looked shocked. "Think about that for a moment, maybe you'll stop being a dictating ass hole." Samhain stormed out of the restaurant, the door slammed shut behind him.

The room went deathly quiet, and all eyes were suddenly on me. Carlos pulled me in close, and I swallowed the lump in my throat. Hunter was staring me; there was a sadness in his eyes. I didn't know who to blame for what happened to Gabrielle, all I knew was that I felt empty, and that person had to pay.

I wanted Ezekiel back, wherever he was. As much as I hated to admit it, Hunter didn't know how to lead such a large group, he was way out of his element. Since he became Leader, shit had literally hit the fan.

* * *

A loud alarm woke me up, and I squeezed my eyes shut as the lights flickered on automatically. When I opened them again, I lifted my head up from the pillow to look around, Carlos's arm moved from around my waist as he sat up with a groan.

"*Danger imminent: please evacuate the facility,*" a robotic voice ordered around the room.

I sat up quickly, my heart raced. Carlos quickly got out of bed, he grabbed my hoodie from the floor and threw it at me.

"Do you know what's happening?" I asked, as I tugged it over my head.

Carlos shook his head as he tugged his jeans on, and looked to the door. The same voice ordered us to evacuate again. I turned my head to read the time 4:50 a.m., I didn't know what the mysterious alarm was.

"We need to get moving," Carlos instructed, extending his hand out to me.

I nodded and took his hand in mine, then slipped out of bed to get my shoes on. Both of us walked hand in hand towards the door to the hotel room.

Out in the corridor there was a spinning red light which made the corridor look like it was filled with blood. The robotic voice ordered us to evacuate a third time, something big must be going off. Boudica from Zone 3 emerged out of her room, hands over her ears, she was wearing an oversized t-shirt as she looked around.

"What's happening?" she shouted over the alarm.

The door opposite mine and Carlos's opened and Xander stepped out alongside Thora—surprisingly. I knew Thora's room was on the floor below ours, so I could only guess why she was here. When another door opened, I turned my head and Daisuke emerged from his room, looking disgruntled from being woken up so early in the morning.

"I say let's evacuate!" Xander ordered.

Nobody protested, Carlos was the one to lead everybody out into the stairway next to Xander's room. This area smelled musty, but another scent made me stop and pull Carlos back—blood.

Carlos looked at me, then at everybody else who were waiting to ascend the stairs behind me. The air was suddenly filled with screaming followed by gunshots. My eyes widened, and I looked behind my shoulder as I took step back.

I froze when I heard the sound of hurried footsteps coming down the stairs, only relaxing when Sung-Jin from Zone 11 came into view, he looked like a deer in headlights, close behind him was Oluchi Zone 2 and Ace from Zone 1.

"What's happening?" Daisuke asked Sung-Jin.

Sung-Jin stopped, clearly breathless by what was happening. "Guards are in the hotel, get to the lower levels, until the bottom." He continued running down the stairs, followed by everybody else.

It was like somebody had turned my feet into blocks of ice, I couldn't move and my breathing became painful after what he just said. I didn't know how long I had been standing on the stairs, but before I knew it, Carlos had to physically carry me down the stairs to get us to safety.

* * *

Carlos put me down when we got to the bottom corridor, I breathed heavily and ran a trembling hand through my hair. Even though it wasn't ever cold in The Rebellion, I was shivering, I looked around while everybody tried various doors to see which one was unlocked. Then a sinking feeling of dread overwhelmed me when I realised we were trapped down here, there was no way out of this hotel with guards on the higher levels. The only thing strange was a set of three mirrors at one end of the corridor.

"We're trapped, there's no way out," I breathed out, feeling tears sting my eyes.

I jumped as a hand was placed on my arm, I looked at Carlos. "We'll be fine, breathe." he told me.

Suddenly a door opened and Xander, Oluchi and Ace piled into a room. I swallowed the lump in my throat, looking at Daisuke as he leaned against one of the walls staring at the ceiling, then Sung-Jin joined him. I looked over at Thora who stood by the mirror wall, she looked deep in thought.

"Guys, we need help barricading the door to the stairwell," Xander called into the corridor as a box spring was shoved through the doorway.

Carlos nodded as he took hold of the box spring, and dragged it into the corridor, Sung-Jin followed behind. Both of them shoved it into the doorway to the stairs vertically. It was slightly too big for a full barricade, which is where Xander and Oluchi came in—both of them used some other pieces of furniture to shove against the box spring to make us more secure. I jumped as gunshots could be heard on the floor above, followed by screaming.

All four of them wiped their hands together, impressed with their handy work, then Ace emerged out of the room, he leaned against the door frame.

"Great work, that should keep us safe until—"

I never got to hear the end of that statement. The walls near the barricade exploded like a volcanic eruption, I was instantly thrown back from the impact, feeling debris raining down on me; the smell of burning and blood was thick in the air. The explosion had sucked all oxygen out of the environment, and had stolen all the light from the corridor. My headed erupted into a heart beat of throbbing pain as I smacked into something hard and metallic.

Immediately my world spun and then darkness.

29

Judas

I was sitting on the floor while I worked with Dad to complete Task 90 outside of the home I grew up in, a large Victorian-style house, which we painted green before the regime came into existence. Dad grunted as he ripped out a weed from the sidewalk, he looked deep in thought as he stared at it.

"What?" I questioned, as I stood up.

"Just thinking, Denmé is exactly like this weed in such a beautiful landscape."

I looked at Dad with a furrowed brow as I picked up a pair of hedge shears, getting to work on cutting back an overgrown bush. My dad picked up an identical pair, and we worked in unison to get it looking pristine.

"Son, do you remember how great St. Herculia was?"

I shook my head. "What was it like?"

Dad smiled as he cut back a large section protruding out into the side walk. "Well for starters, you had freedom. None of these tasks or the barcodes." I nodded as I listened. "You could buy your own plot of land, and do whatever you wanted. Live with your parents until you're eighteen. And in St. Herculia you could travel, do you remember that trip to Tivai?"

I shook my head, but smiled anyway to see how happy it made him to discuss St. Herculia with me. This discussion was just a father speaking to his fifteen year old son, being care free about the topic in hand.

Something hard smashing into my arm made me slip, and I swore under my breath, knowing full well I'd get shouted at for the piece of shrubbery having a huge gaping hole in it. Looking at where it came from, a six-year-old Michael stood there laughing while collecting the soccer ball he had just kicked at me. But before he could get there, I jumped at the sound of a gun shot, watching as the ball deflated.

"Boy!" I turned around to see a guard storming up to Michael, grabbing him by the arm. "You are fully aware our leader prohibits ball games!" the guard shouted.

Michael's eyes glazed over, and he looked at myself and Dad. Struggling to get away from the guard. I glanced at the patio where mum and Gabrielle were sitting on the stairs doing crotchet, a long forgotten habit between the two of them, they seemed oblivious to the confrontation going on.

"He's a child, leave him alone," Dad snapped.

I winced as the guard slapped Michael across the face, he screamed loudly and instantly burst out crying—running into my arms when the guard let him go. I held him against me, running a hand through his hair. He sobbed loudly, I could see an angry red hand print already appearing on his small face.

Suddenly it occurred to me, maybe Olympia was where Michael rightfully belonged.

When I woke up, I groaned, all I could see was the red circular spinning lamp which hung from its wire. I was led on what could only be a sheet of concrete, and the air smelled of burning. Around me, I could hear running water and two alarms blaring—the same voice telling us to evacuate echoed out twice. But something struck out to me, it was the sound of counting. Despite how dizzy I felt, I forced myself to sit up, my world rocked side to side at a delirious angle.

Near me I could see the outlines of two figures, at first they split into four people until I focused, then I noticed one of the figures was doing chest compression's to somebody on the floor. My eyes widened, and I screamed loudly when I realised it was Carlos, covering my mouth with a trembling hand—I broke down crying all over again, backing up into a piece of wall.

The person doing chest compression's, I now recognised as Sung-Jin, he glanced behind his shoulder, then at Daisuke who sat next to him. He became more determined to revive Carlos, I slowly crawled up to them, not caring if my vision was impaired.

"I need to help," I insisted, holding Carlos's hand. "Let me help him. I can't lose him too."

"Sure you can handle it?" Sung-Jin questioned, he had a large cut on his forehead.

I nodded quickly, after a moments hesitation Sung-Jin sat back. I swallowed the lump in my throat, my hands trembled as I linked them together then resumed the chest compression's. My lips quivered as I cried, willing for him to come back. I still couldn't feel his heartbeat, it was becoming more difficult for myself to breathe.

"Please wake up, I need you," I choked out.

I felt a hand on my shoulder. "Judas, let me take over."

"Get the fuck off me!" I shouted.

I sucked in a breath and started to do the kiss of life. I was becoming desperate, I couldn't lose my boyfriend this close to my sister. When I looked up as I started resuming chest compression's, Sung-Jin was watching me silently.

My only relief was when Carlos took that deep inhale of breath. Instantly I kissed him deeply, tasting the saltiness of my tears on his lips. When I pulled away, Carlos was looking at me, he reached up and wiped away my tears with his thumb, I held his hand and cried.

"Don't leave me again," I sobbed, kissing his hand.

"I guess we're even now." Carlos smirked.

I laughed through tears, wiping them away with the heel of my hand, Carlos looked tired and had a cut on his cheek.

"We lost Ace," Daisuke suddenly announced.

My laughter quickly subsided when I looked at him in shock, he pointed to a large pile of rubble where an arm was sticking out. My stomach rolled, and I had to fight everything not to throw up. When I looked around, everybody else had made it out—Thora held Xander who was unconscious in her lap, Oluchi sat by the mirror wall with her knees brought to her chest.

The sound of movement brought my attention to the wall of mirrors, the middle one moved to one side to reveal an ominous black tunnel—only lit by the warm glow of candles. A musty scent filled the air. My heart skipped a beat as a black silhouette filled the tunnel, their heavy foot steps echoed around the walls.

"You could say, Zone 7 went out with a bang," Samhain exclaimed as he came into view, scratching behind his ear.

Daisuke stood up and got to him in three steps, I jumped when he slapped Samahin across the face. I watched as Samhain squared his shoulders then let out a low growl as he touched his cheek.

"You got one of us fucking killed, you fucking nut case!" Daisuke shouted in his face. "Carlos almost died, you know Judas is already on suicide watch!"

I furrowed my brow and looked at Carlos, this was news to me, however Carlos just held my hand. Sung-Jin suddenly stood up, and so did Oluchi.

"I'm not a fucking nut case, thanks Daisuke. Now all of you fuckers, get a move on. You can thank me later!" Samhain shouted down the corridor.

Nobody moved, the adrenaline I had built up from reviving Carlos quickly faded and was replaced with a debilitating dizziness, my head pounded against my skull and even my vision kept going blurry. I wanted to be sick from it.

"What about Xander?" Thora asked weakly, there was a large cut on her leg and shoulder. When I looked at Xander he was still unconscious. "Who's going to carry him? We're all injured in some way."

Samhain looked over at everybody in the corridor, then he clicked his fingers. "Joseph, help me."

I froze, looking down at Carlos, he nodded in approval letting go of my hand. When I tried to stand up, I fell back down—my whole vision blurred and I retched from the queasy feeling in my stomach. I covered my mouth, and turned away from Carlos in case I actually threw up.

"I can't." Covering my mouth with trembling hands as I almost threw up again, feeling Carlos's hand on my back. "I feel too dizzy."

"Fine, Sung-Jin can help carry him. I'll carry Carlos," Samhain responded.

When I pushed my hair away from my face, I placed a hand on my forehead. "Can you get somebody to turn off the two alarms?" I managed to choke out.

I heard the crunching of shoes on the debris. But I wouldn't dare move my head in this moment. "There's only one alarm ringing, Judas," Oluchi told me.

My eyes suddenly felt extremely heavy, and almost instantly, everything went dark for a second time.

30

Nadine

I winced as I extended my arm out in front of me, instantly it burned where the main source of the injury was—it burned down to my fingers which tingled like I had just sat on them for an hour. Though I could move my arm a small amount, I preferred not to use it other than these small exercises the doctors had instructed for me to do, after Ezekiel made me go to the doctors office. Ezekiel rolled over to his side, and watched me, he was shirtless and his eyes glistened in the morning light.

His room was small, but it was what he needed as a temporary stay. All the walls were white, and there was a closet with barely any clothes in at the foot of the bed; even a full-length mirror where I could see myself laying next to Ezekiel.

"Is it still painful?" Ezekiel questioned.

"Yeah, but at least I can move it more," I held the comforter to my bare chest, looking at the window where a sliver of light shone like a spotlight on us both.

"Doctors said it'll take four weeks to heal, it'll get better," Ezekiel said, then he kissed me. I smiled, and kissed him again.

I let out a laugh as Ezekiel pulled me close and started kissing my neck, I could feel his hand travel up my thigh and rest on my hip. I moved so I found his lips, and kissed him deeply with my hand on his cheek letting the comforter fall off me. When he kissed my chest, I arched my back and bit my lip. Suddenly our spotlight of morning sun was eclipsed by a shadow, I turned my head to see somebody standing outside of window looking into the room, I screamed and sat up, wrapping the comforter around me again. Ezekiel looked at the window, and swore under his breath.

The figure continued to stare into the room, I was breathing heavily and swallowed air. I watched Ezekiel move to the end of the bed, and picked up my discarded towel from the night before. He wrapped it around his hips as he stood up.

"Close the blinds," I whispered.

Ezekiel nodded as he approached the window, peering through the gap in a stealthy way. He swore under his breath again. "It's a Denmé guard," he whispered.

My eyes widened. "Close the fucking blinds."

He grabbed the pull chord, and lowered the blinds down so the room was as dark as night. My heart was racing, and I felt a sinking feeling in the pit of my stomach.

I jumped when something soft was thrown at my face, only relaxing when I realised it was one of Ezekiel's shirts, as I slipped it on I dropped my grip on the comforter and brought my knees up to my chest.

"What a fucking pervert," I spat.

"Has Michael said anything about The Educators?" Ezekiel asked as he got dressed.

I sucked in a breath, and pressed a hand to my thumping heart. "No, he says they stay outside his house, but cops won't do anything."

Ezekiel let out a laugh, and placed his hands on his hips while shaking his head. "Is that normal in this country?"

"More normal than you think." I sighed. "What do we do now?" I asked.

He breathed out, biting his lip as he looked around the room. "Try to go about our normal day, warn Michael and try to come up with a plan."

I nodded quickly, wiping a lone tear from my eye. I was so mad I was shaking, how dare my dad do this to us.

* * *

An hour later I dragged a duffle bag of laundry down the basement stairs of Ezekiel's apartment block. Down here it smelled funky, I couldn't describe it. As I passed the white painted brick walls and then the whirring boiler; I got to the laundry machines.

Opening one of the washing machines, I started to put all my dark colours inside of it, but the feeling of being watched was like a heavy weight on my shoulders. There was nobody there when I turned around. Swallowing air, I closed the door and waved the money card in front of the card reader, the balance of one dollar and sixty cents displayed on the screen; as I started to select the wash cycle the feeling of being watched crept back on me. This apartment block was old, so it probably was just the fact I was in a creepy basement which was freaking me out.

But then the smell of cigarettes filled the air, I froze as I pressed the start button, the washer kicked into gear. Then the sound of steel toe boots filled the air. Suddenly I was grabbed from behind, I started thrashing and kicking out, punching anything in my path. Whoever grabbed me put their hand over my mouth, I bit down hard until I tasted blood, a male yelled out and momentarily let me go.

I tried running towards the exit, but the person grabbed hold of me and slammed me to the floor. The air inside my lungs instantly knocked out of me. My eyes widened to see a Denmé guard hovering over me. I groaned and tried to kick out but his strength couldn't match mine, one last move and I thrust my knee into his crotch. He cried out and rolled off me.

My breathing was heavy, and I wheezed out as I tried to get oxygen into my lungs, seeing the guard hunched over on the floor. I tried to back into the wall, but the guard lunged at me, slamming me against the floor again, I screamed loudly and used my one good arm to try and punch him—but he grabbed hold of my injured arm instead and squeezed. I screamed even louder as my arm burned like somebody had just set me on fire, my vision momentarily becoming blurry from the sheer pain.

"Get the fuck off me!" I screamed. Finally getting strength to punch him in the face, he groaned.

I screamed even louder as he squeezed my arm again, I broke down crying. "Where is ID 498765?" the guard snarled.

Using my one bit of remaining strength, I head butted the guard, he cried out as he held his head and I pushed my way out from underneath him. My breathing was even heavier, and my entire arm was now numb. Then a loud bang filled the air, I screamed and shielded my head.

There was more bangs, the sound of something metallic hit the washer and dryers with a loud ping. Then it hit me, somebody was shooting. More gun-shots then the sound of glass shattering, ending with a whoosh and a popping sound which came from the guard. He yelled out in pain as another gun-shot sounded out, bullets coming scarily close to me.

"Stop!" I managed to choke out. "Stop! I'm in here!"

If it was another guard, I had just blown my cover. My eyes widening as another dark silhouette entered the room, they aimed a gun at the guard then squeezed the trigger, I screamed and covered my mouth. The guard cried out, and I heard him wheeze out a guttural shuddering sound like he was choking on liquid. My throat was burning from how much I screamed.

My saviour cradled me against them, and I soon realised it was Ezekiel. I broke down into hysterical crying and held onto him tightly.

"We need to go somewhere," Ezekiel whispered into my ear.

I pulled away, and looked around the laundry room, some of the washer and dryers had bullet holes in them. Even some of the light bulbs had been shot out. Then I looked at the guard with a large red puddle spilling out of him.

"Where are we going?" I questioned, my voice wavering.

"Just trust me," Ezekiel insisted.

I nodded, I let him take my hand and stand me up. "I think I need a doctor."

Ezekiel checked my arm, and I bit my lip to try and not cry out. "Take your medication early tonight okay, don't use your arm."

I nodded again as I wiped my eyes. "Let's go."

* * *

Ezekiel and I had driven for hours, and as he turned down one of the secret import tunnels that lined the border into Denmé, my stomach tied in knots. This felt incredibly wrong, and I gripped hold of the door handle hoping we wouldn't be crossing the border today, that was the last thing I wanted to do. I could hear rocks crunch underneath Ezekiel's car tires as he drove, then at the bottom there was a group of people—The Importers. All of them looked like coal miners with head lamps on their heads, only they were void of black stains of soot. All of them looked bewildered when the cars headlights revealed their location, some gripped hold of a handrail and stood up. They clearly knew what they were doing was illegal, and I was thankful Dad only knew of one of these tunnels.

This tunnel was a far cry from Zone 7's, it was dirty with green slime on some of the walls, evidence we weren't near the capital. I glanced at Ezekiel as he put the car in park, then unclipped his seat belt, checking the time on his phone with a sigh.

"Where are we exactly?" I questioned.

"Zone 4," Ezekiel responded. "Sometimes, I used to leave Denmé and come here to go into St. Pleasant."

I raised an eyebrow, and looked at him as I unclipped my own seat belt. "So that's how you weren't scared shitless of driving me home."

Ezekiel nodded with a slight laugh as he got out of the car, I quickly followed him. I couldn't help but cover my nose at the smell in the import tunnel, it smelled like seaweed and fish. The smell was understandable with St. Pleasant being a coastal town.

When I looked at The Importers they relaxed as they realised it was Ezekiel, it appeared as though they were expecting him. Ezekiel let out a breath as he adjusted his shirt, then started moving. I followed, linking my arm around Ezekiel's as we made our way towards the Importers. Both of our footsteps echoed around the tunnel.

We stopped just shy of the border, and waited as the Importers knocked on a metal door, when it swung open I was surprised when Carlos and Hunter stepped through. I raised an eyebrow at Carlos who looked beat up with a large cut on his cheek, and a split lip—there was no sign of injury on Hunter. Carlos froze when he saw Ezekiel standing there, Hunter carried on at normal speed, he looked tired.

"Ezekiel, you're alive," Carlos exclaimed as he jogged down the stairs, and pulled him into a one armed hug.

"Careful, I've got broken ribs," Ezekiel warned, he nodded and stepped back. "Did you not get my note?"

Carlos shook his head and looked at Hunter, who stood with his arms folded watching us, I noticed Carlos look at my injured arm.

"What happened to you?"

"My dad put a tracking device in me," I admitted truthfully. A sadness overwhelmed Carlos's happy facial expression.

I watched Ezekiel produce some letters from an inside pocket of his jacket. He handed three letters to Carlos, the rest were given to Hunter. I didn't know why Hunter was being so quiet, but he looked through the letters.

"Those are letters from Michael," Ezekiel explained, pointing to the ones in Carlos's hand. "Please send them to Gabrielle, Judas, and his mother."

Carlos looked down at the one for Gabrielle, his eyes glazed over, and a tear ran down his cheek as he looked at the car. My heart skipped a beat, there was something wrong. I had never seen Carlos cry.

He breathed out as he wiped his eyes. "Michael's not here, is he?" Carlos questioned.

Ezekiel shook his head. "It's Friday afternoon, he's at school."

I watched Carlos's throat bob as he swallowed, still looking at the envelope for Gabrielle, then handed the letter back which Ezekiel took after a moments hesitation.

"What's happened?" I asked finally.

"Gabrielle sacrificed herself to save us in Zone 7," Carlos breathed out. "She passed away."

I gasped, and covered my mouth out of shock. "How is Judas?"

"He's taking it pretty hard," Carlos admitted.

"Joseph also has a concussion, because our good pal Samhain decided to play with explosives in four Zone 7 neighbourhoods," Hunter spat out. "Your family is safe, Ezekiel, I checked."

Carlos looked at Hunter. "He blew up The Rebellion to save our lives, it was just a domino effect that there were four neighbourhoods affected."

I didn't know who Samhain was but I looked at Ezekiel as he

stiffened. He looked between Carlos then at Hunter, shaking his head.

"We'll tell Hannah about Gabrielle, thank you," Ezekiel said. "We should get going before Michael returns home from school."

Carlos and Hunter nodded. Then Ezekiel guided me back to the car, one last time I glanced behind my shoulder to see Carlos watching us with a sense of longing. I felt horrible, knowing I had to be the one to tell Hannah her only niece had passed away.

* * *

I tapped my foot nervously underneath the dining table in Hannah's home, my hand trembled on my lap, my nerves were at all time high. As I looked around her kitchen, all the cupboards were made of wood with a grey backsplash by the stainless steel stove. Then my gaze fell on Hannah, she cried as she washed the dishes, on occasion she wiped her eyes with the back of her hand. When I turned to Ezekiel, he sat opposite me, staring mindlessly at the cup of coffee Hannah made for us.

"Even though I never knew her, Michael always told me stories about what she did for him, and I would have liked to have met her at least once before saying goodbye." Hannah admitted.

"She was very clever, Gabrielle got chosen to be a Zone Director," I admitted.

Even though Gabrielle had told me not tell anybody about her being chosen for the role, I felt it was only right to make Hannah feel better. She started smiling as she looked out of the window, but that quickly diminished, and she fumbled to dry her hands as she ran towards the front door.

I turned around as she opened it, Michael was standing on the porch, looking extremely pale. His eyes were glazed over with tears as they ran down his cheeks, Michael's hands trembled on his crutches.

"Please help me," he pleaded.

Then he jolted forward, arching his back as he dropped his crutches. I covered my mouth at the sound of buzzing electricity, he cried out in pain as his body convulsed before collapsing. I tried running towards him, but I fell forward, and gripped the hand rail as something hit my chest. My heart raced when I looked up to see Denmé guards hidden in the bushes.

"Don't do this," I managed to gasp.

When the electricity hit my body, all I felt was pain in every single limb, I heard myself screaming but it was like I was somewhere far away. My world spun at delirious angles, until everything went black.

31

Judas

It smelled like pizza in Zone 8's auditorium from our countless meetings in this place. Since the explosion which happened in Zone 7, it had been a week and my head still pounded, and I felt sick whenever I stood up.

Xander sat next to me on the floor, sobbing on Thora's shoulder, she rubbed his arm and looked at Samhain who sat in an actual chair with his feet up on a desk. He had his arms folded, and was staring at his boots.

"I can't believe Meaty is dead," Xander sobbed.

I turned my head when I heard Samhain snort, he was smiling then he looked up at Xander. "Sorry, but who the fuck names their hamster, Meaty?"

As much as I wanted to shout at Samhain for his statement, I had to remember he didn't understand empathy, so instead I narrowed my eyes at him. He clearly saw because he winked at me with a smirk.

"Maybe because you're a heartless freak, doesn't mean I have to follow in your footsteps," Xander snapped coldly.

"He's your brother, be nice," Thora warned.

I would have never guessed they were siblings, they didn't look too much alike, though now I looked harder they had the same brown eyes and facial structure. It was also highly strange how they both ended up in different Zones, that rarely happened.

When Hunter walked into the auditorium with Kane Bedford, Rebellion Leader of Zone 8, I straightened up. It was strange seeing Hunter with all black hair, which he had recently dyed. Kane had surfer boy blonde hair, cut short and combed over to his right—his grey suit was too small for him, so much so it looked like he was stuffed full of cotton and the buttons were about to pop.

Kane glanced at all of us sitting on the floor, then he instructed with his eyes we should sit on actual chairs. I had no idea where Carlos was, either way I used the wall to support myself, the world spun as I stood up. Once the dizziness subsided, I dragged myself up the steps, and slid into the empty seat next to Samhain.

"Are you happy to sit next to the most hated guy in the room right now?" Samhain smirked while speaking.

I groaned, and pinched the bridge of my nose. "No, but my head is pounding, and if I sit any higher, I will literally throw up."

Samhain shifted in his seat, and stiffened as he looked at something by the door. Following his gaze, my eyes widened to see Carlos looking flustered, his hair a complete mess and his tie was missing.

He approached me, and gave me a kiss on the forehead, I leaned forward so I could feel his warm breath on my ear. "They found Zone 14," he whispered.

I pulled away and looked at Carlos in shock, butterflies filled my stomach and my heart raced. When I looked around me, it only appeared to be Samhain who heard but he stayed silent. Carlos sat on the stairs next to me, his trembling hands ran through his hair.

"What about Taylor?" I questioned.

"Judas, Carlos. Everybody is waiting," Kane exclaimed harshly.

I straightened up, looking at Hunter who seemed tense while

watching us. Within his face I oddly recognised somebody else, now his hair was black, but at the moment I couldn't even begin to think of who. I pushed that thought aside, and instead I hoped Hunter could sense something was wrong, as his duty for being Head Rebellion Leader—Ezekiel would have.

By this point, Kane had been talking for a while, looking at a computer inside the podium proposing crazy ideas. However, I was too focused on wondering who Hunter looked like, and if Taylor was safe to bother zoning into the conversation. Only leaving my mind when Carlos held my hand, I relaxed slightly.

The meeting was long, boring, and drawn out beyond belief. I almost fell asleep a handful of times but I forced myself to stay awake.

"I know we've had a very intense week of meetings, so tonight, you're off the hook. But you do not leave Zone 8 unless the guards discover it. Understand?" Kane announced over the microphone.

All of us mumbled in agreement, Kane looked pleased and nodded, I was thankful to be off the hook tonight and not see the inside of an auditorium or jail meeting room. Then Samhain raised a hand; Kane tensed his jaw but gestured for him to speak.

"Can we get wasted as fuck?" Samhain asked.

"You'll ignore me if I say no," Kane pointed out. "But if you do bother to listen to me, we're going back to Zone 7 tomorrow, so I would rather you don't."

Samhain shifted in his seat, he forced a smile and played with a piece of string on his cape, trying not to look Kane in the eye.

"Everybody apart from Judas and Carlos, you're dismissed," Hunter finally announced.

I stiffened and looked at Carlos, his brow was furrowed, but as we watched everybody pile out of the auditorium. I hoped that whatever Hunter wanted to talk about, it was brief.

JUDAS

* * *

The meeting was just to ask what had gone off in Zone 14, thankfully. But now, I was blindfolded and being led somewhere by Carlos, who kept laughing. It was making me feel more dizzy than I already was, but I occasionally laughed along with him.

"Don't look," Carlos said through laughter.

I could suddenly hear music, like an orchestra playing a beautiful sounding song, and the scent of spaghetti hit my nose. Mixed in there was the sweet smell of roses. My heart skipped a beat, and I laughed.

"Are we having a blind date?" I asked, and covered my mouth.

Carlos let go of my hand, I extended it out in front of me so I could feel him, but all I could feel was air. Then I could hear his footsteps walking around me. "Okay, close your eyes," he whispered in my ear, I shuddered from his warm breath on my neck. However, I squeezed my eyes shut as the restraint of the blindfold relaxed.

I felt vulnerable with the blindfold completely off, I exhaled a breath while waiting for the next instructions from Carlos. More footsteps circled around me. I didn't know what was going on, there was so many possibilities which swam through my head.

"Open your eyes."

Blinking my eyes open, my jaw fell open. We were in a large sports arena, surrounded with string lights. The sound of the beautiful music was coming from a string quartet to my left, and in the middle was a table and chairs with two plates filled with food. I sucked in a breath, I couldn't see any sign of Carlos until he coughed, then I looked down.

Tears stung my eyes when I saw him down on one knee, butterflies fluttered around my stomach, and I swallowed the lump in my throat. In his hands, he was holding up a gold band, a big smile was on Carlos's face. I couldn't help but start crying from how beautiful this was.

"Carlos, what the fuck," I choked out as I wiped my eyes, my cheeks already hurt from smiling.

His smile lit up the room. "For the past three years you have been my rock—"

"Yes," I said with smile.

"Let me finish," Carlos managed to say through laughter, as he took my hand.

"Yes." I smiled at him.

Carlos let out a laugh. "I want you to be my forever. I belong with you forever, and always. Will you make me the happiest man, and let me call you my husband?"

I nodded quickly, he stood up quickly with a beaming smile as he pulled me close. He slid the gold band onto my finger, it fit me like a glove. My lips found his, and I smiled as I kissed him deeply.

All the crap of the past month just melted away, no guards, no strict regime, or Uprising. It was just Carlos and I against the world. While in his safe embrace, it felt like home, always had since we started dating, and now always will be.

"Can we go for a dance?" I asked, kissing him again.

Carlos looked at the string quartet, then at me. "Certainly."

He pulled away from our embrace, took my hand, and walked me over to the empty space in front of the musicians. Carlos pulled me into him with both hands placed on my waist, I crossed my hands behind his back, and we both swayed in time to the music. I pulled him close, my hands travelled to his waist, so I could rest my head onto his shoulder, which resulted in Carlos holding me tighter. I relaxed in his embrace with a sigh. Through his shirt, I could hear his heartbeat which raced from the thrill of the moment. I smiled when he kissed the top of my head.

The only thing which would make this proposal more amazing was getting freedom, to pretend like I wasn't married to Carlos would tear me apart, hurt worse than losing my entire family. He was my light for a better world.

***

We had made our way to the hotel room we stayed at in Zone 8, I kissed Carlos until he laid down on the bed. Straddling him as I kissed him hungrily, feeling his hands on my waist as I unbuttoned his shirt. Only letting him sit up enough so I could throw his shirt to one side. I was breathless as I stared down at his bare chest, running my hand over his defined torso, before I knew it Carlos threw me onto my back—I groaned but let him as he kissed me deeply, while I gripped hold of his hair.

"I love you," I managed to say through kisses, Carlos tugged off my T-shirt and threw it on the floor.

"Love you too," Carlos moaned as I started kissing his neck.

I rolled him onto his back, then looked at his face as I unbuckled his belt. Tugging it off, throwing it wherever his shirt landed. He bit his lip as I unbuttoned his jeans, sliding my hand down his pants, and he moaned loudly when I started massaging his crotch. Carlos gripped hold of the pillow, breathing heavily through moans as he arched his back while I continued.

The sudden sound of clapping made me stop, I turned around to see Samhain standing by the closet smiling at us both with a raised eyebrow. I swore under my breath, and moved my hair away from my face.

"Don't you know how to fucking knock?" Carlos spat out breathlessly, he looked at the ceiling. "Jesus." I groaned, and turned to face Samhain, the feel of Carlos's hand on my back made me bite my lip.

"How did you get in here? Why are you here?" I questioned.

Samhain looked at his hands. "Well the fairy bi-mother spanked my ass and told me two gay guys were about to fuck. So I thought, why not ask to join in." He smiled.

"I wouldn't fuck you, even if I had a gun to my head," Carlos replied.

I laughed as I looked at Carlos, then at Samhain. "The real reason," I pushed, trying to sound more authoritative than I did through laughter.

"Fine, firstly, Hunter called for an emergency meeting," Samhain responded. I groaned loudly. "Secondly, Kane doesn't keep good tabs on his house keeping room keys."

Carlos sat up, looking at Samhain. "I thought we were off the hook tonight," he pointed out, putting emphasis on the annoyance in his voice.

"Well I did too, but the Listed are saying people are flying the St. Herculia flag. So we need to go," Samhain ushered.

I sighed loudly as I leaned over the side of the bed, giving Carlos his shirt and belt. I found my discarded T-shirt and tugged it on as Samhain checked his phone. Then I found my shoes, and slipped them on.

"How have they gotten hold of the St. Herculia flag?" Carlos asked as he buttoned his pants back up, then fixed his belt.

"The older generation most likely." Samhain shifted on his feet as he continued to stare at his phone. "You can continue sexy time after the meeting."

I couldn't help but roll my eyes, as I fixed my hair once I was stood up. Samhain smiled, and headed out of the room, I followed, taking Carlos's hand in the process.

* * *

Out in the corridor, I passed some people I recognised from Zone 14, it still made my blood boil to know the guards had found my home.

To my relief, Taylor was safe as she fell into step next to us.

"So, from what I gather, St. Herculia was the country's name before Denmé?" I asked, mostly aiming the conversation at Carlos and Taylor because they were the oldest in our little group—Taylor being the oldest at twenty-five years old.

"Yes, and some people have started the flying the flag again, even though it has been outlawed for seventeen years," Samhain responded. I furrowed my brow, confused because he was the youngest out of all of us at twenty years old, he was too young to remember this information.

"Could it be something to do with those letters Ezekiel gave out?" Carlos questioned.

Taylor shrugged, and looked at Samhain as he opened a secret panel in the wall. "Could be. Where did it originate?" she asked.

All of us half jogged down the secret passage way, which was only lit by candles. "Zone 7, and now it's in all eighteen Zones."

Samhain stopped abruptly, then looked at us all. For the first time since I've known him, his eyes were dark with fear.

32

Nadine

I struggled to steady myself on the seat as the truck bounced over an uneven road, my wrists were shackled together causing my injured arm to burn furiously, my brace lay discarded on the floor. Outside was dusk, casting dark shadows around the enclosed space, it was just light enough to show what was around me. I noticed that the divider which separated myself, and the two guards in the front seats was unprotected, from the windshield the dark road was only lit up by headlights. Directly across from me, Ezekiel sat there with his head hung low. When he looked up, his eyes were glazed over. Next to me Michael was staring at his trembling hands, tears ran down his face. It smelled like cigarettes, and dirt in here.

"Nadine," Ezekiel hissed, looking at the guards. "Do you have a hair pin?"

I bit my lip, and squeezed my eyes shut as I raised both my hands to run them through my hair. My arm burning furiously with the movement, and my fingers tingled. When the pain got too much, I placed them on my lap, breathing heavily and shook my head out of defeat. Ezekiel looked at Michael.

"Michael," he hissed, Michael looked up at him. "Do you have a hair pin?"

"Totes because I'm a pretty little girl," Michael whispered back with full sarcasm.

I had to bite my lip to stop myself laughing.

Ezekiel furrowed his brow at Michael's language, it was evident he would have never used that in Denmé. I noticed the guard in the passenger seat glance behind his shoulder before focusing on the road, I tried listing all the possible escape routes in my head. Then I noticed Ezekiel's belt glistening in the dim light.

"Ezekiel," I hissed, looking at the guards. He looked at me, I pointed to his belt.

He nodded quickly, moving his hands in a way that could securely grip the belt and get it undone, once he did that, I watched as he slotted the buckle into the key hole and start moving it around. Ezekiel grimaced from the obvious discomfort of the metal digging into his wrists, then with a click his shackles came free. I breathed a sigh of relief.

I held my arms out to him when he leaned forward, and got to work on my shackles, I occasionally checked in the rear view to see if the guards noticed what we were doing. Thankfully, they were oblivious. Feeling the shackles loosen their grip, I relaxed even further, but I had to keep them around my wrist in case the guards noticed.

When I leaned back, Michael whispered into my ear. "Go into my pocket and take out the contents."

I nodded, as I slipped a hand out of the handcuffs, my hand ventured into the depths of Michael's pocket. When I brushed against a pile of used tissues, and receipts I shuddered. After I decided to ignore those, my hand brushed against a cylindrical plastic object. Once I pulled it out, my eyes widened to see a small spray bottle of something, I looked up and checked the rear view again. Quickly hiding the object when the guard checked the mirror.

"What are doing back there?"

"Just getting comfy," Michael replied.

The guard was silent as he focused on the road again. I secretly looked at the bottle in my hand, trying to read the label in the dim light: *Fart Spray X-Tra Strength*. I looked at Michael, then showed the bottle to Ezekiel. His eyes lit up.

When Ezekiel leaned forward, Michael and I leaned toward him.

"Michael, pretend you have a really bad stomachache and you need to poop real bad," Ezekiel instructed. I covered my mouth to stifle a laugh.

Was this really how we were going to escape? Either way it was our best, and only plan.

As Michael composed himself, it was suddenly show time. He leaned against the wall then started groaning loudly, I popped off the lid from the fart spray. Ezekiel made a farting noise with his mouth. The guards started to shift in their seats.

"Ah! It's coming!" Michael groaned out as he clutched his stomach, and shifted on the seat.

"What's coming?" I asked loud enough for the guards to hear.

"I need the bathroom!" Michael shouted to the guards. Ezekiel made yet another fart noise. "Everybody at school said not to eat the chilli, but I ate it anyway!"

"You can wait," one of them snapped.

"No, it can't wait I need to go now!" Michael shouted. Ezekiel made an extremely loud farting noise, I knew it was my queue to spray the bottle around.

Immediately the pungent smell hit my nose, and my eyes stung, I honestly thought I was going to be sick as I retched. My stomach rolled as the smell of actual sewage and rotten eggs wafted through the air, so strong I could taste it.

"Michael, that's disgusting!" Ezekiel choked out as he covered his nose.

"Oh no, it's happening again!" Michael cried out. Despite covering his nose, Ezekiel made another loud farting noise, and I sprayed more for good measure.

The guards immediately pulled the truck to the side of the road as they started retching from the stench; I was trying my hardest not to. First the driver got out of the car, then the passenger and both of them ran out of view.

I knew I was the smallest out of all three of us, regardless of my injury I was the one who had to slip through the divider. Ezekiel nudged my knee, and I went for it. Despite the pain, I held onto the bars which held the canopy of the truck, and I swung my legs through the divider. Lowering my way down, jumping as I hit my head.

When I was in the driver's seat, I could see in the passenger side wing mirror that the guards were throwing up nearby. Coughing while inhaling the stench, I forced my foot on the brake, put the car in drive, and pressed down hard on the accelerator.

The tires squealed, but we were quickly on the move, despite the heaviness of the vehicle and the fact I could barely see over the steering wheel. I could see the guards had started pursuing us, after a short while they gave up and produced weapons.

"Get down!" I shouted to Ezekiel and Michael.

The exterior of the car made loud metallic pinging noises as bullets bounced off. I gasped as my heart thumped against my ribs, my hand trembled—the other hand held against my chest, but I focused on driving; having no choice but to roll down the window to air out the truck, only being relieved when the guards finally gave up fully.

Michael's head suddenly appeared through the divider.

"They're kind of dumb aren't they. Who leaves this thing unprotected?" Michael commented, his question rhetorical. I laughed.

"You stink, go away," I joked, Michael laughed and disappeared out of view.

On the horizon, I saw a glowing city with a thick blanket of black smoke over it, I instantly recognised this place from the copious amounts of news reports. Then it hit me where we actually were.

"Erm, guys, we're not in Olympia anymore." I announced.

Knowing I was back in Denmé put a heavy weight on my shoulders.

* * *

Ezekiel helped guide me through Zone 7, it was in utter chaos with debris strewn on the ground and entire neighbourhoods burning. Some buildings and entire neighbourhoods were reduced to nothing but a burning mass of rubble, the buildings that were standing either had big red X's painted on the door, and most shocking of all I recognised people were flying the St. Herculia flag. I had always found this flag beautiful when I saw it in history books, emerald green with a gold triton in the centre—signifying what used to be the strength of the nation.

I slammed on the brakes when an older woman with wispy white hair stepped into the path of the car holding a rifle, hearing bangs from the compartment behind me.

"Ow," Michael and Ezekiel groaned out in unison.

"Sorry, somebody stepped into the path of the car." I raised my hand out of the open window. "Don't shoot, we're rebels!"

The woman slowly approached the car, she looked at me like I was a piece of meat, several other figures surrounded the truck. I noticed she was wearing the government uniform, and I realised she was staring at my clearly obvious foreign clothing. Once I heard the back of the truck opening, I gasped.

"No, be careful! The one with the cast has a broken leg, and the other has broken ribs!" I exclaimed.

"Which Zone?" the woman asked sternly, pointing the rifle at me after reloading.

My hand trembled, and I swallowed. "We've been kidnapped by guards from Olympia, however, the two in the back are from 7 and 14," I replied. My voice wavered.

"Ezekiel?" I heard a woman exclaim.

"Mum!" Ezekiel responded.

"They're fine, Erin, if Ezekiel's with them."

Erin lowered her weapon, and opened the car door, letting me step out. I immediately went to check on Michael who sat there crying, once I climbed into the back with him, I picked up my brace and secured it place over my arm. Then I tended to Michael, as I sat next to him, I placed my hand on his arm.

"I never wanted to come back here," Michael sobbed.

"I know," I replied.

Once I heard a cough, I looked up to see Ezekiel's mum standing there. She had the same dark complexion, and her brown and grey afro tamed by a thin floral scarf. His mum looked over at all of us.

"Let's take you all to my house," Ezekiel's mum instructed proudly. I could see where Ezekiel got his leadership skills from.

He was the first to jump out of the vehicle, then myself, and soon I helped Michael get down before grabbing his crutches. I was thankful guards let him keep those.

***

From the outside, Ezekiel's parents house was a small but grand home. However, on the inside the furniture was anything but. There was a faded pink sofa in the living room which sat in front of a roaring fireplace, next to it was a gentleman which had some resemblance to Ezekiel sleeping in a red armchair. It was obvious he was Ezekiel's father. A dining table with fruits and vegetables was to my right, then tucked away in the very back was a hint of a kitchen. The house smelled like burning wood.

"Hello, I'm Simone," Ezekiel's mum said with a smile, she extended her hand out to me.

I smiled as I shook her hand. "Nadine."

She moved onto Michael, shaking his hand.

"Michael, ID 498765." He cringed before the last number—Michael hadn't spoken of his ID number since moving to Olympia.

Simone looked at me again. "ID 495718." It was my turn to cringe.

"Oh, so you're both from Zone 14?" Simone questioned, she gestured for us to sit down.

I sighed as I sat on the edge of the sofa. "No, I was kidnapped by guards from Olympia, then Ezekiel helped me get Listed," I responded honestly. Simone nodded as she watched Michael lower himself down.

Simone brushed her hand on her overalls as she looked at her son, Ezekiel helped himself to an apple and took a bite. "When I got Ezekiel's letter with the plan of action, I got to work immediately. But we need Rebellion members to fully implement it, they're difficult to find."

"What plan?" I asked, sitting next to Michael.

"First was the Herculia flag, second was setting fire to the guard houses. But the third is taking down Ms. Sanchez."

I looked at Michael when he started laughing. "I'd rather shit on my hands and clap, than join in with all of this," Michael responded. Simone gasped and covered her mouth. "I want to go home."

"Olympia's done wonders on him," Ezekiel said sarcastically from the dining room with his mouth full.

Simone sucked in a breath then clapped her hands together. "I think you should all get some sleep; you must be exhausted. Michael and Ezekiel can stay in his old room, and Nadine, you can sleep in

Rachelle's old room."

"Who's Rachelle?" I asked.

"My younger sister," Ezekiel replied.

I nodded and followed Simone once she started walking away. "Up these stairs."

As I made my way up the stairs, each one creaked under the weight of our feet. The house was clearly very old. Once we were on the landing, there was a door at the top of the stairs, and another one with a porcelain sign saying *bathroom*. We both made a left, and walked to another door at the front of the house.

Simone opened the door, and turned the light on. I stepped into a room frozen in time, all the walls were baby pink, the saddest part were the dusty children's toys sitting in the window bay waiting to be played with, even a doll house. The bed was white with frilly pink bedding.

"Rachelle's not been in this room since she went to a work camp at eleven, she's twenty-five now," Simone explained with a sadness in her voice. "I'll get some fresh bedding, and you can wear some of my night clothes tonight."

"Thank you," I replied.

Simone smiled as she left the room.

* * *

I forgot how uncomfortable the beds were in Denmé; it was like sleeping on concrete. Turning on my side, I stared at the creepy stuffed animals staring at me, and the glow of the flames outside the window. Despite the room being warm, I felt stone-cold knowing I had let The Educators take me again.

A knock at the door made me look behind my shoulder, Ezekiel came into the room, and I faced back to the window and sighed.

"Can't sleep either?" he asked in a hushed voice. I felt the bed sink down as he climbed inside of it. I shook my head, his strong arms pulled me close.

"Ezekiel," I said as he started to kiss my shoulder. "What are we?" I asked, turning to face him.

He looked a little taken aback. "I'd like to think we were a couple."

"I thought so too, just we've never officially said it," I admitted.

Ezekiel let out a laugh, then kissed me. "Will you be my girlfriend?"

I nodded as I kissed him back. "I'd like that."

After kissing him again, I turned back to the window, closing my eyes willing for sleep to come. But Ezekiel's hand pushed my hips into him, feeling something hard against my back, he trailed a line of kisses on my neck and along my shoulder. My toes curled, and I bit my lip, letting a moan escape my lips.

"What are you doing?" I whispered, and opened my eyes to look at him.

Ezekiel drew an invisible line up my thigh with his finger, running his hand along the waistband of my pants, he hesitated to go lower. "I might be wanting to make you feel better, if you want."

I bit lip as he kissed my neck, I took his hand and guided it into my pants. "Yes," I whispered as I kissed him.

He moved his hand into my underwear, then placed his leg in between mine, and I arched my back and moaned loudly when his fingers entered me.

My grip on the pillow tightened as I moaned while feeling Ezekiel's fingers pump inside of me, sending waves of pleasure through my body, I relaxed into him. I let him take me away from the events of today, I closed my eyes as he sucked on my neck.

"Fuck me," I moaned.

I felt deflated when Ezekiel stopped, and slid his hand out of my underwear—I was now turned on to the max. Only getting the satisfaction I craved when Ezekiel pulled down my pants, and underwear, I helped him get them off and threw them on the floor as I kissed him passionately. He guided me onto my back, and got between my legs, I kissed him as I tugged off his shirt then watched him take off his pants. I looked into his eyes as he kissed me again, I could feel him against me and it turned me on even more.

Ezekiel gently took my injured arm from my chest, I sucked in a breath as he moved it so my hand was was pressed onto his back. Though I could move it, I chose not to most of the time. As quickly as the burning sensation presented itself, it subsided, only left with a tingling sensation in my fingers.

"Are you okay?" he asked as he kissed my neck.

"Yeah." I gasped and bit my lip as he nipped at my skin, I pressed my other hand on his back.

"Ready?" he asked before he gave me another kiss.

I nodded, gasping as he thrust into me, my toes curled against the sheets. Ezekiel pulled out of me, then thrust me into me again. I moved my hips along with him, and moaned loudly, letting him place his head on the pillow I was led on. He did it again, and I arched my back as a loud moan escaped my mouth, I could feel the muscles on his back move with each movement. My moan was clearly fuel to an already burning fire. Ezekiel moaned as he went harder, each thrust driving him deeper into me, I dug my nails into his shoulder and scratched down as I cried out his name in pleasure. He kissed me roughly as he carried on, the bed made a creaking noise which I was sure the rest of the house could hear, but I couldn't care less. Then he slowed down, I shuddered as pleasure rippled through me.

"I'm not hurting you, am I?" he breathed out.

I shook my head. "Ezekiel," I gasped as he suddenly resumed, fucking me even harder than before, the pleasure he was giving me was like a quickly rising river.

We were both covered in sweat, as I brought his mouth to mine and we kissed as he worked me in all the right ways. I moaned into his mouth, his breathing became more heavy by the second. Pulling away and arching my back as I hit the climax, I moved my arm from Ezekiel's back and grabbed the sheets as I let him fuck me while I came. I breathed heavily, biting my lip as he carried on. A few moments later, he came in me, fucking me and moaning loudly as he rode out his own orgasm. Then he led against me.

Exhaustion took over my body, my eyelids heavy like I could pass out at any second.

"Did you enjoy that?" Ezekiel breathed out as he gently took my arm from his back, placing it back on my chest, then he led next to me.

I nodded quickly, as I kissed him.

* * *

At breakfast the next morning, I yawned and rubbed my eye with the heel of my hand, as I bit into a piece of toast. I looked around the table, Ezekiel's dad I had seen the night before sat at the end of the table reading a newspaper, he had the same jaw line and brilliant blue eyes as Ezekiel, Simone sat next to him eating some cereal. Only now did I realise most of Ezekiel's features were from his mum, and it suited him. My gaze fell onto Michael, who was silent, looking tired like he didn't get any sleep.

When Ezekiel rubbed my thigh, I jumped and hit the table with my knee, it made a loud clattering noise as the cutlery jumped. My body was still sensitive from last night. I narrowed my eyes at Ezekiel who smiled. Then I realised all eyes were on me.

"Is everything okay?" Ezekiel's dad asked as he looked up from his newspaper.

"Yeah, I just fell asleep for a minute," I lied. When I glanced at Ezekiel, he was silently chuckling to himself.

Simone looked around the table. "Okay, so how are we going to find The Rebellion? Jackson?" She looked at her husband.

Jackson shrugged, his gaze burned into his son and I.

"Its not a case of how to find The Rebellion, it's a case wondering where they are. I know Zone 7's Rebellion is obliterated, half The Rebellion facilities have been discovered," Ezekiel explained, turning off his flirtatious demeanour. "I say we start at Zone 8, it's the closest one that's not been discovered."

Michael looked at Ezekiel, there was a sense of fear clouding his brown eyes.

"Are you coming too? You're practically part of The Rebellion now as Ezekiel and me." I drank some of my coffee. "And Judas."

He shifted on his seat, casting a look at Simone and Jackson. "I'll think of it."

"Well we need permits to get into Zone 8, those could take weeks," Simone pointed out, glancing at us.

"No, we don't; we just need a car," Ezekiel responded as he ate some cereal. "And bolt cutters."

Michael was evidently becoming more agitated while he fidgeted in his seat. I looked at him, then my heart skipped a beat, he looked too out of place in Denmé, after dying a strip of his hair blue. If he was going to go with us to finding The Rebellion we would have to lay low.

Just when I thought I had finished fighting guards, we had just planned to go into the storm.

33

Judas

"We need to get into government-issued clothing and survey Zone 7 again," Samhain instructed, pointing to the map of Zone 7 that was pinned to a pool table.

I yawned but moved my hair from my face as I leaned forward, looking at the map.

"But we're going with weapons this time," I insisted.

Samhain nodded as he moved a red marker, indicating the fires raging in neighbourhoods, and placed it in a box. I knew the Uprising was bad, however each day new fires sparked up in neighbours as Our Leader was becoming desperate to flush out The Rebellion. Even worse somebody had took it upon themselves to burn down guard houses, I had heard the suspect trapped the guards inside so they were now at half capacity.

Boudica stood up and surveyed the map, her dirty blond hair hung from her left shoulder. My heart ached as it reminded me of Gabrielle, she always wore her hair like that. As I pushed the thought away, she moved more red markers into the box.

"I feel like we need to discuss this with Hunter," she said, tapping her thumbs on the pool table.

"Fuck Hunter, where was he when the hotel got raided. He also knew the the situation when you went to patrol the path to the castle, yet still made you go out without weapons," Samhain snapped. "Zeke wouldn't have allowed that to happen."

"Everybody knows Ezekiel hates being called Zeke," I pointed out.

"All the more reason to call it him," Samhain replied with a smile. "Realistically, we need to speak to whoever is flying the St. Herculia flag."

I felt bad for deceiving Carlos and pretending I wouldn't do this, but it needed to happen. Hunter had taken it upon himself to try and return to normal, and stop fighting. However, Samhain had been prepared to fight from the start. Despite him being an actual head case, he'd done more for The Rebellion than anybody. Our Leader stole my home, my father, sister and almost my fiancé, I couldn't sit and wait anymore.

"Everybody, get changed. Bo, get the car, I'll get the weapons, and Joseph you help clear this up. Meet us above ground in fifteen," Samhain ordered.

Boudica nodded, then hurried out of the room, he followed quickly behind her. Despite being shocked Samhain was willing to go above ground, and risk detection, at the end of the day it wasn't out of character for him. Samhain lived life on the edge. As I cleared the rest of the red markers and placed them in the box, then I rolled up the map. I climbed onto the pool table, moving a ceiling tile and placing both items in there, where nobody would look.

* * *

As we left the sprawling metropolis of Ashford, Zone 8 I had never seen Samhain in government uniform, it was incredibly weird to see. I noticed he had placed a stick on tattoo of a barcode on his arm, it was still shiny from moisture.

"Does that thing even scan?" I asked.

Samhain glanced at it. "It should do, I got it off somebody in a morgue." He laughed, obviously lying.

"You're fucked up," I responded with a laugh.

I glanced at Boudica in the backseat, she was smiling and covered her mouth.

"We're going on a trip in our favourite piece of shit!" Samhain sang loudly as he drummed his hands on the steering wheel.

It was true, we had stolen and hot-wired a Task 21 vehicle, so it was indeed a piece of shit. The car slowed to a stop as we approached the barbed wire fence which separated Zone 8 from Zone 7, Samhain put the car in park and took off his seatbelt, the cold air from outside hit me when he exited the vehicle. He was humming along to himself as he went to the trunk. I looked behind my shoulder at Boudica, she shrugged as another wave of cold air hit us, neither of us understanding what Samhain was doing.

He hummed as he walked around the vehicle with garden shears in his hand, the ends had been sharpened into an ominous point which could kill somebody. I shuddered. However, Samhain quickly got to work cutting the fence away, his movements seemed effortless. Eventually there was a large hole in the fence, large enough for our car to fit through.

Samhain got back in the car, and handed the shears to Boudica, she hesitated looking at the pointed edges before placing them in the foot well. The car roared to life as he drove into Zone 7.

***

The streets of Zone 7 scared me like never before. I noticed Samhain was making extra effort to avoid burning debris in the streets, as we turned down neighbourhoods we passed rows upon rows of charred remains of houses which could be seen for miles. My eyes widening at the flags hanging from the windows, and the red X marks on the doors.

"If we infiltrate the castle, I just thought of a great idea," Samhain finally announced with a wicked smile.

I turned my head to him, and noticed Boudica even leaned forward, her arms resting on both front seats. "I'm listening," Boudica responded with a smile.

"My little friend, Carbon Monoxide. Once you put that through the castle vents, guards will be sleeping like a baby," Samhain said with such enthusiasm it unnerved me, I was painfully throw into the door as he swerved around a pile of bricks.

"No. Let's not, carbon monoxide kills people," I warned.

Samhain looked at me. "Wait, it does? Oops." He put a hand to his mouth to suppress a laugh.

I glanced at Boudica and Samhain in shock. "You haven't used that before, have you?"

"Maybe once or twice," Samhain replied while scratching the corner of his eye. "Okay, I may have used that on all the guards in Zone 13 when they found The Rebellion's oubliette."

"The fuck is an oubliette?" Boudica asked with a furrowed brow. "And guards found Zone 13?"

"An oubliette is a secret dungeon which drops people down to their inevitable doom of starving to death. Yes, technically speaking guards found Zone 13, but they've never properly gotten inside because of the oubliettes which protect it. Now the guards who are down there are either having a wild as fuck orgy, or reverting to cannibalism, there is no in between." Samhain explained in a matter of fact way, like it was a completely normal thing to talk about, not messed up at all. Even Boudica looked horrified.

I sucked in a breath as I ran a hand through my hair when Samhain pulled to the side of the road in front of a standing house. It was a white brick property flying the St. Herculia flag proudly.

"Let's try this house," Samhain said with an enthusiastic attitude.

I unbuckled my seat belt as the engine died then got out the car. The smell of burning hit me instantly causing me to cough, Bouidca got out of the car with Samhain getting out last. He skipped over to the wooden door, and gave three strong knocks, then waited. An old woman with white wispy hair answered.

"Good morrow, ma'am. We're here to talk to you about our Lord and Saviour, Jesus Christ," Samhain exclaimed. I tried not laughing when I saw how confused this poor woman appeared. "Okay, really, we're here to ask you about your St. Herculia flag, do you mind if we come in and ask some questions about it?"

The woman looked over at all three of us, she still looked incredibly confused, but she slowly nodded and opened the door wider for us to enter.

* * *

All three of us sat on the woman's faded white sofa; she came in with a tray balancing glasses of water on it, I said *thank you* under my breath as she placed each individual one on the coffee table. Once she was finished, she smoothed out her overalls and sat on a matching faded white love seat. Her home was as small as it looked on the outside, a small living/dining space then a kitchen in the back with stairs leading to the second floor. Inside it smelled like burning wood, and apple pie.

"What do you to want to know about the St Herculia flag?" the woman asked, looking sceptical, from the corner of my eye I could see the flag billowing in the wind.

"How did you obtain it?" Boudica asked softly, her hands linked together on her lap, giving the woman a smile.

The woman looked at us as she sipped water. "Unlike you three young people, I was much older when the regime came into existence, it was hidden in my attic along with other St. Herculia remnants.

"What made everybody start flying the flag and painting the marks on their door?" I asked, looking at Samhain then Boudica.

"Simone Kenwood received a letter saying to start it, she spread it around our reading committee we hold every Tuesday," she said with a smile. "She's trying to track down The Rebellion."

My attention picked up to hear the name Kenwood, I looked at Samhain to see if he had any input on doing anything. Suddenly the house shuddered followed by a loud boom which erupted outside, the woman grimaced, Boudica looked around then looked at her hands.

"Perfect, we know her son, can we get her address please?" Samhain announced. Another boom outside made the house shudder. "I think she'll be happy for The Rebellion to come to her."

The woman nodded, and hurried off quickly to get a pen and paper.

* * *

Simone Kenwood's house was in a more central location of Zone Seven. Outside it was a white two-story brick building, its black door had a red painted X on it, I could see children's toys from a lost childhood in the upstairs bay window. From the outside it looked like a normal family home, but we knew it wasn't.

All of us exited out of the vehicle and made our way up the stone path, Boudica smoothed out her hair and smiled at me, I watched Samhain knock loudly three times on the door. He smoothed out his overalls, and waited.

"State your name and your occupation," a woman's voice called from inside.

Just as I about to say something, Samhain responded. "Ben Dover, Ruler of Anal Cavities." He scratched the back of his head, then shrugged while widening his eyes.

My jaw fell open, and I started laughing, Boudica even turned around and crouched down. I noticed her body shudder as she also started to laugh.

"Your real name and occupation," the woman's stern voice didn't waiver with laughter.

"Judas Wells, Rebellion Leader," I finally said once I composed myself.

"And the others?"

I turned around, somebody was watching us from the downstairs bay window. "Samhain Roach and Boudica Reynolds, Rebellion Leaders," I responded.

Almost immediately the sound of various locks clicking, and a bang against the door filled the air. It flew open revealing a dark skinned woman with a brown and grey afro, I tried not to gasp at the rifle in her hand.

"Get in," she said quickly, pulling Samhain inside. I followed quickly behind.

Once we were all inside, the woman slid the bazillion locks into place, using a crank to seal us in with metal slats. "We're here to speak to Simone Kenwood. We are very close to your son." Samhain stood taller as he looked around the home.

Just like the old woman's home, it smelled like burning wood. As I walked deeper into the home, it looked like your average place to live, the fire in the fireplace was almost completely burned out. The person watching us was an older male, he looked similar to Ezekiel with the same blue eyes.

"I was not expecting The Rebellion to come to me," Simone said as she disappeared into the kitchen. "I just sent Ezekiel, and some of his friends to track you guys down."

Samhain made himself at home by sitting on a faded pink sofa, I stayed standing not wanting to come across as rude, Boudica stood next to me. The house rattled as another boom filled the air outside.

"What is all that racket? It's not us doing that today," Boudica asked, folding her arms across her chest.

Simone came back into the room with a tray of cookies. "Our Leader is basically blowing up any homes flying the St. Herculia flag."

I nodded. "So you're saying Ezekiel is here? Who were the friends he was with?"

Carlos had already told me that Ezekiel was in Olympia so hearing he's back in Denmé unnerved me. I sucked in a breath.

"A woman named Nadine, and a teenager named Michael. They got kidnapped from something called The Educators last night, and we rescued them."

My whole world tilted to one side, and I had to use the sofa to steady myself. I felt like the room had been sucked clear of oxygen. Oh my god, this couldn't be happening, I held my chest feeling my heart pounding. If Michael was in Denmé, where was he now.

34

Nadine

When the truck bounced over debris, I had to hold onto the grab bar to maintain balance, worried the seatbelt couldn't hold me. My heart raced in my chest, burning buildings were a blur as we sped past. Their flames licked the blue sky. It was a far cry from what I was used to seeing about Zone 7 on the news, and that night when Ezekiel took me up on the roof during my time in The Rebellion.

My eyes widened when I saw several guards step into our path, forming a human barrier against us. Ezekiel's jaw tensed as he pressed down on the accelerator, I got pushed back into my seat. I couldn't help but scream as a bullet smashed into the wind shield, the crack spider webbing through the glass.

Ezekiel pushed me down, so my head was between my legs, I shielded my head and tried to focus on my breathing. I jumped as more sounds of smashing glass and pinging of bullets on the door battered the vehicle.

"Be careful," I exclaimed, hoping Ezekiel would be okay. The truck lurched forward and roared as loud a series of bangs from the front hit the car, then the vehicle bounced heavily like going over speed bumps. "What did we hit?" I asked as I kept my head down.

"Guards," Ezekiel announced.

Suddenly the truck lurched forward and lifted into the air as it hit something hard, then the engine started to roar as Ezekiel floored the accelerator. I sat up with the sudden realisation something was wedged underneath the truck, I could smell oil burning as he kept trying. All the truck did was rock. I felt sick when I looked around to see we were completely exposed at a T-junction, the windshield had seen better days. But all I could focus on were the guards coming at us from the right, their guns raised.

"Ezekiel, we need to move," I said sternly.

"No shit," Ezekiel grunted as he put the truck in reverse, again we just rocked. "Fuck!" he shouted as he hit the steering wheel.

I screamed loudly as the passenger door opened, a guard grabbed me and unclipped my seatbelt, then flung me to the ground. My injured arm burned furiously, and my fingers tingled—my other hand ached, so did my knees and head. I coughed as I curled up. When I heard the truck speed off, my eyes widened.

"Ezekiel!" I screamed.

My scream cut off as a steel toe boot slammed into my stomach. I coughed and held it tightly as I fell on the floor. Before I knew it, the guard straddled me, his huge weight taking my breath away, then he grabbed me by my throat—squeezing even more air out of me. I started coughing, and kicked with all my might, my vision going blurry as my throat burned. The guard had a feral look in his eyes, as he smiled sadistically, I smacked his leg but it was no use.

I noticed there was a knife on the guard's belt, I tried to reach for it, but he smacked my head on the cobble stone road; pain erupted through my skull. Anger and adrenaline filled my veins, so much so I pulled my arm back and forced my fist into the guard's Adam's apple. He started coughing, and let go of my throat enough for me to sit up and grab the knife. The guard quickly recovered, and returned to squeezing the life out of me.

While coughing, with all my remaining strength, I jammed the knife into the guard's leg. He screamed out in pain, and let go of me.

I wheezed loudly and coughed, getting my first oxygen-filled breath, my lungs burned from being deprived of air. The guard drew his fist back, and was about to swing for me, but I thrust the knife into his hand. He cried out, then a loud gun shot filled the air and landed directly into his skull. I almost retched when some of his head splattered on my face—tasting his blood on my lips. The guard stiffened as his eyes glossed over, I pushed my way out from under him quickly as he slumped forward. Blood leaked out of him and onto the ground. More gun shots filled the air, and I noticed there was a pile of bodies on the side of the road which weren't there before.

Suddenly a truck came speeding into view, and the passenger door opened, and my eyes widened to see Michael in the driver's seat.

"Get in!" he shouted.

I looked around to see Ezekiel was the one shooting the guards. "Ezekiel!" I called out to him. He gestured to the truck as he fired at more guards.

As I pushed myself up, I got into the vehicle, Michael handed me a cloth and I wiped my face. When I pulled it away, I shuddered at seeing pieces of skull and brain on there. Michael quickly floored the accelerator, I wondered how he was driving with his injured leg, but I didn't care. In the wing mirror I could see Ezekiel running behind the car, eventually grabbing hold of a grab rail on the exterior, and pulling the back door open. Once he was inside I broke down crying.

"Why did you drive off?" I sobbed towards Ezekiel, feeling dirty from the ghostly feel of the guards hands around my neck, and the crap on my face. My stomach rolled.

"I needed to get Michael and a weapon," Ezekiel admitted. "It pained me to see you pinned down, I couldn't sit back and watch, they were going to kill you."

The tires screeched as Michael made a sharp turn down a neighbourhood, my injured arm burned as I pressed into the door, I choked on tears then turned to Michael. "Why the hell are you driving in your condition?" I questioned, as I wiped my eyes with the heel of my hand; the cuts on my hands stung from the tears.

All Michael did was glance at me, turning the car to avoid debris.

"When we became a couple, I thought you'd protect me!" I eventually shouted at Ezekiel.

"I killed the guard who was strangling you, didn't I?" Ezekiel shouted back. "Believe it or not, I was protecting you!"

"Take me back to Ezekiel's parents house," I snapped at Michael.

"What do you think I'm doing." Michael responded coldly.

I coughed, and held my stomach which was a heartbeat of pain from being kicked. The events of what just happened were unbelievable. All I wanted right now was a shower, and to forget everything.

* * *

I didn't talk to either Ezekiel or Michael for the rest of the ride home. As we walked up the path to his mums house, Ezekiel pushed me against the wall and kissed me. His hands gently around my waist, a tear rolled down my cheek as I kissed him back, the anger and fear I felt fading away.

"Please don't be mad at me," he said in a hushed voice, his warm breath on my lips.

I pressed a hand to his back, and kissed him again.

"Erm, guys I kind of want to go in the house to throw up," Michael said, leaning against his crutches.

I pulled away, and looked at him. Suddenly the door opened, and a guy with a shaved head in Denmé uniform stepped out, I was shocked by the marble textured scar which travelled from his ear down to the base of his neck. Ezekiel straightened up immediately, and looking surprised by this persons appearance.

"Ezekiel, babe, how are you doing?" the guy exclaimed, holding his arms out with a smile. I looked at Ezekiel with a raised eyebrow.

"Samhain," Ezekiel replied coldly. So this was the infamous guy Carlos and Hunter mentioned, the person who blew up Zone 7's Rebellion, yikes. Ezekiel took me by the hand, and led me into the house. "What are you doing here?"

Once we had all gotten into the house, Samhain shut the door behind us, and used the crank to seal us, then he smiled at us both. "Well, Hunter's being a little bitch and wants us to stay underground, go back to normal. However, I'm not going to be a little bitch, I'm going to fight for my fucking freedom."

There was a scary aura about Samhain, but at the same time, I strangely felt safe around him. I was quite shocked by his boldness about getting safety.

"Typical," Ezekiel said under his breath. "Just you here then?"

"No, Boudica and Joseph too," Samhain said as we walked towards the living room.

I furrowed my brow, something must have gone off for Judas to be part of Samhain's miraculous plan away from Carlos, I knew about his sister but this was out of character even for him. When I saw myself in the mirror, I looked like actual crap, my hair was messed up and there were red hands around my neck, even dried blood splatters were on my face and overalls.

As soon as we were in the living room, Judas stood up immediately, his jaw fell open to see me and then Michael. His eyes glazed over as soon as he saw his brother. Then it hit me, I hadn't told Michael about Gabrielle.

"Michael," he gasped. "You look so…different."

I watched Michael nod with a pout, and a shrug, moving to sit on the sofa. "How have you been?"

Judas wiped tears from his eyes, he looked older, dark circles were under his eyes which indicated he hadn't been sleeping. "Do you know about Gabrielle? Carlos told me he told Nadine and Ezekiel."

I watched Michael shake his head, he shifted on the seat then fixed his overalls. The look he gave Judas was quizzical.

"We never got to tell him," I admitted, looking at my feet.

"Gabrielle passed away," Judas managed to say before he broke down crying.

Michael looked between us all. "No, you're lying." His eyes glazed over and his lips quivered. "Please tell me you're lying, that this is a joke." Tears rained down his face now, and he wiped them away with the back of his hand.

"I wish, I was," Judas replied as he wiped his eyes with trembling hands.

Michael cried out, covering his mouth as he leaned forward. A woman with dirty blond hair quickly came over, and wrapped her arms around him. That must have been Boudica, though she didn't introduce herself. Michael sobbed loudly on her shoulder.

My gaze fell on Samhain who leaned against the wall, staying quiet as he looked around the living room. A single tear rolled down my cheek, I quickly pushed it away and exhaled a breath.

"What happened to your neck?" Judas asked after composing himself enough to talk properly.

"Guess," I replied, glancing at Michael as he cried.

He rolled his eyes, and shook his head—due to how the guards handled me in Zone 14, he knew all too well what guards were capable of. Ezekiel wrapped an arm around my waist, then gave me a kiss on my cheek, Judas seemed surprised but smiled.

"I'm going to get a shower, I feel like I just waded through sewage," I announced to everybody.

Then I left the room, I was so tired I had to practically drag myself up the stairs.

* * *

The warm water around my neck was soothing, I could already feel bruises forming on my skin. As I ran my hand through my hair, I took in the moment of tranquillity, no guards, no Denmé. Just me, myself, and my thoughts. It had been so long since I had been in Denmé that my hair was now shoulder length, though I missed my red hair every day I welcomed the change, I embraced it as a reminder of my time here. I couldn't believe how much had changed in the last month, sometimes I couldn't recognise myself.

"Nadine, can you help me brain storm something?"

I screamed at the male voice in the bathroom with me, covering my mouth as my heart ricocheted around my rib cage. When I looked where the voice came from there was a dark silhouette through the curtain.

"Who's there?" I asked, my voice trembled as I looked around. Thankfully the shower curtain was protecting me.

"Samhain, but anyway." I heard the toilet lid being brought down with a clink. "Do you think what I'm doing is correct? Everybody says I'm being crazy."

"First, answer my question. Why are you in here, while I'm in the shower?" I spat.

"People are more willing to listen to me this way," Samhain admitted.

I scoffed out a laugh from how weird and awkward this situation was. "That's kind of sad, do you always do this to women?"

"Will you please answer my question? I have no intention of coming near you." Samhain sounded tired.

I looked around the shower as I ran shampoo through my hair, exhaling a breath. "Honestly, it's a better plan than Hunter's—"

I stiffened when I heard the bathroom door open. "Get the fuck out," I heard a woman snap. "Seriously, what the hell is wrong with you?

"We'll discuss this later," Samhain grumbled. I heard his footsteps on the bathroom floor.

"Sorry, Nadine!" the mysterious woman called into the bathroom.

I heard the bathroom door close, followed by a scraping noise until the lock clicked into place. Was that Boudica who had come to my rescue? There was something about Samhain I couldn't put my finger on. Even though I felt utterly creeped out by him for what he just did. I hoped he realised it was wrong.

* * *

An alarm blaring outside the house woke me up, Ezekiel stirred, and his eyes fluttered open. When the alarm died down, it came back. I pushed myself up on my elbow, despite how tired I was I looked at the flames on the horizon licking the night sky. Once the alarm died down a second time, I noticed there was a voice echoing around the street, the bed shifted as Ezekiel got out, and approached the window. Cold air which smelled like charred wood filled the air as he opened it.

"This is an important announcement. All Rebellion personnel are hereby summoned to visit me, your Leader, at Zone 7 Courthouse within forty-eight hours. Failure to comply will result in the bombing of your facilities." I recognised that voice anywhere—Ramona Sanchez.

My stomach tied in knots as the same voice repeated itself through the air, Ezekiel quickly closed the window and made his way across the room, opening the bedroom door and slipping out. I got out of bed, wrapping the robe Simone had given me around my body before I exited the bedroom. Out on the landing, Judas emerged out of Ezekiel's old room followed by Michael close behind.

As I jogged down the stairs, Boudica was looking up the stairs biting her nail, when I entered the living room Samhain was staring out of the window. My mind thought back to the discussion he and I had earlier, I realised he was correct in getting those who would comply above ground.

"Can we get Michael back to Olympia?" Judas questioned as he jogged down the stairs, he looked behind him as he watched Michael limp down the stairs.

"We tried yesterday, The Rebellion in Zone 7 is dead, we can't access it," Ezekiel finally admitted. He rubbed between his eyes to wake up.

Boudica gasped, and looked at him. "What do you mean you can't access it?" I only just noticed she had a splattering of freckles on her nose. "There's a manual override for power cuts."

"Follow me," Ezekiel instructed. "Michael, do you want to stay here?"

Michael nodded, and sat on the stairs. Before I knew it Ezekiel was leading us all down a corridor toward the kitchen, stopping at a door underneath the stairs, when he opened it I realised there were stairs down to a basement.

When I glanced behind my shoulder as I descended down the stairs, everybody was behind me, it was unbearably cold down here but I carried on following Ezekiel to the back corner where the washer and dryer sat. He pushed the dryer away from the wall, then crouched down as he pushed a concrete slab away revealing the dark confines of one of The Tunnels, Ezekiel stood up to grab a flashlight from a nearby shelf before lowering himself down.

As I lowered myself down, Ezekiel guided me with his gentle hands on my waist, my breath caught in my throat when I was face to face with him. But I forced myself to keep moving as Boudica started to lower herself down, Samhain was next then Judas.

After we all were securely down, we were on the move. For a short while we walked in almost pure darkness, with only a small flash light to guide our way, until we came to the metal door blocking access to The Tunnels. Ezekiel opened a secret panel in the wall which revealed a keypad, he keyed in the code, to my disappointment it did nothing. The door didn't budge. He tried again, but it was met with the same result. He swore under his breath. We had tried this earlier, but Ezekiel clearly hadn't given up all hope. Samhain pushed forward and tried the code, but even that produced nothing. We were officially screwed.

"So that's it, Zone 7 ceases to exist," Boudica muttered under her breath.

"Do you think Zone 8 will have heard the announcement?" Judas asked. His eyes wide with fear.

"Yeah, they would have, Our Leader wouldn't just broadcast that in Zone 7," Ezekiel replied. "So what's the plan now?"

Suddenly it felt like all oxygen was sucked out of the air like I was in a vacuum, dirt fell on top us, and I cupped my hands over my ears when a bone rattling bang filled the air. My heart skipped a beat when I smelled the strong scent of burning wood. Everybody else had cupped their hands over their ears to protect themselves.

As I looked around our group, I quickly realised something was very wrong.

35

Judas

I pushed past everybody quickly, gripping hold of the lip of the hole we climbed in from and pulled myself into the basement of Ezekiel's parents house. Once I brushed myself off, I then jogged my way to the basement stairs, the smell of burning grew stronger by the second and above me I could hear a loud commotion. I skidded to a halt at the basement stairs, a black waterfall of smoke cascaded down the stairs like a hand of death. My heart hammered against my chest, I swallowed the lump in my throat, and pulled myself up the stairs.

"Michael!" I shouted, covering my mouth as the smoke sucked all oxygen out of the air, it tickled the back of my throat which made me cough. My vision going black aside from an orange light to guide my way. "Michael!" I screamed.

Suddenly the crackling of flames filled the air as I got to the top of the stairs. I tried the door but it was swollen shut, the metal door handle was warm to the touch. Holy shit. As I leaned against the wall, I kicked the basement door as hard as I could.

"Michael's safe!" If it wasn't the smoke stealing the air out of my lungs, it was the sound of Carlos's voice. "Try to get this door open!"

"Carlos!" I shouted, pressing myself to the basement door to listen to him. "The door's swollen shut."

"Try to force it open," Carlos instructed.

Giving up trying to kick the door open, I forced my entire weight against the door and to my relief it came free after the third attempt, I fell into Carlos's arms. When I looked around, it felt like an oven in here as flames roared when they escaped out of the living room, black smoke filled the ceiling. Carlos took my hand, and quickly dragged me out of the house.

"Come on," Carlos ushered.

"Are you okay? What happened?" I asked, instantly coughing, I couldn't breathe.

"I'm fine. After that announcement, we had just arrived in time to see Our Leader set off another trebuchet," Carlos explained once we were out in the street.

Michael was sitting on the hood of a car, I ran up to him and threw my arms around him. Not caring if he almost lost his balance. I was thankful to see he had nothing more than a cut on his forehead. When I turned around, I gasped at how extensive the damage was. The entire left side of Simone's house was flattened along with the entirety of the neighbouring house. Out of shock I fell to the ground, I cried out when a freezing bucket of cold water was thrown over me.

Thora came into view, holding the bucket in her hands. "Sorry, not sorry."

My teeth started chattering, I looked up when Abrianna handed me a bottle of water. Despite my trembling hands, I unscrewed the cap and drank generously. When I looked around, I noticed almost every single Rebellion Leader, when Ezekiel, Nadine, Boudica, and Samhain filtered into the street was present. Only people missing were Hunter and Kane.

Nadine ran up to me, concern in her eyes.

"Are you okay?" she choked out while coughing, black soot covered her cheek and arms.

I nodded, when Oluchi threw a cold bucket of water on Nadine, she tensed up and gasped loudly. She let out a wheeze.

"All of you might be burned, you can't bust ass if you're covered in blisters," Abrianna explained. Throwing more water on me.

Ezekiel and Samhain were getting the same treatment from Sung-Jin and Daisuke.

"What is everybody doing here?" I asked Thora, who was busy looking at the burning house.

"Kind of realised Samhain was right," she replied. "So we got out. Kane and Hunter don't know we're here."

Nadine shivered violent, her hair stuck to her face. However, she nodded as she looked around.

"We need to get off the street, some of us are Unlisted, they'll get caught otherwise." Oluchi pointed out.

I watched as Oluchi, Abrianna, and Thora looked at each other, all of them nodded then ran up to Ezekiel to see what to do next. It was like they had telepathy or something. But I sat there, waiting to dry off with the warmth from the nearby fire while everybody else made a plan of action.

* * *

Carlos's hands held my waist as I climbed down the ladder from the roof of the gas station. I was thankful this was one of the only Zone 7 Rebellion facilities not closed off. Most gas stations had been taken over by The Rebellion, they all fell into a state of disrepair when Our Leader banned vehicles, except for those used by the government.

All the shelving units in this gas station had been removed, the only sign they were in there to begin with were their outline on the green linoleum. It smelled like coffee inside of here. When I looked at the cashier desk, the bullet proof shield was completely opened and now used as a desk. The only comfort we wouldn't get caught in here was all the windows and doors welded shut with metal plates.

Sung-Jin helped Daisuke carry in a folding table from the storage room, then Oluchi helped Harold and Esmerelda from Zone 17 distribute sleeping bags. I watched Carlos walk away to help Liberty from Zone 12.

I approached Michael, sitting on a torn up sofa, tears rolled down his cheeks as he looked at his hands. I crouched down next to him, and placed my hand on the arm of the sofa, he looked up at me.

"You should sleep," I suggested.

"Sleeping won't bring Gabrielle back," Michael admitted. I nodded, and swallowed the lump in my throat.

"At least try," I replied.

Michael looked up at me, then behind my shoulder. "Somebody wants to speak to you."

I followed Michael's gaze, Samhain was standing nearby, he moved his head to indicate we had to talk in private. With a sigh, I looked at Michael as I stood up, then followed Samhain.

* * *

Samahin had led me into the bathroom, it smelled funny in here, but it was pretty much the only place to talk in private. The floor felt sticky beneath my feet. He turned on the lantern which sat on the wash basin, lighting the room in a white light. I gasped as Samahin locked the bathroom door.

"What are you doing?" I hissed, reaching for the lock.

"Don't unlock it, we need a serious talk," Samhain ordered.

I reluctantly folded my arms over my chest, and turned around to see Samhain sit on the toilet, resting his chin on his hands. After a couple moments, I crouched on the floor, not wanting to sit down fully because of the stickiness.

"What's so important we need to be inside a locked bathroom?" I asked.

Samhain let out a breath as he played with the lace on his boots. "I think tomorrow we should be extra vigilant," he announced.

My eyes widened, and I looked around, despite knowing it was only us in here. He wiped something off the overalls he was wearing.

"In what way?" A sinking feeling made it feel as though my stomach was being sucked into the earth's core.

We were interrupted when a knock sounded at the door, then it thudded as somebody tried to push it open. "What are y'all doing in there?" I recognised Alana's Southern drawl through the door.

"Helping Joseph make a hot kinky video for Carlos's viewing pleasure. Do you have any baby powder?" Samhain called through the door. The sound of her walking away, filled the air.

I started laughing, as I raised an eyebrow in his direction. He seemed unfazed by what he just said as he looked at the floor, clearly waiting to see if we were truly alone before speaking again.

"As I was saying, I just have a bad feeling about tomorrow. Dirty Sanchez has known about The Rebellion all these years, and now she wants us to visit after finding its location? Something smells off."

Slowly I nodded, while I considered this for a minute, either way he had a point. Our Leader had known about The Rebellion's existence for the past ten years, mostly as a result of past Rebellion Leaders rescuing the Unlisted, and partly from Samhain.

"What happens if something really wrong happens?" I questioned.

"Then we'll have to improvise, go against whatever plan Zeke pulls out his ass," Samhain looked behind my shoulder, his jaw twitched. "This conversation doesn't leave this room."

Another knock sounded on the door, I used the wash basin to stand up, and unlocked the door. Carlos was standing on the other side, he leaned against the door frame.

"That leather nurses outfit looked so good on you," I said to Samhain as I left the bathroom. His jaw fell open, and he started laughing.

Carlos furrowed his brow, looking between Samhain and I until I gave him a kiss on the cheek then took him by the hand.

I guided Carlos towards the section of the gas station, which had been turned into the sleeping area while I had been talking to Samhain. As I passed by the sofa where I had left Michael, he was curled up asleep, somebody had placed a blanket over him. A smile crept over my face to see Nadine asleep wrapped up in Ezekiel's arms.

There were two sleeping bags in the far right corner next to the cashier desk, a perfect secluded area for myself and Carlos which I made my way over to.

"Samhain wasn't actually doing anything in the bathroom, he just had to vent out what's on his mind," I assured Carlos as I sat on my sleeping bag closest to the wall, I unzipped it so I could climb in.

Carlos nodded. "I know. Just find it difficult to trust him, there's rumours he does ritualistic shit, so didn't want you to be involved in that." He unzipped his sleeping bag, and got inside of it, I nodded. "Why did you go with Samhain earlier, and not tell me about it? I had to check records to see potential places you three could have gone." His voice was calm, but I knew him well enough to know he was disappointed.

I exhaled a breath. "I'm sorry, I thought you wouldn't support my decision," I answered truthfully, knowing deep down it was partly about my sister.

"Of course I would have supported you, it's why I asked to marry you," Carlos held my hand.

"I'm sorry," I said again.

He kissed my hand. "It's okay, I'm not mad. You're safe that's the main thing."

"I love you."

"Love you too," Carlos replied as he kissed me.

I snuggled into him, wrapping my arm around his chest and used it as a pillow. He wrapped his arm around my shoulders. As I closed my eyes, I was thankful sleep came very quickly.

* * *

I woke up with a gasp, my heart hammered in my chest, and my breathing was heavy. My cheeks felt stiff from dried tears on my skin, it felt like my cheeks would crack if I did so much as smile.

Close by, I could hear muffled voices, as I sat up Alana was standing to the side of a green plastic box talking to everybody. I noticed there was a table filled with food and drink behind her, the smell of coffee even stronger than before. Alana looked up at me, smiling as she saw I had woken up.

"Nice of you to join us, Judas; help yourself to some breakfast," she instructed. I nodded and wriggled out of the sleeping bag. "Now we're all present, I can begin our meeting."

That was one thing I always appreciated with Ezekiel as the Head of The Rebellion—nobody got left behind. If he was the one leading us when Gabrielle was taken from me, he would have called off all meetings until I felt strong enough to come back.

As I stood up and approached the breakfast table, I jumped when I felt a hand on my back, Carlos suddenly coming into view.

"Are you okay?" he asked, Carlos picked up an apple and bit into it.

"I had a bad dream," I admitted, wiping a tear from my cheek. "Are you okay?" I picked up a piece of bread, and a banana. Dumping a pile of bacon into the weird mixture.

"Much better now I've heard your voice," Carlos replied.

I laughed, and shoved a strawberry into his mouth just to shut him up. He laughed as he took a bite. "Your flirting is more cheesy than that right there," I commented, pointing to a tray of various different cheeses.

Carlos threw his head back as he laughed even harder, despite his mouth being full.

"Alright, meeting is starting," Alana called out.

I held Carlos's hand as he guided me to a spot at the back of the gas station. When I sat on the floor, I placed my plate in front of me and tore off a bit of bread then took a bite. The bread was still warm, clearly freshly baked and it had a buttery taste to it despite having none on it.

"We split up in two teams at first," Alana proposed, my chewing slowed at hearing this; the last time we split up my sister happened. "Team One, is going down into The Tunnels, and safely transporting Nadine, Ezekiel, and Michael home in Olympia. Team Two, I'm requesting you to head straight to the court house."

I saw Michael straighten up on the sofa he was sitting on, he glanced at Nadine and Ezekiel who were sitting next to him.

"I'm not leaving," Nadine called out. "I want to help."

"If Nadine's not leaving, I'm not either," Ezekiel announced sternly.

Alana looked taken aback, and looked around the room. "If both of you aren't leaving, how is Michael going to get home?"

Good point. All three of them looked at each other.

"I've still got my cellphone, if that helps," Michael announced. I raised an eyebrow, he was so different now it shocked me. "I know who to call."

Alana soon nodded, casting a stern look at Nadine and Ezekiel. Maybe both of them were making a dumb decision by staying in Denmé. "Fine, Michael leaves."

I gasped and covered my mouth, feeling a sudden lump in my throat as I pushed the plate away. Michael didn't look too happy, but he appeared to relax after Alana said it. If it wasn't painful enough to lose one sibling, losing both—despite one being alive—would break my heart. Carlos rubbed my back.

Samhain stood up. "I volunteer for Team Two." He bowed, then sat down.

For a moment, Alana tapped her chin while she thought this over. "Okay, I'm appointing Samhain Roach as Leader for Team Two, you're all going into the thick of it, if any shit goes down he's your guy, considering his track record." She moved her hair behind her shoulder. "For Team One, I request Carlos Peres. He's like a brother to Michael, so it'll make him feel comfortable when he goes back."

Daisuke stepped up with a clipboard in hand, tapping a pen to it. "Alright, for Team Two with me and Samhain." He smiled. "Judas Wells, Xander Roach, Thora Paxton, Oluchi Adorette…"

My whole world shattered in that moment, all the sounds from the room fell into silent muffled voices. Suddenly feeling extremely sick, I pushed myself off of the floor and ran to the bathroom—the only place I knew I could get away.

36

Nadine

Up close, the courthouse was beautiful. Once you ignored the green and gold dome roof with a gaping hole in it from when somebody blew it up. I noticed the walls were a brilliant white marble with pristine pink veins running through them. The statues I had seen, which held jade green goblets of light above their heads, lined the marble staircase. In the air was a strong smell of burning, masking the scent of the red roses which grew on vines up the walls.

Samhain decided to split the group of nine Rebellion leaders into groups, some of them were sent to assist Zone 13 Rebellion citizens in the Uprising, others were sent to assist normal citizens who agreed to help. The rest were sent to start fighting, like Judas and Ezekiel. While I walked alongside Samhain, I looked at Daisuke and Thora—we had been chosen specifically to represent The Rebellion as he met with President Sanchez.

One of the Zone 13's Rebellion citizens named Mhairi had let me borrow her clothes, it felt amazing to get out of Denmé uniform and wear something comfortable. Even if I could feel the gun pressing into my back, which sat in its holster around my waist; concealed by my T-shirt. I was grateful Mhairi and I were the same size.

Feeling an arm loop around my elbow, I looked at Samhain, a smile crept along his face as we ascended the marble staircase. In his hand was a wooden staff, and a goat skull sat on his head; I could see why everybody called him an insane person.

I tried to get out of his grasp, but he held tighter "I have a boyfriend," I warned Samhain.

Samhain chuckled then looked at me. "Friends can have their arms linked, can they not?" He questioned.

I sighed as I gave into him. "You still haven't apologised for trying to see me naked in the shower," I pointed out.

He furrowed his brow then scoffed. "If I was trying to do that, I'd at least move the shower curtain, which I did not. I may be fucked in the head, but I have morals."

"Still. What you did was wrong."

Samhain sighed. "Anyway, us having our arms linked, shows we are strong as a united community. Despite the Zones being designed to separate us, and resent each other. Which isn't the case in The Rebellion. You may not notice it, but the guards are watching."

I looked around but it appeared to be only us around, was there something Samhain could see that nobody else could? Despite the pain it caused me, I gently tapped his arm with my free hand, my fingers tingling as I touched the material on his cloak. He oddly smelled like sage.

At the top of the stairs were two large green doors, both with golden lion heads on the handles, I looked at Samhain for guidance, then looked at Daisuke and Thora—both nodded with reassuring smiles. Samhain pushed his goat skull down to conceal his face, then we pushed open the doors.

* * *

Three guards guided us into a grand room which smelled like cupcakes, I gasped when I looked up to the ceiling—an oil painting depicted a war amongst angels laced with ornate gold. Our footsteps echoed on the black and white marbled floor. I looked at every single wall which was covered in floor to ceiling book cases of ancient crumbling books, some were missing their bindings. When my gaze fell onto the large oak desk in the middle of the room, my throat went dry as I laid eyes on President Sanchez. She looked even more grotesque in person, her hair was slicked so tightly back that it thinned out her cracked face; even her military uniform looked like it was ironed onto her skeletal frame. When she looked up and smiled at us, it was all teeth no lips, her dark eyes glistened.

"Wonderful." Even her voice was more nasally in person. "These must be my Rebellion. Please state your Zones."

"I'm Samhain, Zone 13. Bethany, Zone 14. Daisuke, Zone 18 and Thora, Zone 9," Samhain said on our behalf. I was thankful for that.

I found as I grew more nervous, I dug my fingers into the fabric of Samhain's jacket. Could that be the real reason why he had made me hold his arm? Pushing that thought aside as President Sanchez scanned all of us with that wicked grin, her red leather chair creaked as she leaned forward.

"How kind of you to lie about Bethany's Zone. You know as well as I do she's an Influencer," she snarled. I froze when she pointed that out. "Did an Influencer make you start The Rebellion?"

Daisuke went to step forward, but Samhain tapped his staff on the ground which made him stop. Samhain sucked in a breath. "The Rebellion was established thirteen years ago, My Leader—way before Bethany even entered our great nation. She had no influence on The Rebellion's actions; it was your oppressive laws."

President Sanchez gasped, then let out a laugh which sounded more like a cackle, as she placed a hand on her chest. "Keeping you safe is oppression?"

"I'm the orphan you wanted dead at four years old, is that not oppression?" Samhain's voice was scarily calm.

When President Sanchez smacked both her hands on the desk, and stood up I jumped. Then I stiffened when I heard the doors behind us open.

"Mother. Here is the latest report for The Rebellion."

I recognised that voice. When I looked behind my shoulder, my jaw fell open and I tugged on Samhain's sleeve so he could also see who it was. As the person approached the desk, Thora and Daisuke's mouth came open when they saw *Hunter*.

"Ah, yes. Samhain, Daisuke, *Nadine*, and Thora. It was nice of you to abide by my mother's request to meet us here," Hunter spoke calmly with a smile. In his arms he cradled a large stack of documentation, his hair had been dyed black and sat in a mess at the base of his neck. "I thought Judas would be here."

"Why do you keep calling Our Leader *'mother'*?" Thora squeaked, I noticed she was reaching behind her back for her weapon.

President Sanchez placed a hand on Hunter's arm. "Hunter here is my illegitimate child. As an experiment to see how The Rebellion was rescuing my orphans, we sent him into an extermination camp and let him be raised as what you call an Unlisted. He's been my greatest weapon ever since."

I couldn't breathe, this was all too much. Even as Samhain dropped my arm with a low growl, he turned toward the door, ready to leave. "If you leave, I will get the guards—"

"Get the fucking guards! We have more people than your worst fucking nightmares, you dried up useless bitch!" Samhain screamed across the room. I was frozen in place, immediately terrified of his sudden change in personality.

Hunter stepped forward, his hands up to signal he meant peace.

"Samhain, calm down, it's okay."

I jumped out of the way as Samhain grabbed Hunter, and slammed him into the nearest book case. He produced a knife which he held against Hunter's throat. "Tell me one thing, traitor," Samhain growled. "Were the stories of you being beaten a lie?"

When I heard the click of a gun, I noticed Daisuke and Thora had produced their weapons, both aimed their guns at President Sanchez and Hunter. I fumbled to do the same, but found it surprisingly difficult with one arm. Daisuke stepped forward, and switched my gun for his, I gave him a thankful nod and aimed it at the door in anticipation for the guards to barge in.

"I'm Our Leader's son, they wouldn't touch me," Hunter snarled.

A hard fist drove into Hunter's face, and he cried out. "But I would, you fucking vermin." Samhain punched him again.

Everything inside me wanted to scream as I saw Samhain aim the knife to Hunter's cheek. It was like something had possessed him and turned him into something dark. Hunter screamed as Samhain ran the knife down his cheek three times, panting from the obvious pain.

"Samhain, no!" I managed to choke out.

I jumped as Samhain punched Hunter again. I was so fixated on him beating Hunter to a pulp, I didn't notice that guards had opened the doors.

"Run!" Daisuke shouted.

As I tore my gaze away from Samhain's reign of terror, guards were approaching with their arms outstretched. Their boots like thunder against the floor tile. I fired my gun four times, some went down, but I was outnumbered.

I made my way out into the corridor, ducking out of the way and avoiding them as they lunged to catch me. Once I was at the top of the stairs which led down to the exit, I realised my path was blocked, all the guards were congregating in the lobby and piling up the stairs with their guns out. Then it became obvious, my only plan of escape was to go up.

***

As I pushed open the roof access door, I stumbled out onto the roof panting from the exertion of running, my throat felt like it was closing as I tried to get more oxygen desperately into my lungs. Seeing a broom propped up against the wall, I grabbed it and rammed it into the door handle, and backed up. I had just enough ground between myself and the guards to make a plan.

When I looked to my right, there were domed roofs. When I looked to my left it spread out into a flat platform, I could easily run across, and jump onto the roof of the adjacent building. That seemed my most promising line for escape, I stiffened when the door behind me started to rattle and something heavy was smashed against it. My time had ran out.

I started running at full speed, my legs burned from climbing up all the stairs to the roof and now this. Even my arm was burning while I tried to keep it in place as I ran. I briefly glanced behind my shoulder as I heard the door burst open, then voices called after me as stones crunched beneath my feet. The smell of burning growing stronger from somewhere unknown.

The bangs of gunshots made me wince, and I tried to shield my head. I skidded to a halt at the edge of the roof, when I realised the jump to the adjacent roof top was much, much larger than it looked at the door.

I screamed as something hit my shoulder, a burning sensation overwhelmed my entire body.

Before I knew it, I was falling.

***

I landed inside a net, which sank down. My arm burned furiously, and I could feel something warm and wet trickle down my spine. The world around me spun and I felt paralysed from the burning sensation on my left side, my fingers felt like electricity would shoot out of them. The idiots hit my already badly injured arm, I grimaced and pressed my hand to my forehead and cried out.

Tears rolled down my cheek, as I looked above me, the sky's were blue aside from the grey clouds forming to blanket it with rain. I could smell the earthy, wet scent of it as I lay here. Actually if I stayed here long enough, it would be easy for the Rebellion Leaders to rescue me.

However, the sound of tearing and a sudden lurch downwards made me tense up. My heart hammered against my ribs. I could see the net was becoming frayed under the weight of me.

Another tearing sound as the net was losing its substance. Another lurch towards the ground.

No. No. No!

The entire net gave out from underneath me. I screamed loudly as I started falling, only managing to twist my body enough to grip hold of what's left of the net with my good arm. The material dug painfully into my skin.

I was now stuck in a limbo, dangling half way to safety, and half way to death. When I looked down, the ground spun, and I cried out again from the pain in my arm and started sobbing.

My stomach lurched as my fingers started slipping, I screamed again, trying to secure my hand in any other way.

"Help me!" I screamed.

At this point I didn't care if guards cut the net from my grasp, or if by some miracle a staff member in the courthouse broke out of their alliance with President Sanchez. I sobbed loudly as I looked up at the sky.

"Just help me," I pleaded to the sky.

"Nadine!" a familiar voice shouted. Looking around, I couldn't see anybody. "Down here!"

When I looked down, I felt deflated to see Samhain just out of reach, he rolled up his sleeves as he stood on the marble handrail, then held his arms out to me.

"I can't move my left arm!" I shouted to him. My fingers trembled from trying to hold my own strength.

Despite my vision being blurred from crying, I noticed Samhain nod in my direction, and ran a hand down his face. I saw him exhale a breath. "Stop crying, and swing your way over to me, I'll catch you!"

"I don't trust you!" I groaned as I slipped again. "What if you drop me?"

"We'll figure that out if it happens, now do as I said!" Samhain shouted. My heart skipped a beat knowing there was a possibility he could drop me.

Either way he was my only hope.

With every bit of remaining strength, I gripped hold of the net tighter, and began the attempt to swing over to Samhain. It took exactly three attempts of me swinging towards him, with my injured arm screaming in protest, until I felt confident enough to let go.

As I hurtled through the air, the momentum made my breath catch in my throat, I squeezed my eyes shut and I had to push aside the fact I was completely at mercy of Samhain's actions.

Once I felt somebody's arms embrace me, I dared to open my eyes, as Samhain and I crashed onto the balcony. When my shoulder hit the concrete, I screamed loudly and broke down into a sobbing mess from the burning pain which shot down my spine. I felt like I could pass out. When it subsided, Samhain was scarily close to my face, I could feel his warm breath on my face. I grimaced again as another ounce of burning pain shot down my spine, I started trembling. Around us I could smell blood, and there was an even stronger smell of fire.

"See, I didn't drop you," Samhain said with a laugh as he straddled me, I was too weak to tell him to move. I grew concerned when he held his arm to his chest, it was misshapen from an obvious break.

"I'm sorry," I said through chattering teeth.

"I think the correct term you're looking for is thank you," Samhain replied, his smile vanished when he glanced at his injury. "Besides, you fell ten feet, give or take. It was going to happen."

A deep tiredness made my body feel extremely heavy, the world rocked like a boat battling a rough sea, my stomach churned as the cold air washed over me making me feel sick. The chattering of my teeth wasn't helping. "Thank you," I told him slowly, when I pushed aside the urge to throw up. Groaning and squeezing my eyes shut as more burning pain shot down my spine.

Samhain's smile returned when I opened my eyes. "If I knew you fell for guys that easily, I would have told Ezekiel to get in on the action sooner." Quickly I punched his thigh as hard as I could. "Ouch."

"That wasn't funny," I spat at him.

Just as I was about to rant at him, I screamed and squeezed my eyes shut as the burning pain suddenly made me feel like I was being torn in two—it was worse than any I had experienced thus far—both my arms were now tingling, even my legs. I broke down sobbing, trying to breath through it, but breathing made it worse.

A child suddenly came into view when I opened my eyes again, was I hallucinating from the pain? Why was a child here in the first place? As I wiped my eyes free of tears, I noticed the child had short purple hair, and two grotesque scars on either side of his mouth. Samhain rolled off me, his face was like stone, he glanced in my direction as he tried to stand up.

"Help?" the child mumbled, there was something wrong with his speech.

Samhain looked at the child, then nodded. "Nadine, this is Fionn, he's a recent Unlisted rescue; guards cut his tongue out so we're teaching him how to talk again. I'm going to find the other Rebellion Leaders, stay here until they arrive."

The child smiled and waved at me. I shuddered at the thought of guards doing that to an innocent child, all because he didn't have parents. I turned my head slightly as I watched Samhain slip through an open window, he disappeared entirely after closing it. A strange emptiness filled the air, even with Fionn with me.

"Sky is pretty," Fionn exlcaimed. I turned to look at him, then looked at the sky which had now turned grey.

"The sky is pretty," I repeated slowly, swallowing the lump in my throat.

"Rain coming," he announced. "It is good for hurting bad men who hurt me."

37

Judas

I sat in the back of a stolen SUV from Our Leaders house, somebody named Mhairi was driving and the tires squealed around corners. Her white hair flying about from the open sun roof. Ezekiel looked out of the wind shield to see the direction we were headed to, guards were everywhere trying to fight off people who attacked them with a variety of weapons.

There was a child in the passenger seat from Zone 13, Mhairi had said his was Fionn. He was an Unlisted child, where guards were dicks and cut out his tongue. I was thankful he didn't seem too fazed by it. As I looked at the gun in my hand, it felt unnaturally cold to the touch.

My eyes widened as guards came into the path of the car, guns aimed at the windshield with a sternness in their stance, before they even had a chance to pull the trigger Mhairi cackled loudly as she floored the accelerator, and smashed into them. The SUV bounced over their bodies with a satisfactory roar.

"Play time, boys!"

Ezekiel glanced at me, and I gave him a forced smile in return. I was unnerved by the fact Mhairi was as equally messed up as Samhain, it was terrifying. More guards came out of nowhere, this time Ezekiel stood up through the sunroof and started firing. His aim was so precise guards went down like a line of domino's. From the corner of my eye, I noticed Fionn staring at me, he had two large scars on the side of his mouth, and short purple hair—dyed, of course. I mouthed *what* to him, and he motioned a gun in his hand, sucking in a breath, I pointed to Mhairi.

He tapped Mhairi's arm. "What do you want, bud?" she asked. He motioned the gun again, and Mhairi pulled open the glove compartment, showing a horde of weapons. "Take your pick."

"Hold up, you're letting a *child* shoot a gun?" I spat. Bewildered by the fact she was open to this idea, but I had to come to the realisation this was normal, especially with an Uprising fuelled by the majority of Zone 13's Rebellion.

Fionn climbed out of the passenger seat, and crawled out of the window onto the hood of the car, he crouched there, weapon aimed and he started firing.

"You should see him with Ninja Stars, he even scares me." Mhairi laughed. I had to admit he was a great shot.

Soon enough, Fionn climbed up to the roof of the car to join Ezekiel.

"I'm out, give me bullets," Ezekiel announced, handing me his gun, which I swapped for mine as I replenished the bullets, already there were several cuts on his hand.

Guards were very clearly outnumbered, with the horde of The Rebellion and regular citizens kicking their asses. The car roared as Mhairi slammed into a long line of clueless guards, they all went down like human bowling pins, she laughed from the enjoyment it gave her.

Ezekiel sat back down, breathing heavily and clutched his side. Up on the roof, Fionn was the lone assailant, he laughed with each hit. My eyes widened as the court house loomed over us, there was no slowing the car down, we were going to have to drive through it.

"Brace!" Mhairi screamed.

Fionn dropped back into the vehicle and crouched down.

Immediately the SUV smashed directly into a set of glass doors which led into the court house, I held onto the grab handle as the car spun at dizzying angles. The tires screeching on the floor tiles. When it came to a stop after smashing into a staircase, I felt extremely sick. Once I climbed out of the sunroof of the SUV, I dropped down onto the black and white marble floor titles, looking at Mhairi as I straightened up. She whipped the air with a charred black whip she had carried out with her. Fionn climbed out after me, followed by Ezekiel who still held his side, he grimaced in obvious pain. As I looked around, there were no guards—it was far too quiet for the courthouse.

We were in a grand entrance way, above us was an oil painting framed in gold of *The Seven Deadly Sins*, which I had read about during Task 105. The staircase we smashed into was gold and marble which spiralled up three levels, lining it were statues of people holding jade green goblets of light above their heads, I was stunned into speechlessness at its beauty.

"Now, that is how you make an entrance," Mhairi exclaimed as she moved her hair.

She looked like she was made of glass, her skin was pure white, and her eyes a brilliant blue, and crystal-white hair. Even her eyebrows and eyelashes were pure white where make up hadn't covered them.

I jumped at a loud metallic crash which echoed around the foyer, the sound of breaking glass sounding like a wind chime on the floor, when I turned around I froze to see Hunter in the middle of the now crumpled up vehicle.

When I approached him, Hunter was gasping for air, blood rained down his face not only from his nose and lips—but from three large cuts on his cheek, like a bear had just clawed at him. Some of his hair had also been cut off. I looked at Ezekiel, he furrowed his brow as he stood next to me.

"Mummy," he wheezed out. A tear rolled down his cheek, turning a rust colour as it connected with his blood.

"Hunter, what are you doing here?" Ezekiel questioned, raising an eyebrow.

"Samhain attacked me. I didn't do anything, he just flipped out," Hunter gasped out. "He needs murdering. Those are the rules aren't they, for hurting another Leader?"

I narrowed my eyes, and looked at Ezekiel who folded his arms over his chest. When I glanced at Mhairi she shook her head with a laugh. Everybody knew Samhain wouldn't attack a fellow Rebellion Leader without good reason—even if his relationship with Hunter wasn't the best. The sound of loud boots thundered through the staircase, I tensed at the thought it was a guard.

"What kind of pathetic excuse of a twenty-five year old calls their mum, mummy?" Samhain snarled at Hunter, with a bloody knife in hand. "Instead of throwing my name under the bus, why don't you grow some fucking balls, and tell them what kind of pathetic excuse of a human you truly are." He wiped his knife on his cape.

"Mummy!" Hunter cried out. I glanced behind my shoulder to see Mhairi smiling.

"Whoever was leader before Ezekiel, they didn't do a good job at screening this scum bag. He's been a government spy since he joined The Rebellion. Bet you didn't know Our Leader actually had a son!" Samhain shouted.

Suddenly everything clicked into place. The reason he was here right now, how the government found out about Nadine, how each District was going down one by one. Especially his reluctance to fight. Now I understood why Samhain attacked him, and I saw red.

"Kill him," Ezekiel instructed coldly before walking away.

It was never anticipated that one of the people trying to keep The

Rebellion a secret would be a government spy. The Rebellion rarely executed people, but it was one of the golden rules if anybody gave the government its secrets.

"No!" Hunter screamed.

With one single gunshot, Hunter's brain splattered across the shiny crumpled metal of the SUV, I pressed a hand to my mouth to try and not retch. Once the queasy feeling subsided. I looked around to see who had shot him—Samhain had a knife, Mhairi had a whip, I lost mine, and Ezekiel was walking way too much to bother using his gun. Only person left was Fionn, when I looked at him, he was smiling boldly with the gun still aimed.

Samhain growled and stormed back up the stairs. I looked at Ezekiel, who was now walking back up to us, he looked like he wanted to say something but was holding back, his eyes fixed on anything other than Hunter.

"If you were Nadine, where would you be?" Ezekiel asked, scratching his neck.

"Roof access." Daisuke suddenly said from the top of the stairs, covered in blood as he trudged down to us. "She ran to the roof."

Without hesitation Ezekiel bolted up the stairs, followed by Mhairi and Fionn.

"You might need this," Daisuke said as he handed me a bloody gun.

"Thank you." I took it from his hand, shuddering at its warm slimy coating.

Shortly after I followed the rest of the group upstairs.
Ezekiel kicked open the rooftop door, I breathed heavily and swallowed thin air as I leaned against a wall while trying to regain strength. My thighs and lungs burned; I definitely wasn't doing that again. Pushing myself off the wall, my eyes widened, instantly holding my gun out as several guards patrolled the area.

Suddenly the smell of kerosene hit my nose as Mhairi set her whip on fire, she smiled wickedly as she glanced behind her shoulder whilst she moved the whip around. It was only now I had noticed we were down one person. Fionn was nowhere to be found. Alongside the kerosene smell, the earthy damp smell of rain filled the air.

Ezekiel had his gun out as he surveyed the area, only stopping as Mhairi dragged the fire whip along the pebbles beneath our feet which made a noise I knew would alert the guards. Which was apparently the plan, as they all aimed their guns at us with wicked smiles.

"Oh hasn't Our Leader given us a treat. Hello, ID 498763 and ID 008249," the nearest guard to me snarled. I jumped out of the way when he fired his gun at me, the bullet thankfully hit one of the bricks on a nearby wall. The weapon I had dropped glinted at me as it lay in the pebbles, the urge to get it was strong, but if I did I'd be a dead man.

"That wasn't a very nice way to play." Mhairi pouted, fluttering her eyelashes, her voice had switched to something childlike.

"We don't know who are you are, little lady," the same guard snarled.

"Your worst fucking nightmare," Mhairi snarled back as her voice returned to normal, before the guard even had chance to think she whipped him.

I could feel the heat of the whip just from standing nearby, as it honed in on its target—the guards uncovered face. His skin bubbled on impact, the guard screamed out as he fell on his knees.

All the other guards stood nearby, I noticed they all looked shocked, and struggled to maintain composure as they looked at each other while adjusting their guns. Except for one guard who actually threw up. Mhairi hummed a nursey rhyme as she spun the whip, making it look like a tornado made of fire, it whooshed through the air.

"Put your weapon down, we'll run," one guard squeaked out.

"Fuck that, she's one woman," another snapped, and held his gun out to her.

Instantly she whipped him, it licked at his fingers which resulted in him dropping his weapon with a scream of agony. The smell of burning human flesh sent a chill down my spine.

Mhairi cocked her head. "You didn't play nice, so I'm not going to play nice. Now *why* won't you play?" she screamed.

I had to turn around, not being able to watch anymore of her assault on the guards, I had to place a hand on my stomach which rolled uncomfortably as I could hear sizzling sounds followed by screams. The air quickly filling with the smells of blood, kerosene fuel and a charred meat smell like a BBQ of human meat. I knew Samhain was bad, but Mhairi was a hurricane type storm to be reckoned with.

The screams grew into a crescendo, with the smell of charred meat growing stronger by the second, and loud thuds with the crunching of pebbles filled the air. I had to squeeze my eyes shut. Was this ordeal ever going to end?

38

Judas

Once Mhairi took down the final guard, I turned around, the queasy feeling in my stomach strengthened when I saw the mass of bodies. They were still alive, and twitching, their skin already blistering. From the distance, there was a sudden eruption of explosions and gunshots, the smell of fire growing stronger.

"Now we can look for Nadine," Mhairi said as she picked up a gun, and shot every guard dead.

I nodded after shuddering, and followed behind her, hoping Nadine was safe and alive. There wasn't many exits on this rooftop, so I hoped she was both. A blood curdling scream made me stop in my tracks, and I looked at everybody else in our group. My heart started racing, all of us waited if the scream was going happen again.

"It came from that direction," Ezekiel exclaimed as he pointed to a flat part of the roof.

All of us headed in that direction, on a mission to see where the scream had come from and who it belong to. We stopped when another scream erupted through the air. It sounded female, which made me think of the worse. I hastily made my way to the edge of the roof, as Ezekiel and Mhairi spread out, looking between the A/C vents.

There was a gap to another part of the courthouse but it wasn't big enough to jump across, when I leaned over the edge, at first I saw the anti-bird net which spanned the width of the gap. Then I noticed something was very wrong. Not only was blood coating the material, but there was a giant gaping hole. Directly below was a balcony, relief washed over me to see Nadine laying there, with Fionn at her side—however, my heart skipped a beat when I noticed a large pool of blood seeping out of her and she was grimacing in pain.

"Shit, Fionn!" He looked up at me. "Which floor?" Fionn held up three fingers. I nodded. "Meet me down stairs!"

I turned around, and started running towards the stair case, my boots crunched on the pebbles.

"Where are you going?" Ezekiel called out to me.

"Nadine's injured on floor three!" I shouted to him.

* * *

I climbed through the window Fionn guided me to, and crouched next to Nadine. My trembling hands extended out to move her, but I quickly pulled back after the realisation she could have fallen from up there. My gaze fell on Fionn who returned to sitting next to her. Nadine was shaking, her teeth chattered as she grimaced.

"Oh my god, where does it hurt?" I asked, completely at a loss for what to do, hoping the question would let me know if I could move her.

Nadine looked to the window, as Ezekiel entered the balcony, he climbed over her then held her hand for comfort. Ezekiel ran a hand over his face, he looked just as terrified as I felt.

"Wound on her." Fionn tapped his shoulder. His voice was nothing more than a mumble for obvious reasons. "Sam catch her."

That gave me all the answers I needed, I quickly took off my jacket—the bitter cold biting at my bare arms, and gave it to Nadine. "Bite onto this, it's going to hurt." Ezekiel raised an eyebrow at me. "I'm going to move her to assess the damage, on the count of three. One…Two…Three."

I placed a hand on Nadine's stomach then slowly moved her onto her side. Nadine arched her back as a scream erupted out of her, muffled only by my jacket. Flashbacks of my sister clouded my thoughts, after sucking in a breath and shaking my head, I could see the bullet through the hole in her shoulder. Nadine was panting, and groaning into my jacket, I looked at Ezekiel, she clutched his hand so tightly her nails dug into his skin and her knuckles were white.

As I lowered Nadine back down, she sighed out of relief, her shivering had intensified significantly. I ran a hand through my hair as tears stung my eyes, and I looked around at everybody on the balcony. How were we going to get her out of this. I didn't feel comfortable carrying her through the window, her blood would give away our location. Yet, that may be our only option.

The metal clanging, brought my attention out of my thoughts, and to the edge of the balcony where a ladder was coming towards us. My gaze followed the ladder back up to the roof, were we going to have to go back up there? I didn't realistically want to.

Mhairi leaned over the edge. "A helicopter is coming to rescue us! Come up!"

Several other Rebellion Leaders surrounded Mhairi, I breathed a sigh of relief to see Carlos amongst them. The one person I needed right now. As more flashbacks about Gabrielle filled my mind, I did the hardest to swallow the lump in my throat and not get upset about it. I had a job to do.

"Ezekiel, you carry Nadine up the ladder, I'll follow behind you," I instructed, as I closed the window, jumping at the sound of explosions nearby.

"You've got this guys!" A male called down.

"I believe in you babe, you can do this!" Carlos shouted down.

Those words made me close my eyes, and break down crying. I realistically wasn't strong enough, mentally, to be doing this so close to losing my sister. So many flashbacks were hitting me right now, that I thought I would lose my mind. I sucked in a breath, and wiped my eyes—I had to do this.

"I'm sorry," Ezekiel told Nadine as he picked her up.

Nadine bit down on my jacket as he slid his arms underneath her body, her agonised scream muffled by the fabric, Ezekiel moved her over his shoulder, then held her by the waist. I slowly stood up as he made his way over, and gripped the ladder. She looked at me, as she panted into my jacket.

"You'll be fine," I assured Nadine as Ezekiel started his ascent.

I stayed on the balcony as they continued their climb, as more explosions filled the air, I tensed but tried to stay calm. When I looked around Fionn had disappeared again, where he could have gone to was anybody's guess. Once I looked up to see Ezekiel and Nadine disappearing from view, I knew it was my turn to climb.

* * *

At the top, I stumbled into Carlos's arms, giving him a kiss and moved his hair from his eyes. The feeling of his hands on my waist just made me feel safer, even though this entire situation was enough to put anybody on edge. Ezekiel had placed Nadine on the floor, it was evident she had passed out as my jacket fell beside her and she looked as though she was asleep. I tensed as more explosions sounded nearby, they sounded like they were getting closer.

Then the heavens opened and rain started pouring down on the roof top, I gasped and looked up to the sky, this was going to cause some issues with our escape route. My attention was brought back to Carlos.

"Did Michael get back safely?" I asked as I kissed him again, then pulled his denim jacket around him so he wasn't cold from the rain.

Carlos looked behind my shoulder, I followed his gaze but nobody appeared to be there, I looked at his face with a raised eyebrow. He slowly nodded, and pulled me in close, I was grateful my one remaining sibling was away from all of this. I didn't want to let go of Carlos, even though I knew we would have to fight to get out of this country.

"Well, isn't this a nice family reunion," a voice said nearby.

I froze as I let go of Carlos, and looked at them. Our Leader stood near us with a gun aimed in our direction, surrounded by guards.

39

Judas

I shifted to face Our Leader directly, several other Rebellion Leaders surrounded me, guns aimed at her and the guards. The rain was getting heavier by the second, and it looked as though Our Leader could snap at any moment from how cold the air was becoming. I could see my breath whenever I exhaled—her military uniform turning a shade of moss green. She smiled wickedly at all of us, giving the guards a glance behind her shoulder.

"We have a full house," Our Leader snorted, we didn't have a full house—Samhain was missing. Her gaze fell on Nadine. "Oh that's a pretty sight."

Ezekiel glared at her as he tended to Nadine's wounds, I bit the inside of my cheek and took a step forward but Carlos pulled me back. I glanced at him, he quickly shook his head as he held my hand, when I turned back to Our Leader she was glaring at us.

"We aren't going down without a fight, give us freedom, or we'll force you to give us what we deserve," Abrianna shouted.

"People cannot spend their lives living underground because you're fucked in the head!" Sung-Jin shouted.

I was the first to cheer, which made everybody else cheer with me.

Abruptly cut short as Our Leader fired, sending a bullet directly into Nolan's chest, the Rebellion leader of Zone 5. He was dead before he hit the ground, his eyes glazed over where he lay. All of us who had weapons returned to aiming them at Our Leader. We doubled their numbers, it would be an easy fight.

A cold chill went through me, not because of the rain, but because of the three bell tolls which rang out over the city. My eyes widened to see a fireball hurtling towards us at full speed. The smell of kerosene fuel growing stronger by the second. I didn't know how to react until I spun around, and pulled Carlos to the ground. Using my body as a shield.

The impact was so loud I felt it in my bones, the whole roof shuddered underneath me, and I shielded my head. Debris rained over me, and the smell of burning was like somebody had just poured fuel onto an already burning bonfire.

* * *

As I looked up from the explosion, the entire walkway that used to house the door to the stairwell was completely obliterated. The rain bounced off me, I shivered from how cold I was, but I breathed heavily. Adrenaline pumped through my veins.

Our Leader was on the floor, I watched her push debris off of her while she stood up. She stumbled as she grabbed her gun and aimed it at all of us, Our Leader was panting from how furious she clearly was. The guards surrounding her were now down to three. Our Leader's hair had fallen out of the ridiculously tight bun she always had, black curly hair waved around in the wind. Blood seeped out of Our Leader's ears, and a large cut on her forehead. Behind her the rooftop fire raged.

Immediately she squeezed her guns trigger, I gasped when she hit

Esmerelda from Zone 17 in the head. The oldest and last remaining founder of The Rebellion. She jolted at first, then quickly fell to the ground; if it wasn't for the hole in her forehead, you'd mistake her for being asleep.

Once I stood up, I held Carlos's hand to help him stand up, when I heard the bang, I pulled him out the way. My eyes widening to see a bullet lodge into the wall where we were both standing merely seconds ago, I turned around to look at her.

"ID 498763, I'm shocked you helped an Influencer stay in this country. Considering your father's track record," Our Leader mocked with a laugh, reloading her gun.

Without thinking, I grabbed the gun out of the holster on Carlos's belt and aimed it at Our Leader, my breathing heavy as anger took over me. "You murdered my father in cold blood, you fucking bitch. He was innocent," I growled.

"Babe," Carlos warned. I ignored him, and tried to focus on stopping my hands trembling.

She waved her gun at me while laughing. "Your father burned down government documentation in that fire, and you know it, you had it planned." She scoffed and paced in a circle. "Honestly, the very idea of his innocence is stupid."

I wanted to growl and scream at Our Leader, trying to manipulate me into believing my father was not the one innocent. My grip on the gun tightened. "My father wasn't even around at the time of that fire! He was at home, with my mother. You left three kids without one of their parents!" I shouted.

Just as she was about to reply, a sense of dread overwhelmed me as another three tolls from a bell echoed through the air. From the shadows, several ropes flew through the air, strategically wrapping themselves around the remaining guards' necks, then pulled them out the way. The sound of their screams echoed around the rooftop.

Only now did I realise there were people from Zone 13 standing in the shadows. Another gun shot, and Abrianna went down, I gasped and covered my mouth.

Our Leader cackled loudly. "And you grew up to be a dirty homosexual, should it be ID 494011 next on my list of people to shoot?"

I tightened my jaw as she aimed the gun at Carlos. "Not if I do it first," I snarled.

Before I could even squeeze the trigger, I jumped as a loud gun shot came from the side of me, a bullet landed straight into Our Leader's side. She didn't cry out, instead her eyes widened as she pressed her hand to the wound. I turned my head, my jaw fell open as Michael stepped out of the smoke with a rifle in hand.

"That's for manipulating me," Michael snapped, rage in his eyes.

My breathing suddenly became more rapid, this was not happening a second time. No, I wouldn't let it happen a second time.

I watched Michael pull the trigger again. She dodged out of the way of that one.

Our Leader narrowed her eyes at Michael, then pointed the gun directly at me. "Nobody shoots me."

I squeezed my eyes shut as she pulled the trigger, the sound of the gun shot rippled through my bones. My eyes opened in shock, and I felt like all the air was sucked out of me when Carlos screamed. I swallowed the lump in my throat, and slowly turned around to see Carlos on the ground clutching his arm as blood trickled out of the wound, pure rage tore through me. A low growl from deep within me sounded out. My grip on the gun tightening in my trembling hand. I once again aimed the gun at Our Leader—her eyes widening at the inevitable.

"That's the last of my family you're hurting, bitch." Squeezing the trigger, the recoil sent jolts up my arm but I held my ground. Despite hearing Michael shout my name, it only took the edge off of my anger, when it hit Our Leader's shoulder. She gasped and looked at her arm, narrowing her eyes at me.

I kept shooting for everything she had taken from me.

My name. Bang.

Tears clouded my vision, so I had no idea what I was shouting at or if I was hitting Our Leader at all. The smell of blood growing stronger. My lips quivered, and I tasted the saltiness of my own tears on them.

My father and sister. Bang. Bang.

My freedom. Bang.

Each fire of the gun ebbed away at my anger. My hands trembled, but I didn't let it stop me from shooting.

My friends freedom. Bang.

As the gun began to click, I sobbed loudly, I didn't want to stop. A gentle hand wrapped around my arm. "Judas, come on; you need to stop now." It was Carlos. I kept firing through sobs even though I was out of bullets. "Come on, it's over now."

When I felt Carlos's hand wrap around the gun and pull it down, I fell to the ground—I threw the gun across the roof in anger. I couldn't breathe, I wheezed loudly as I sobbed. The reality of what I had just done sinking in. I rocked back, and forth trying to get oxygen into my burning lungs. Our Leader's body was on the floor, several bullet holes splattered her skeletal frame, even the puddle beneath her was a crimson red—turning a rust colour as it mixed in with the rain. I screamed into the air as I held my chest. Never before had I felt so empty.

Every single emotion I had been holding in, came out like a tsunami, Carlos's arm wrapped around me. I choked on tears, as I pressed a trembling hand to his injured arm, he sucked in a breath as I did so. *Just think.*

"I'll be fine," he ushered as he kissed my forehead.

"No," I choked out. "I need to help you."

As I took my belt off, I fumbled to secure it above his injury. It would have helped if my hands weren't shaking so much.

Carlos placed his hand over my hands, I stopped and looked into his eyes, they were glazed over from tears as he smiled at me. "I'll be fine."

He grimaced as I eventually got it secured and pulled it tight, I swallowed the lump in my throat as he kissed my lips, the kiss feeling like it was the last we'd ever share together. The thought broke me even worse than before, sobbing loudly as I pulled away, and squeezed my eyes shut as the tears flowed freely. Carlos pressed me into his chest, and let me cry.

It was over. From today onward, we had an opportunity to rebuild Denmé into a free, and truly safe society.

40

Nadine

Waking up with a gasp, I tried sitting up, but my arm burned furiously, so I laid back down and exhaled a breath. I was staring at a metal ceiling until my dad came into view, my eyes widened and a lump formed in my throat. Despite all the pain, I sat up quickly and backed into the wall.

"How are you feeling, sweetie?" Dad asked, he crouched next to me, then tried running a hand through my hair. I quickly smacked it away.

"What the hell are you doing here?" I practically shouted. Looking around the metal box room we were in, I quickly realised all The Rebellion Leaders were staring at us, except for Judas and Carlos, who were both sleeping on a nearby bed, even more surprisingly Michael was asleep on the floor. Both Ezekiel and Samhain were missing. "What have you done with Ezekiel?" I snapped.

Dad licked his lips and looked around, moving his tie so it became loose. "ORS rescued them all, they're only in Olympia for a short period before going back to Denmé," Dad explained, as he reached for me.

"Get away from me," I snapped.

Dad shook his head and sat down on the bed next to me anyway.

I brought my legs up to my knees and wanted to run. "Nadine, I'm sorry, but I just saved your life—"

"She said, get away dude." I looked up when I heard Thora's voice. She stood close by with her arms folded over her chest and anger in her eyes. "What's he done to you?"

With a sigh, I replied "This guy is my dad. He's the reason The Educators kidnapped me. Without consent he put a tracking device in my arm so I could find Judas and take him back to Olympia. But my dad hasn't admitted it yet." I cringed when Judas approached us. He stood next to Thora, looking at my dad with just as much hatred. "And he's also the reason The Educators kidnapped me the second time, along with Michael and Ezekiel."

The sound of heavy footsteps on the metal floor filled the air, Samhain stood next to Judas, his face stern. When I saw the purple cast on his arm, my stomach tightened, I did that to him. Samhain nodded his head as indication for my dad to start talking.

"Fine, yes I did all of those things but I had a job to do at first. But when Nadine cut me off, and wouldn't let me explain I got desperate. So, knowing how much she bonded with Michael, he was the easiest to target out of her friends," Dad explained.

I noticed Judas's jaw tense, then he looked at me. "Stand up," he instructed sternly, not taking his eyes off my dad.

Slowly, I stood up, the whole world suddenly spun at a delirious angle. As I started falling, I felt an arm wrap around me. Judas grunted, and my breath caught in my throat when I fell into his embrace. But his arms were strong around my waist, ensuring he didn't touch my injured arm.

Judas turned me around, and we were heading for the bed which he slept on with Carlos moments ago. As we approached Carlos was also awake now, and tapped the empty spot next to him with a smile—I wondered where the bandage on his other arm came from.

As Judas slowly freed me from his support, he took my hand, and gently lowered me down.

I jumped at the thud which echoed out of the room, even Michael had woken up, the sound came from where my dad was sitting on my bed. Samhain had him pinned against the wall, and was saying something to him I couldn't hear. Never before had I seen my Dad squirm out of fear, Thora remained in place, smiling while watching the situation unfold.

After a few moments, Dad ran out of the room in a panic. I could see the sweat dripping down his face. Despite how crap I felt, I tried standing up to get back to my own bed, but I felt a gentle tug on my shirt to stop me.

"I don't recommend standing up for a while," Carlos suggested. I turned to look at him, and he gave me a reassuring smile, I sank back so the cold metal pressed against my spine. Wincing out of discomfort. "Ezekiel's in the shower. You've been out for about four hours since Our Leader was killed."

My eyes widened to learn that President Sanchez was dead, and I felt a sick sense of joy as a result of it. I was a little too happy about this news, but terrified of what this meant for Denmé's future.

The glint of ring on Judas's left hand made me do a double take, then I looked at him and then Carlos. My eyes widening as everything clicked into place, I started smiling for them both.

"Am I invited to the wedding?" I smiled at them both.

"Shush, we haven't told anybody yet, didn't think it's appropriate," Judas replied. I looked at him with a smile. "But, yes you are."

Carlos laughed, and for a moment there was a peaceful atmosphere in the air.

* * *

A week later, I was curled up on the sofa with a spare duvet wrapped around me with Payton at my feet. She scooped fries into her mouth, with the floor littered with our take out containers from a trip to Freddy's.

The news came on the TV, flicking through footage of the aftermath of Denmé's Uprising. The destruction was in all eighteen Zones, and the news coverage tried their best to show all of them. Most neighbourhoods were flattened to nothing but charred remains, with only outlines of what used to be there burned into the grass.

Payton grabbed the remote, and started flicking through the channels while chewing on a piece of lettuce. She only stopped when one of the news reports was covering something I recognised immediately; The Rebellion.

Somehow the reporters had accessed Zone 7, and it looked like a sunken cruise ship, with thigh-deep water which people were wading through. Furniture bounced against walls, and there was a distant beep of smoke alarm batteries signalling they were running out. There was no electricity, so the people on screen used headlamps or torches to guide their way. My heart ached to see the apartments and the mall.

"Alright, movie time, we're turning this shit off," Payton announced, as she ate the discarded pickle in my burger container.

I instantly felt deflated when she changed the TV's input device, and started flicking through the movies on the USB we had plugged in.

Denmé's future was still uncertain, but so far, they had a lot of rebuilding to do, there were still no new updates on who the new leader would be.

* * *

Six months had gone by since the fall of Denmé's regime, summer had officially arrived in Olympia. As I sat in a secluded area of Harrowell

Beach, surrounded by sand dunes. Payton was sunbathing in our section of the beach which wasn't protected by the parasol above my head, as I watched Michael play in the sea I hugged my knees to my chest. The humid Summer air making sweat run down my tank top.

"I got it," Ezekiel called as he approached us with a paper bag in his hands, sand kicked up as he approached us both.

I crossed my legs, and shifted on the towel beneath me to make room for him. He sat down, and dived into the bag. Even Payton propped herself up on her elbows, pushing her sunglasses away from her eyes; recently she had dyed her hair a turquoise blue which made her blue eyes pop.

"Do you think he'll like this?" Ezekiel said in a hushed voice.

In his hands was a white box with a red bow, then he lifted the lid, I gasped to see a photo frame with a family picture inside. It was of Michael and Judas's family from when they were younger.

"Yes, oh my god. How did you get that photo?" I asked, looking at Michael who was oblivious to our conversation, Payton was smiling at it.

"His mum emailed it to me," Ezekiel replied, he put the lid back on and shoved it into the bag.

People in Denmé got WiFi and cellphones last month, we had to get their email addresses and phone numbers from old fashioned letters. I was happy I could still talk to my friends in Denmé now that Ramona Sanchez wasn't an issue.

Today we had not only come to Harrowell specifically for Michael's birthday, the thirteenth of June, but we also came here to find out the results of Denmé's first election in eighteen years. All of us were on edge, hoping that another asshole wasn't voted in this time round. I doubted it.

"Michael!" Payton called across the beach, he looked at us, and she waved him over.

I watched as he made his way over, the beach was packed with all people wanting to soak up some sun while the Summer was at its prime, as I picked up Payton's battery powdered fan I tried to cool myself off to no avail; it just made me feel more hot.

Michael crouched down next to us, eventually falling onto the sand, he laughed and shifted so he sat with his legs crossed like Ezekiel and I. From here I could see the scar from where he had been shot, I forced a smile.

"A little birdy told me you're fifteen today," Ezekiel announced as he handed over Michael's gift.

Michael dived into the bag, and produced the box, then looked up at all three of us with a smile as he took the lid off. The smile vanished when he looked down and his grip on the box became tighter. Michael's eyes glazed over, and a single tear rolled down his cheek, he exhaled a breath and wiped away his tears.

"Jesus guys, we wanted to give him a birthday present, not a mental breakdown," Payton spat, as she grabbed the sun cream and started to top it up.

Michael laughed. "It's fine, I love it. Just home sick, you know."

Everybody nodded, then I felt my phone buzz in my pocket. When I pulled it out, I looked at what it was, my eyes widened to see the notification on my lock screen.

"Guys, check your phones!" I announced.

At first everybody looked at me, I gestured for them to do as I told them to. On my phone there was a picture of a man who looked extremely humble and kind, he was older with white hair. The new president of Denmé was President Maxwell.

"I wanted him to be President," Ezekiel said with a smile.

Michael started beaming while he looked at his phone. Denmé was one step closer to true freedom.

NADINE

* * *

A year after the regime of Denmé fell, I grabbed my suitcase off of the concourse and put it onto the luggage cart. I watched Ezekiel as he found his own suitcase, then got Michael's for him. Michael had a satchel bag slung over his chest, and he was texting furiously as he slowly made his way over to us, pushing emerald green hair from his face. Ezekiel cupped the small of my back and pulled me close to give me a kiss. I smiled, but I stepped back when I heard a loud sigh from Michael.

"Are you ready?" I asked. Michael nodded.

Glancing behind my shoulder as I heard Ezekiel start pushing the cart, I turned and followed him, pulling my green coat around me and zipping it up. There was a big poster as we exited the luggage concourse reading, *'Welcome to Newton, St. Herculia!'* We passed through the double doors into the Arrivals Hall, and saw people lined up alongside the fence waiting for loved ones while holding signs up. The air was electric with bustling conversations. It was a joyous occasion for those involved. Even for us as we had come back for a special occasion indeed.

At the end, there was a man in a black business suit holding a sign that read *"Kenwood + Ellis + Wells."* That was for us.

"Hello," Ezekiel said as he approached the guy.

"Welcome, Kenwood and friends," the man said as he turned and escorted us through the Arrivals Hall. The man turned left, away from the parking lot I thought we were going to. "Usually, The Mayoress doesn't personally drive people into town, you must be special."

I laughed, and so did Ezekiel as the gentleman scanned a key card which opened up some doors which looked like the wall.

We entered a secret parking lot where a black SUV was waiting, my jaw fell open, and I felt amazed by it, following the gentleman to the back of the SUV, he opened the trunk and started loading our suitcases into it. Seeing the silhouette in the driver's seat, they turned around, and I waved at Taylor; correction Mayoress Ashby. Her once green hair was now a beautiful auburn that complimented her eyes. During the Uprising, I heard from Judas that Godfrey McRitchie was decapitated by some people from Zone 13—a happy *accident*.

Climbing into the back next to Ezekiel, Michael sat on my left and shut the door. For obvious reasons, there was a silent security guard next to Taylor, as the car rolled forward—we were on the move towards the actual town of Newton.

Outside snow fell gently onto the ground, making me feel colder than what I actually felt in the warm interior of the car. I couldn't believe how busy the highway was.

"I've literally just busted my ass this morning, I fell on ice while going up to my office," Taylor explained with a laugh. I heard Ezekiel snort and laugh while shaking his head. "I can't believe that Judas and Carlos are getting married in two days; it's insane."

"This is the first time I've been back in Newton in over a year," Michael admitted as he looked at his phone.

Taylor looked at Michael in the rear view, she gave him a warm smile. "It's changed a lot, I hope you fall in love with the town how it is now."

Michael scoffed. "I doubt it."

"I bet you ten bucks," Taylor replied.

"Make it twenty, and you have a deal." Michael laughed. Then he staired out of the window clearly lost in his own thoughts.

* * *

This felt weird being back in Apartment Block East. It had now been turned into holiday suites; even weirder Taylor had assigned me my old apartment. Everything had been modernised inside, there was a large TV on the wall with a large three-piece leather suite. The kitchen was replaced with sleek black cabinets and stainless steel appliances. Everything was the same aside from an added second bedroom. I was in shock.

It was like the regime never happened. But it did happen the barcodes on our arms were a permanent reminder.

Ezekiel pressed me against the wall, his hands on my hips and lowered his head down to me so our lips were inches away. I could feel his warm breath on my lips as I stared into his crystal blue eyes.

"Being back here is weird," I admitted, wrapping my arm around his shoulders, feeling his muscles through his shirt.

"But it's nice we now have freedom," Ezekiel admitted, I sucked in a breath as he brought his lips down to mine and we shared a kiss, I tightened my hold on him and ran my hands through his dread locks.

A knock at the door made us pull away from each other, and Ezekiel smiled as he approached the door, when he opened it Judas and Carlos filtered into the apartment cheering and holding up bottles of alcohol with red cups, I laughed as I watched them approach the three-piece suite—Michael sauntered in a couple moments after, hands shoved in his pockets. He smiled at me.

Just as I was about to walk over to them, the loud bang from a wine cork made me yelp and cover my ears. Suddenly the sound of explosions and gunshots filled my head, everybody around me replaced with Denmé guards laughing and sneering. My breath caught in my throat, then my arm burned furiously for the first time in a year.

I jumped and stepped back as Ezekiel touched my back, everybody around me had returned to normal and they were all staring at me. Tears rolled down my cheeks, and my breathing was heavy like I had just ran a marathon.

"Are you okay?" he asked, his face painted with concern.

I slowly nodded, as I approached the coffee table, grabbing a red cup filled with alcohol and chugged it down like it was a shot. When I finished with a cringe as my throat burned from the alcohol, Carlos was staring at me with a raised eyebrow then looked Judas.

"Being back here is harder than I realised. I'm fine," I lied.

As Carlos poured me another drink, I just wanted to enjoy this night with my friends, tonight was a celebration of everything that had happened over the past year. I wasn't going to let my flashbacks of Denmé ruin that for me.

41

Judas

A week had passed since we beat Denmé's regime, and not much had changed in that time frame. The only changes were the curfew being lifted, and no guards monitoring our every move. Carlos and I were finally allowed above ground, even Archie and Adriel checked our files, all charges had been cleared. It felt wrong to be up here.

While completing Task 72, I stood outside the bookstore where Richard got shot just shy of two months ago when Nadine came to town—it felt like a life time ago since that day. Holding the ladder, I watched Carlos at the top whilst he tore down one of the posters where Our Leader stood on a mountain pointing to a golden horizon; *Tasks Are Good* was written at the bottom. I stifled a laugh. Today there was no putting any new posters up, or using the scraper that was provided to us, it was a bittersweet moment.

The poster fell at my feet, so I scooped it up and shoved it into a duffel bag which hung across my chest, all posters today were going in the incinerator. Even though our relationship was still illegal, when Carlos got to the bottom of the ladder he pulled me in close and kissed me, which made me smile and my cheeks became warm. I picked up the ladder, and we both walked in unison to the next location.

"You know, when we started the Uprising, I didn't expect to still be doing tasks a week after we won," Carlos grumbled as I extended the ladder out again.

I looked at his arm brace, and blinked back tears. "You can tear this one down, if you want to with your arm."

Carlos shook his head as he held the ladder in place. "No, it's good for anger management, so your turn."

I nodded and made my way up the rungs. At the top, I tore down a poster of Our Leader sitting on a throne, staring into your soul with the words *We Are All Equal* at the bottom, I actually laughed at this one. Actually, Carlos was right, it was good anger management to tear these down.

"Even though we still have to do tasks, at least we don't have to put any of this bullshit back up," I replied as I climbed back down.

Carlos nodded, and shoved the crumpled up poster inside the duffle bag. Despite everything being the same, everything was oddly different as well. Denmé had no government anymore, and Zone 13's Rebellion had decapitated every single Zone Director so none could take over Our Leader's position.

But I prayed life would change soon, I didn't go through the Uprising to have it staying the same way.

* * *

Life changed drastically when the eight month anniversary of Denmé's Uprising rolled around. Not only were tasks now abolished, but so was the government uniform, extermination camps ceased to exist, and food regulations were lifted which allowed us to eat processed food. However, the strangest concept I couldn't get my head around was the abolishment of Zones. These were replaced with something called counties as Denmé itself faded out of existence and returned to being St. Herculia. Slowly, the new government was helping Unlisted integrate into society as they started moving everybody out of The Rebellion, it was being shut down while they checked its structural integrity before turning it into something called a museum. And the best part, I could finally get married to Carlos legally.

As we walked hand in hand through the threshold of a glorious manor house on the outskirts of Newton, Taylor's high heels clicked on the stone flooring as she led us inside, recently she had dyed her hair a beautiful auburn colour which matched the figure hugging grey dress she was wearing. Last month she had been elected as Mayoress of Newton, so there was a couple of security guards dotted around.

My jaw fell open to see how grand this home was, a beautiful real wood staircase sat to the right of the entrance which led to so many rooms. What I could see to my left was a dining room, and to my right was a modern, and sleek kitchen. I was amazed Taylor could afford a second house, something like this was something Carlos and I couldn't afford in our wildest dreams.

"Your second home is beautiful," Carlos gasped while looking around.

Taylor checked her phone as she led us deeper into the home, and stood inside a beautiful sun room, the wrought iron had been painted green and there were beautiful white tiles on the walls—there were hand painted flowers on some of them.

"Actually, this isn't my home," she admitted, as she held up a set of keys. "This is yours."

My jaw fell open, and I looked at her with a raised eyebrow. "Taylor, we can't take this, what the fuck." I scoffed and swallowed the lump in my throat.

"You both need somewhere to live, it's the least I can do as my adoptive brothers. Think of it as an early wedding gift." She smiled, showing her brilliant white teeth.

I looked at Carlos, whose lips quivered as tears rolled down his cheeks. Seeing him cry, had me crying. I stepped up to him, and embraced him. We had been living in Carlos's apartment for the past eight months, we simply couldn't afford anything else.

"Thank you," Carlos choked out.

* * *

A year after the fall of Denmé, I stood in mum's house looking over the seating chart of my wedding reception. Hearing footsteps approach behind me, Michael was in the doorway eating a grilled cheese, Michael always came back different, now his hair was emerald green. But despite this he even looked more masculine, he had defined muscles now that really made Michael look older.

Due to Mum still having her Olympia dual-citizen status, that got passed onto her children so Michael could live there all the time he wanted, I also had that privilege but Carlos's job held us back.

"Michael, where do you think Nadine and Ezekiel sit? Like here, where they are now?" I asked, pointing to a table near the family table.

The floorboards creaked with Michael's approach, and he leaned in and nodded. "That looks about right." I put a thumb up with a smile.

Michael took another bite of grilled cheese and walked away. I heard another set of footsteps— it was Mum, who fanned herself while looking flustered. "So, one of my babies is getting married in two days, and I still haven't figured out how to wear my hair."

I laughed, looking at Mum in stained sweatpants and a sweater, her hair a mess, and it broke my heart to see more grey coming through.

"Let the hairdressers surprise you," I announced. Mum nodded and disappeared back into the kitchen

I admitted defeat on the seating plan, and I sat on a nearby sofa. Running a hand through my hair, I looked at Michael. He was looking at his phone when it buzzed and flicked through it. I shook my head at him, texting away to clearly his friends back in Olympia.

I looked at the oil painting above the fireplace. It was our family photo, three smiling children with Mum and Dad. Every now and then, my heart broke at realising how much Gabrielle was missing, she would have loved to get her first car, try pizza for the first time, or even get a chance to have a real education.

Despite her not being here, I knew on that seating plan I had left a seat reserved for Gabrielle.

42

Judas

Carlos and I had separated from the wedding reception that was going on nearby; instead, we were slow dancing on the bank of Newton's river to the sound of the random cars driving past. Despite being Winter, I felt warm inside from the copious amounts of alcohol in my system, pulling Carlos in close. He sucked in a breath as he stared at me, my hand firmly on his back.

Leaning down, I kissed him and felt his arms move around my neck. Another kiss, and another, we both started laughing as our kisses became sloppy. Only stopping when we heard the crunch of the frozen grass next to us, turning my head, I saw Nadine approaching us.

She hugged her arms and looked cold despite the fluffy jacket she was wearing to cover her arms. I slipped off my blazer and held it out to her with a bold smile. "My lady."

Nadine laughed and slipped my blazer on, Carlos extended a hand out to her. "Care for a dance, Miss Ellis?"

I watched her place her hand into Carlos's with a smile, he spun Nadine around, making her baby blue ball gown dress glow in the moonlight. All three of us laughed, and I fell sideways into Carlos, he laughed as he caught me. I could feel his hand supporting me by the waist as he kissed me.

"Nadine Ellis, the girl who kicks ass!" I shouted.

* * *

Back inside music blared out of speakers, tables were pushed to the sides around the dance floor, and people were dancing—most were ex-Rebellion Leaders. As I made my way through to my assigned seat, I glanced at people sitting at tables eating or taking a break from dancing, I noticed Thora asleep with her head on a table, laughing when Xander took a photo of her.

"Is she okay?" I asked him.

Xander laughed. "Perks of being a new parent."

I laughed, they brought a daughter into the world three months ago.

When I collapsed into my seat, I took off my tie and smiled. Once Carlos sat next to me, I laughed as I wrapped the tie around him and pulled him for a kiss. Then I took in all his perfect features, I couldn't believe he was now my husband. As I heard the click of heels, I looked at Nadine's friend Payton, who approached us with a glass of champagne in hand which she took a sip from.

She arrived last night, I couldn't help but wonder if she was tired.

Behind Payton, I could see both Ezekiel and Nadine dancing together in each other's arms, I was happy they had found each other during such a dark time in our lives.

"Are you both ready for me to show you around Olympia while staying in my dad's lake cabin?" Payton questioned, throwing her midnight purple hair behind her shoulder while taking another sip of wine.

I nodded and felt the butterflies in my stomach. It was nerve wracking going to Olympia for my honeymoon, but I could explore something new.

"What's the best thing Olympia has to offer?" Carlos questioned.

Payton held the champagne glass close to her heart. "Me, of course—well, me and a good lobster, you have to try that."

I had never eaten lobster before, it was banned during the regime.

As nervous as I was for this new chapter in my life, I was excited for it to begin.

Thank You

L.J. Kerry hopes you have enjoyed your journey through the world of Denmé and Olympia.
If you'd like to get Listed in the hands of more people, please leave a review on: Goodreads, social media, or where ever you think is necessary.
By leaving a review, you not only help L.J. Kerry as a small author, but you also help get this book in the hands of more readers.
Thank you for reading and spreading the word.
I hope you have an awesome day!

Denmé Task List

Task 1: Border Security

Task 3: Laundry

Task 5: Grocery Store Stock Replenishment

Task 10: Church Maintenance

Task 11: Housing Maintenance

Task 12: Courthouse Cleaning

Task 14: Mail Service

Task 15: Trash Collection

Task 16: Landscaping

Task 17: Teacher (<u>Permanent</u>)

Task 12: Chauffeur Service

Task 50: Street Cleaning

Task 72: Leader Posters

Task 90: Yard Work

Task 105: Church Service

About the Author

L.J. Kerry born in Sheffield, England. She has always loved to read and write from a young age, some of her favourite genres are Urban Fantasy and Dystopia.

Now living in Derbyshire, England. L.J. Kerry likes to spend her free time (aside from reading or writing) playing video games, travelling and learning new languages/cultures.

You can connect with me on:

- https://twitter.com/LJKerryBooks
- https://www.facebook.com/LJKerryBooks

Printed in Great Britain
by Amazon